AN *A*CQUAINTANCE
WITH *D*ARKNESS

AN *ACQUAINTANCE* WITH *DARKNESS*

Ann Rinaldi

Gulliver Books

Harcourt Brace & Company

San Diego   New York   London

Requests for permission to make copies of any part of the work
should be mailed to: Permissions Department,
Harcourt Brace & Company, 6277 Sea Harbor Drive,
Orlando, Florida 32887-6777.

Gulliver Books is a registered trademark of
Harcourt Brace & Company.

Library of Congress Cataloging-in-Publication Data
Rinaldi, Ann.
An acquaintance with darkness/Ann Rinaldi.
p.   cm. — (Great Episodes)
"Gulliver Books."
Summary: When her mother dies and her best friend's family is
implicated in the assassination of President Lincoln, fourteen-
year-old Emily Pigbush must go live with an uncle she suspects
of being involved in stealing bodies for medical research.
ISBN 0-15-201294-X
[1. Body snatching — Fiction.   2. Physicians — Fiction.
3. Lincoln, Abraham, 1809–1865 — Assassination — Fiction.
4. Washington, D.C. — History — Civil War, 1861–1865 — Fiction.]
I. Title.   II. Series.
PZ7.R459Ac   1997
[Fic] — dc21   96-51008

Text set in Electra
Designed by Lydia D'moch

C E F D
Printed in the United States of America

For my husband,
the wind beneath my wings

JOHNNY

APRIL 3, 1865

I KNEW THINGS were going to be bad when I heard the knock on the door early that morning.

Nobody was up yet. I remembered that Mama and I were the only ones living in the house now. Ella May, our house-girl, had left yesterday. Ella May was a freed woman, just up from slavery. Nobody could keep freed men or women. They couldn't even keep themselves, they were so confused. Ella May told me she had thought freedom meant that Mr. and Mrs. Lincoln were going to give her two new shifts. "My old mistress give me two new shifts a year," she said gloomily. "She take care o' me. Gov'ment supposed to take care o' me. Better I go back to my old mistress."

"Don't go back," I begged her. "I'll make you a shift. Two, if you want. It's just that I've been busy taking care of Mama."

But she up and left. And our boarder, Mrs. Paxon, left—because I couldn't do for her and Mama and go to school, too. And now I was here alone. With Mama dying.

I couldn't think for a minute. The house was cold. The fires had died during the night. And it was raining. All it had done was rain this spring. Washington was crying. Four years of confusion, pain, crowding, and mistrust, with half the people on the streets carrying knives and guns and the other half crazy. Four years of scavenging for food. If I were a city I would cry, too.

I got up, put on my robe, and went out into the hall. "Who is it?" I called over the banister, just like my daddy had taught me back home in Surrattsville. "Always ask who's knocking, Miss Muffet," he'd say. My daddy always called me Miss Muffet, not Emily. He'd raised me on the Brothers Grimm and taught me all life's important lessons from fairy tales and nursery rhymes.

Here in Washington I'd already applied much of what he'd taught me. I had to. All kinds of unsavory people walked the streets. Oh, we were used to the Blue Soldiers and the Free Issue nigras like Ella May, who overran the city asking for the forty acres and a mule that they said "Mister Linkum" promised them with freedom, but now it seemed like every other person was a stranger, an interloper, an outlander who had come to prey on us.

Maybe it would be a boarder at the door, I thought. Out of the goodness of her heart, Mrs. Mary sometimes sent us a boarder when she couldn't accommodate the stranger who knocked on her door in the middle of the night.

"What goodness?" Mama would ask. "What heart?" She hadn't spoken to Mary Surratt since that woman's brother foreclosed on our house in Maryland when Mrs. Mary's husband died, over two years ago now. And they were girlhood friends. We lived over the creek from them in Maryland. And now we lived at 543 H Street. And they lived at 541.

"The same goodness that made her find us this house," I'd remind Mama.

"A small enough favor, since they took our other."

"Mrs. Mary still didn't have to find us this house," was always my reply. "It wasn't her idea in the first place, to take our old one."

It did no good. I could never make peace between them. Mama was going to die without ever speaking again to Mrs. Mary. Would I do that to my best friend? (Who was my best friend? Annie Surratt, Johnny's sister). No, I wouldn't.

I paused in front of Mama's room. She was still sleeping. Good. I started down the narrow stairs, wishing I had forty acres and a mule right now. What I would do with them, I didn't know. But I'd do something. Anything would be better than living here in this narrow, sad little house, with the rain pouring down outside and Mama dying. I couldn't blame Ella May for leaving.

"Who is it?" I asked again.

"It's Johnny," came the muffled answer from the other side of the door.

How had I known it would be Johnny? The same way I'd always known he'd be down at his daddy's tavern–post office–store of an afternoon, back in Maryland. I was just a skinny little kid back then, down in Prince George County, and I'd get the feeling he'd be there. And he would be, too, standing on the front porch talking politics with his daddy, the squire, and the other planters who'd come to jaw away the afternoon.

"Just a second." When had he gotten back? He'd been gone since the end of March. And I hadn't seen him since a week before, when he took me and Honora Fitzpatrick to Ford's Theater. Honora boarded with his mother. She was nineteen. We sat in box number 10.

The president's box! Up so high over everyone else! The draperies were silk brocade, the seats crushed velvet; the chandeliers sparkled overhead. Johnny wore a blue military cloak. Where had he gotten it? Where did he get anything he had these days? His large revolver, his bowie knife, the two horses he kept at Howard's stables.

Everyone looked at us that night, wondering who we were. I wore my blue silk moiré. The play was *Jane Shore*. And then John Wilkes Booth stopped in, and I thought Honora would swoon. Booth was a matinee idol. All the girls were crazy for him.

More knocking. "I'm coming!" I stumbled down the narrow steps. Johnny hadn't spoken to me since that night at the play. The next day he rode off with six men, one of them Booth. I went over with a pie to show my thanks for the theater. He wouldn't look at me; just rode off.

Annie took the pie. "If any harm comes to my brother because of that scoundrel Booth, I'll kill the man," she said. She had Booth's picture in her room. Signed.

How had Annie gone from thinking Booth was a matinee idol to wanting to kill him? And what did it have to do with Johnny? Booth was pure Secesh, loved the South. So did all the Surratts. So did half the people in Washington. Mrs. Lincoln herself had had four brothers killed fighting for the Confederacy. You couldn't sort things like that out anymore. And you couldn't kill people for it, or there wouldn't be anybody left in Washington.

I saw Johnny's shadow through the frosted glass of the door. I unhooked the latch. A cold blast came in.

"Hello, Emily."

"Hello, yourself."

"Don't be like that."

"Like what?"

"All huffylike and contentious."

"I'm not huffylike."

"Well, you're contentious."

I smiled. Johnny could do that to me, always. Make me smile no matter what was going on around us. But still, I wasn't about to let him off that easy. "What do you want, Johnny?"

"To come in out of the rain."

"You are in."

"Not all the way."

I moved back in the hall. He came in, and I closed the door. "What's the matter?" I asked.

He took off his hat. He was nothing if not polite, Johnny Surratt. How could he be anything else, with all that fancy schooling? St. Ignatius's here in Washington, then St. Mary's outside Baltimore, and finally St. Charles's Seminary near Elliot Mills in Maryland. He was once going to be a priest. But that was all before the war, when his family had money.

"I'd offer you something hot," I said, "but the stove isn't started. Ella May's gone. Left yesterday. It's only me and Mama now."

He nodded. "What will you do?"

"Take care of Mama. There isn't much else to do."

"How is she?"

"Not good, Johnny."

He nodded and looked at his hat in his hands. "I recollect when my daddy died."

"So do I." I'd been there. In their villa in Surrattsville

when his daddy was laid out in the parlor, surrounded by white candles, white roses, dimness, and Johnny crying.

"I wish I could stay and be with you," he said.

"You haven't spoken to me in three weeks."

He looked abashed. "I've been busy, Emily."

Doing what? I wanted to ask. Only I didn't. These days you didn't ask what a person was doing. People weren't what they had been before the war. They did strange things to survive. For a while Johnny had a job with the Confederate mail service, running letters and God knows what-all else South, skulking through Union picket lines, crisscrossing creeks, reaching Pope's Creek, Maryland, in six hours, crossing the Potomac, then on to Port Royal on the Rappahannock River, then crossing that river with only eighteen miles to an open road to Richmond.

But he was doing something else now. His new job took him North. To Canada. To New York. He'd brought me back a darling pair of gloves from New York. They had eighteen buttons on each cuff. Better than Myra Mott at school had. And you had to go pretty far to best Myra Mott. Johnny got the gloves in a Fifth Avenue shop. He'd seen John Wilkes Booth and his famous brothers in *Julius Caesar* at the Winter Garden.

"I'm going away, Emily. I came to tell you."

"You're always going away."

"I may not be back for a long while. The war's ending. You know that. The Confederacy is dying."

I didn't care about the Confederacy dying. The Confederacy never should have been born, as far as I was concerned. My daddy died fighting it. The Confederacy had ruined everything. But Johnny believed in it. So I didn't argue the point.

"Dying," he said again. "You can hear the death rattle. Petersburg has fallen. Richmond is being evacuated. People are going crazy out on the street. Don't go out if you can help it."

"Richmond? My aunt Susie lives in Richmond."

"I know. I delivered all those letters to her, remember?"

"Mama wants me to go and live with Aunt Susie after she dies."

"That's why I'm here. To tell you you'll have to make other plans."

"What other plans? There's nobody else, except Uncle Valentine. And Mama and he don't get on, you know that. She says he's crazy."

"Everybody is crazy these days."

"She says he does things I wouldn't want to know about."

"So does everybody else. So do I."

"Do you, Johnny?" I peered into his handsome face earnestly. I was fourteen. He was twenty. But I'd loved him for years, ever since he used to take me into the store, away from all those jawing planters on the porch, and give me peppermint candy. He taught me to swim, too, in the creek back home. I was like a little sister to him, no more. I knew that. It wasn't enough, no. But beggars can't be choosers, Daddy always told me.

"Dr. Mudd holds your uncle in high esteem," he said.

"Dr. Mudd?"

"You remember. From Charles County. I told you how Booth wants to buy a farm from him down in Maryland."

Booth again. I looked at Johnny. He was wearing a new suit of clothes. Gray. Good cloth. I know cloth—before she took sick, Mama had worked for Elizabeth Keckley, Mrs.

Lincoln's personal seamstress. Was he getting things from Booth, then?

"I'm here to tell you that my mother says you can come and board with her when your mother dies," he said.

I looked up quickly. "At your house?"

"Well, I won't be there anymore. But you can have my room. Mama would be glad to have you. So would Annie."

"I couldn't pay thirty-five dollars a month board. Mama hasn't been able to work for a while now and our money is giving out."

"Mama says not to worry about that. You know she feels responsible that my uncle Zad foreclosed on your house."

I was going to cry, I was sure of it. And then I started.

"Don't, Emily, please," he said. He pulled out a handkerchief and gave it to me. I looked at it. It was so fine.

"Annie made it for me," he said. "Last Christmas. From cloth laid away before the war. She made me seven of them. You see how she put my name on the corner? And the day of the week?"

I nodded. "This one says SUNDAY."

"Yes. You can keep it. I want you to keep it," he said.

I wiped my face with the handkerchief. Next thing I knew, Johnny had his arms around me. Like a brother would do if I had a brother. Which I didn't. He patted my shoulder and held me until I stopped. Then he reached into his pocket and took out some gold coins. "Take these," he said.

"Twenty dollars! Oh, Johnny, I couldn't! You need them."

"I have all I need. And I'll get more. Take them now, I said."

I looked at the gold coins in my hand. Where had he gotten them? Nobody I knew had so much gold to give away

8

in Washington these days. What had he done to get them? I did not want to know. I sniffed. "Thank you."

"I've got to go now, Emily. There's things I've got to do. Pack. Exchange some gold for greenbacks. They go farther, where I'm going."

"Where are you going?" I knew I shouldn't have asked.

He smiled. "Maybe I'll write. But not right away." He opened the door and peered out into the early-morning street, looking to see who was out there. Nobody was. How different he was now, having to sneak about. How different from the Johnny I'd known in Maryland, whose father's house had eleven rooms, who rode blooded horses, whose manner and bearing were so sure and elegant.

"Johnny!" I grabbed onto his sleeve. "Take care of yourself."

He hugged me again. "We must do the best we can, Emily. We have to find our own way, all of us. And do the best we can. At whatever comes along. Doesn't matter what side we're on. It won't be easy for anybody." He released me. "Things are going to be even crazier than they have been when the war ends. You don't want to go down-country to Richmond, Emily. Stay with my mother. Promise me that, so I know you'll be all right."

I nodded and gulped my tears.

"I've made arrangements with my friend David Herold, who works at Thompson's Drug Store. Whatever you need for your mother, he'll send over. No charge."

Herold was one of his scruffy friends. Johnny had been running with a lot of scruffy friends lately. Mrs. Mary was worried about him.

Then he kissed me on the forehead and went out the door.

I watched him go. He turned in the cold rain and waved, then he hunched his shoulders and walked away.

I would never see Johnny Surratt again. I just knew it, the way I know things sometimes. Didn't I know Daddy's name would be on the list of those killed in the battle of Chancellorsville?

I knew, too, that something bad was going to happen to Johnny. I shivered, closed the door, and clutched the handkerchief that said SUNDAY, and went back down the hall into the tiny kitchen to start the stove for breakfast.

2

A STAR AT NOON

MY MAMA HAD MOMENTS in her sickness when she rallied. Sat up, even walked around. Then she started talking. Mostly it was about Daddy.

"It was what he set out to do, get himself killed. Because he didn't want to come back and face things. Left me here to face them alone."

Or: "He failed at everything but war. Just like General Grant. No wonder he went to fight for the North. They belonged together, him and Grant." Never mind that Daddy never met Grant. That he was with General Hooker at Chancellorsville, a Union defeat.

There were days she said such mean things about Daddy that I had to make an excuse and leave the room.

Should I tell her Richmond was falling? I wondered. Her

sister was there. I was confused. "Don't ever act on your thoughts if you're confused, Miss Muffet," Daddy had told me. "Wait until your mind clears."

And then, on April 4, Elizabeth Keckley came around and confused me more.

She came in the fancy barouche that the White House let her use, with the matched black horses. And with Jehu, the White House coachman. . . . She'd sent him around to take us to the inauguration in March. But Mama was too sick to go. So I went alone. It was raining. The streets were full of mud, but Jehu took me to the exact spot of the grandstand where Mrs. Keckley's "girls" who worked for her, sat.

Now she came bearing gifts: canned sardines and oysters, slabs of cheese, pickles, honeyed ham, bread. She was angry about the freedmen she'd just visited for her Relief Society.

"Living in shacks!" She drew off her kid gloves. I took her lavender cape and hung it on a peg in the hall. "They huddle together talking of the good old times on the plantation."

It wasn't as if she'd never seen them before. She visited them all the time on Murder Bay, on the lower stretches of the Washington Canal.

Mama said she was Mrs. Lincoln's confidante. She never left the woman's side when little Willie Lincoln died.

I took the foodstuffs into the kitchen. Elizabeth Keckley followed. "You shouldn't have brought food," I protested. But I was glad for it. Now I wouldn't have to dip into the twenty gold pieces Johnny had given me for a while.

"It's left from last evening's reception. Such a waste, all that lavish entertaining. The president eats nothing. Apples on occasion. He's wasting away. I take the leftovers to Murder Bay when I can. But this morning I thought of you and your mama. How is she?"

"No better."

"My best seamstress." She sighed.

My best mother, I thought.

"The dress she was working on is finished," I assured her. "I stayed up late doing the hem. And I'll finish the flounces on the other Mama was doing if you want."

"Wonderful! You're getting to be a regular little dressmaker. Would you like to be in my employ when your mama passes on?"

I pulled out a chair for her and set down two cups. The water was boiling for tea. I fetched it. I poured carefully and spoke the same way. "I never thought to become a dressmaker."

"What did you think to become?"

"Nothing yet. I'm only fourteen."

"When I was fourteen, I was sent from home to live with my master's eldest son and his wife. I was their only servant. I did the work of three."

But you had no choice, I wanted to say, *you were a slave.* I didn't say it.

Elizabeth Keckley was nigra. But not like Ella May. There were two kinds of nigras in Washington. The contrabands, who came expecting forty acres and a mule. They were trained only "to the hoe," as people said. At first the white people welcomed them. But now there was a lot of bad feeling. There were never enough rations for them. In winter many died in their shacks. Nobody knew what to do. *We fought the war for this?* You could see it on people's faces.

Then there were the regular people of color who had been in Washington for years. Many of them now resented the contrabands, because they disturbed the order of things. And because the whites were beginning to mark no difference between the contrabands and the nigras who had education and jobs, like Elizabeth Keckley.

We learned about the problem in school. "Who will bear the increased taxes for schooling the contrabands?" Mrs. McQuade asked us. "When the war ends, who will get the jobs? Who will have a place in the new order of things? Think, girls, think!"

Girls who attended Miss Winefred Martin's School for Young Ladies were supposed to think. Mama said Daddy had always wanted me in a school like that and had set aside money for my schooling. "I honored his wishes," she'd said. "I just want you to know that."

Elizabeth Keckley was awaiting my answer. "Do you mean for me to come and work for you right away?" I asked.

"I fill my openings right away. I must. I have other important clients besides Mrs. Lincoln. And with the war ending—well, next fall will be a brilliant season."

"I have to finish school. My daddy wanted it. He paid for me to do so."

"A person goes to school to find a means of support. I am offering you that."

"Daddy said a person goes to school to learn how to think."

She stirred her tea. "I and my race have not had the luxury of that."

She'd had a hard life. Mama said she'd lost a son in the war, a half-white son, her only child. I knew, too, that she'd purchased her own freedom. That was no small accomplishment. Yet I knew she would never understand why I didn't want to become a dressmaker.

I didn't quite understand it myself. What would I do when Mama passed on? All I had were the many vague ambitions

14

and desires that Daddy's lessons and my schooling at Miss Winefred Martin's had instilled in me. And Johnny's twenty gold pieces.

I knew there was more in life than taking up occupation with the needle. Mama had set out every day for work with no joy. And come home with less. I wanted to do something else with my life, something fine. I didn't know what it was yet, but I knew I could do it if I set my mind to it.

I felt the knowing in my bones sometimes. The surge of desire to accomplish. The opening up of possibilities. The connection to dreams. It pounded in my blood at given moments.

"You must harness those feelings," Mrs. McQuade had told me. "Focus them on your goals like you focus a telescope on a star. You must work hard and study."

"Where will you live?" Elizabeth Keckley was asking.

"I don't know yet."

Her yellow-green eyes fixed on me. Cannon from one of the many fortifications around the city would fix on you with less accuracy. "I can find you a room with the family of one of my girls, if you wish."

It would have been so easy to say yes, I'd take the job, I'd live with the family of one of her girls. I could always have got Daddy's tuition money refunded by the school. Then I'd have had that plus the money from Johnny. But then the rest of my life I'd have been unable to see beyond the seam I was working on.

"Did you notice how the sun came out just as President Lincoln got up to speak on Inauguration Day?" she asked.

I said yes, I did.

"Most people remarked on that. I saw something else. I

saw the star that came out in the heavens. It was noon. It was a brilliant star. It was the noonday of his life at that inauguration. It was a sign, a summons from on high."

Now she sounded just like Ella May, who saw omens at the drop of a hat. The morning she left she'd said she was going not only because the government didn't give her two shifts but because there was a curse on the street. Bad things would soon happen here, she'd said. A curse on H Street? I'd laughed. The people here were so dull they would welcome a curse or two.

"We don't all get a star at noon," Mrs. Keckley went on. "The rest of us have to muddle through and find our summons from on high where we can. The trick is to answer it when it comes."

The trick for me right now was getting through Mama's death. I thought it a bit presumptuous that Mrs. Keckley thought her offer my star at noon.

"There is not always a star at noon, Emily. There is not always a star. But when a summons is given, we should take it."

"I appreciate the offer, ma'am. I would like time to study on it."

She set her cup down. She stood up. The broad shoulders in the black silk dress with the lace collar were straight. She was not accustomed to having her wishes disregarded, I could see that. "I hope you are not thinking of living with the Surratts," she said.

I stared at her. "I don't know yet where I shall live."

"That woman allowed her brother to take your mother's house. There is a serpent in the breasts of those people. Once serpents take up residence in a domicile, they do not vacate the premises."

I sighed. *For all your accomplishments*, I thought, *you are still like Ella May.*

"And now I will pay a short visit to your mama. Is that tea for her?"

I'd fixed a tray. "Yes."

She reached for it. I handed it over. "Don't tell Mama that Richmond has fallen," I said. "Her sister is there. It would cause her needless worry."

The yellow-green eyes met mine. She nodded in compliance. "We are all people of contradictions," she said. And then she said something else. "We all, at some time in our lives, have an acquaintance with darkness. It will pass." Her silk gown rustled as she went out into the hall and up the steps.

Half an hour later, when she left, she kissed me. "You will always have me for a friend," she said. I watched her get into the barouche and drive off. *Another friend*, I thought. *Suddenly I have friends all over the place.*

Standing on the front steps, I looked over at the Surratt house. Annie was just going up the walk. She'd been shopping. Her arms were full of bundles. She smiled and waved. I waved back. *Serpents in the breast*, I thought. And I laughed.

3

ℋNCLE VALENTINE

TWO DAYS LATER Mama was having one of her rallying days, so she said it was all right if Uncle Valentine came to call. He'd sent a note around. There were matters he needed to discuss, he said.

I got her out of bed, dressed her in a good morning gown, fluffed up her hair, and gave her a goodly supply of clean handkerchiefs. She was spitting up blood. I knew she would want to conceal this from Uncle Valentine, what with him being a doctor.

"A noted surgeon," Mama called him. She said it with mockery. I did not understand why. Uncle Valentine had gone to school at the University of Edinburgh, in Scotland. For most of the war he worked long hours in Washington military hospitals. He now taught at the National Medical College. And did experiments in his laboratory there.

For as long as I could remember he had been looking for a cure for the Wasting Disease. I did not know what this disease was. But he was obsessed with finding a cure for it. Mama said he sometimes took in people off the street when he thought they had it.

"He studies them," she said. There was contempt in her voice. Mama also said there was no Wasting Disease. Even while she coughed up blood and wasted away in front of me.

"He claims his wife died from it," Mama said. "What she died from was drinking rum distilled through lead pipes."

The day Uncle Valentine came to call there was a parade outside our windows. Washington paraded if President Lincoln got over a cold. Still, I couldn't very well keep the fall of Richmond from Mama. The day was clear and bright for the first time in weeks. From outside came the sounds of cannon firing, people celebrating, bells ringing, soldiers marching.

When I told Mama about Richmond, she sighed. "So the war will soon be over, then. I am glad I lived long enough to see it. Have there been any letters from my sister?"

"No. But I'm sure it's just that she's too busy, Mama," I said.

"You can't go to Richmond to live now. She'll have all she can do keeping her own body and soul together." She seemed resigned. "Where will you go?"

"Mrs. Keckley has offered to find me a place." I didn't tell her the Surratts had offered, too.

She nodded. "Elizabeth is a good woman. I'm lucky to have her as a friend...Emily, you must promise me something. When I die, don't let my brother have anything to do with my body or the funeral."

I almost dropped the fresh daffodils I was arranging in a vase. "Mama, please don't speak of dying."

"I am dying, Emily. We all know it. So you must promise me."

"I promise, Mama."

"He'll want to arrange things. Run things. And do things. He has no rights. I want that understood. When I die, send for the reverend. He is to see to it that I am buried in a lead coffin."

"Yes, Mama." I did not like this talk about lead coffins and dying. But she was set on being morbid this first sunny morning in weeks.

"Now take me downstairs. I will receive Valentine in my parlor. Not in my bedroom, like an invalid."

Somehow I managed to get her downstairs without letting her fall and kill herself. I had just about propped her in a chair in the parlor and lit a fire in the grate, to ward off the chilliness of the room from so many days of rain, when Uncle Valentine arrived.

He was a half hour late. And agitated. In the hall I took his stovepipe hat. It was just like Mr. Lincoln's. And he wore a shawl around his shoulders like Lincoln, too. Uncle Valentine adored Lincoln.

"Horse racing on E Street!" he said. "Within a stone's throw from the Congressional cemetery! Have people no respect?"

"Whose funeral were you attending?" Mama asked.

"Nobody's funeral." He stepped into the parlor. "Haven't I a right to go to the cemetery and visit the grave of an old friend?"

"What old friend?" Mama asked.

"Does it matter?" He handed me a package. "For the flower of H Street," he said. Then he kissed me. "Hello, Emily, how are you, dear? How is school?"

"Fine." He liked me. I was not a coquette, he said, like most Southern girls. I did not bat my eyelashes and pretend helplessness. Who did I have to bat my eyelashes at? How could I pretend helplessness? I'd been Mama's mainstay.

Before we moved to Washington I didn't really know him. Since moving here I knew him only from his visits to Mama, which always had undercurrents of arguments. It came out in one of those discussions that it was through him that I'd been accepted into the fancy Miss Winefred Martin's. You had to have family connections to get into the school. Uncle Valentine knew the headmistress, Miss Martin herself, from when he'd been young. And had cleared the way for my acceptance.

Many times he wanted to take me somewhere: to the opera, to the Baptist church on Tenth Street to hear Adeline Patti make her Washington debut, to the National Theater, to Harvey's for oysters. Mama would never let me go. "He wants to steal you away from me," she'd say. "He has no children of his own. He has always envied me you."

"Are you keeping up with your lessons?" Uncle Valentine asked.

"Yes, sir." He had made arrangements with my school so that I could study at home for a few days, since Mama was failing. He'd spoken to Miss Martin about it. "But I'm no flower, Uncle Valentine," I said.

"You're a flower about to bloom. You're just waiting for the right time."

My daddy would have said that. I missed my daddy. That

was part of why I liked Uncle Valentine. I needed to hear things like this from a man I could look up to. But I liked him, too, because he kept coming to see Mama, in spite of her insults. And because he was debonair. He had a flair about him that bespoke a man of the world. He was an important surgeon in Washington. He had led the fight to get the offal cleaned from the streets to prevent disease. He knew influential people. Young medical students considered themselves lucky to get into his classes. Everyone respected him. Everyone but Mama.

He loved baseball almost as much as he loved Abraham Lincoln.

"They're the same," he'd say. "In baseball, three strikes and you're out. Lincoln's had his two strikes already, his crazy wife and his bad generals. All he needs is one more and he's out."

He would not conjecture what the one more was.

"How are you, Mary Louise?" He stood in front of Mama, bowed, took her hand, and kissed it. Then he held on to the hand.

"Don't take my pulse, Valentine," Mama said. "I have my own doctor."

He released her hand and sat down. I brought him his usual glass of wine. He sipped it and regarded Mama. "Has Dr. Dent been around?"

"Last week."

"Does he have you on the same medicine?"

"Yes."

"It's not doing you much good, Mary Louise."

"I'm much better," Mama insisted. "I'm up and around today and feeling much better."

"Your eyes are too bright. Your face is feverish."

"She's run out of medicine," I blurted out.

"Emily!" Mama chided.

But I didn't care. "I've sent a note around to Thompson's for more," I said. "A man is bringing it this afternoon."

Uncle Valentine slipped a hand into his pocket, withdrew his billfold, and put some money on a small table.

"We don't need that," Mama said quickly.

"Don't be foolish, Mary Louise."

"We have money, Uncle Valentine," I said. We didn't; I did. But neither Mama nor he knew it. Mama's pride wouldn't let her deny it, of course. "And anyway," I added, "Thompson's won't charge us."

"Not charge you?" He scoffed. "Thompson's charges everybody twice what their medicine is worth. Why has he suddenly developed this altruistic streak? In honor of Richmond falling?"

"In honor of my friendship with Johnny Surratt," I said. "Johnny made the arrangements. His friend works for Mr. Thompson."

He scowled. "Surratt?" He seemed to be searching his mind for something. He set down his wineglass. But he said nothing.

"Johnny and Emily were always friends," Mama told him. "You remember. From Maryland. He's been like a brother to her. You know his mother and I went to school together."

"That fancy girls' school. It gave you notions, Mary Louise."

"All girls have a right to notions," Mama said.

"You haven't spoken to his mother since her brother foreclosed on your home."

"I won't deny the children their friendship. Neither Mary nor I protest it. But it's over now with Johnny. He left the other day on a long trip."

23

I'll say one thing for Mama. She has always allowed me my friendship with Johnny and Annie. She was defending those friendships now. Of course, she would defend my friendship with the Devil himself if it meant going against her brother. Still, I thought this as good a time as any to tell her I'd been invited to live with the Surratts.

"My friendship with Johnny isn't over," I said. And I told her about the invitation. To my surprise, it wasn't Mama who was upset by it. It was Uncle Valentine.

"You can't be meaning to let this child go and live with the Surratts, Mary Louise," he said.

"I'm glad to know she has people to care for her."

"She has me."

"Don't start that again, Valentine."

"I'm your brother! Her blood uncle. You'd rather have her live with strangers?"

"Mary is still a dear friend to Emily. She runs a good boardinghouse. Her daughter, Annie, is only a few years older than Emily and like a big sister. Emily can't go to Richmond now. And she needs to stay here and finish her schooling."

"She can live with me," Uncle Valentine said again. "For once in your life, Mary Louise, listen to me. You never did before."

"I know. And I married Edward. He wasn't a good provider. And we lost our home."

"Edward was a good provider. It just wasn't enough for you, Mary Louise. You were too much the Southern belle."

"I never was!" Mama said. But she preened, nevertheless, tossed her head; and for a moment I could see the remains of the Southern belle my uncle accused her of being. "You may be right about me," she sniffed, "but you are not right about the Surratts."

24

I fetched a tray of tea and poured Mama a cup, then put honey in it. I feared for her. She was using all her strength to best Uncle Valentine. Tomorrow she'd be spent.

"Don't argue," I pleaded.

"We must settle this," Mama told me. Then she turned to her brother, and it was as if I were not even in the room. "You may know baseball, Valentine. And sickness. But you do not know people."

"I know of the Surratts," he said. "They are trouble."

"Trouble?" Mama even managed a laugh, though she near choked on it and I had to give her water and pat her back. Then she waved me away. "Trouble? And you are not?"

"I have honest dealings, Mary Louise."

"Honest, indeed!" Mama smiled. It was a smug smile, as if she knew something. "I am too close to the grave to have you mince words with me, Valentine."

"I won't mince, then. The Surratt house in Maryland is a stopping place for blockade runners, spies, and no-'counts."

"We know Johnny has run the blockade. He's Secesh. We are at war, Valentine."

"Dr. Mudd, a colleague of mine in Maryland, told me of them. John Wilkes Booth made a trip down there with Johnny Surratt. Booth claimed he wanted to buy a farm from Mudd. Mudd thinks Booth just wanted to get to know the lay of the land."

"What is wrong with wanting to know the lay of the land if you are going to buy a farm in Maryland? I wish my Edward had learned the lay of the land."

"Why would anyone venture into Maryland now, with such devastation there, to buy a farm? The Surratts are up to no good, the lot of them. Something evil is brewing there."

"Evil," Mama repeated.

"Yes. I know evil when I see it."

"You should," Mama said. "But you are wrong this time. You may object to Booth as an actor and therefore not desirable company for young girls, but with Johnny gone, I doubt if Booth will be coming around anymore. You go out of your way to distress me. If there is nothing else you can say to convince me that Emily should not live there, you should hold your tongue. I know you want her to live with you. But I do not wish it. And it distresses me that you would attempt to tarnish the name of my old friend to secure your own ends."

"It distresses me that you are so angry because I want to give your daughter a good home. And try to keep her from having me as her protector, even after you are gone."

I could stand it no longer. "Stop fussing," I said.

They both looked at me as if they'd forgotten I was there.

"I love you both." My voice broke. "I really do love you, Uncle Valentine. In spite of what Mama says. I can't bear to see you arguing all the time. I always wanted a brother. Or a sister. And you two have each other and all you do is fight!"

There was shocked silence. I got up. "I'll fetch your coffee, Uncle Valentine," I said.

"I can't stay for coffee."

"You'll stay!" I almost shouted it. "It's dear. Twenty-one cents a pound! I got it at market yesterday and you'll stay. And stop fussing! Both of you!"

He stayed. I brought out the coffee and some peach cobbler. I'd made it that morning. They didn't argue anymore. Uncle Valentine started telling us how he'd summoned the police, and the sporting men who'd been racing their horses on E Street had been arrested for reckless driving.

I wasn't listening to him. All I was pondering was what

he'd said about the Surratts' house. And how evil was going on there. And Ella May's words about there being a curse on the street we were living on. Then that serpent-in-the-bosom business that Elizabeth Keckley had spoken of.

Could all these people be wrong? I shivered, then looked up and saw Mama was failing. "You'll have to go, Uncle Valentine," I said.

He left. I walked him into the hall. He put on his stovepipe hat, his coat and shawl. "You're a good girl, Emily," he said. "A fine girl. You know your mind. I hope you'll sort things out for yourself and not hold against me anything that your mother has said."

"I won't," I promised.

"Are you going back to school soon?"

"Yes. I'd like to go back after everything is over."

"Your mother could linger for weeks."

"Well, I must find someone to come stay with Mama during the day. Ella May up and left, and I'm alone now."

"I'll send over Maude. She can spare the time."

"Thank you, Uncle Valentine."

"If you come and live with me, I'll not be overbearing. I'll not tell you what to do, but I'd be honored to have you. Think on it, Emily."

I said I would, to please him. But I never intended to live with him. Oh, he had a lovely house on a fancy street. . . . I'd never been inside. Mama had pointed it out to me once. Who would not want to live in a house like that?

"Let me know if your mother worsens," he said.

I promised that, too. He left. I never thanked him for the violet water.

4

ROBERT

MAMA TOOK TO HER BED the day after Uncle Valentine's visit and never got out again.

It wasn't his fault. He had done what any brother would do, come to visit her. If I had a brother and I were dying, I'd want that.

Mama coughed and coughed so. And got weaker and weaker. Sometimes she lay so still I thought she'd died on me. But then she would start coughing again. Her forehead was hot, her hands clammy, her breath shallow.

I got frightened and ran to the Surratts' to get a servant to take a note to Dr. Dent. He came around, but there was little he could do. He wrote an order for more medicine. Again I went to the Surratts', and got a servant to take the order to Thompson's Drug Store.

Then I waited all afternoon. But Johnny's friend David Herold never delivered the medicine.

I went to the Surratts' a third time. A servant ushered me in. Mrs. Mary was in the parlor.

So was John Wilkes Booth. I stopped short, seeing him. He was pacing back and forth. He looked disheveled, angry. Like an alien thing in that dainty parlor. "Damn them, damn them," he was saying. "Damn all the talk of surrender! Couldn't Lee have held on?" He directed the question at me.

Was he rehearsing for a play? Was I supposed to answer?

"So many times he had the Federals cornered. Doesn't he understand the importance of the kill?"

I did not know my lines. I stood, dumbstruck.

Booth looked right at me, his eyes burning. "The fools! All of them! Don't they know what will happen once Lee surrenders?"

"What is it, Emily?" Mrs. Mary asked.

"I need someone to send a note to my uncle's house. Mama's taken a turn for the worse."

"Of course." Then she turned to Booth. "This girl's mother is dying," she said.

"We're all dying," Booth said. "Some sooner than others, that's all. Some not soon enough!" Again he looked at me. "Do you study Latin in school?"

"Yes," I said.

"Then tell me this, is *tyrannis* spelled with two *n*'s or two *r*'s?"

I liked it. It had passion. Not like so many of the milksop plays here in Washington. But I didn't think it would get past the Union people.

Mrs. Mary didn't like it. "Enough, Wilkes," she said. She

called him Wilkes, not John. Annie said it was the name of some famous English ancestor.

Mrs. Mary called a servant and had my note delivered to Uncle Valentine. Then she saw me out. "Let me know how your mama fares," she said. Then she went back into the parlor, where Booth was still ranting and swearing.

Uncle Valentine sent medicine—calomel, rhubarb, and opium.

He also sent Maude. She was a short, heavy woman with hair tied back in a bun, and glasses on the edge of her nose. She looked like somebody's mother.

Not mine. My mother had never looked or acted like anybody's mother. My mother acted like a Southern belle. It was all she'd ever wanted to be. A Southern belle. It had nothing to do with politics or being for or against the Union. She just wanted to play the part, be taken care of by everybody, have Negroes waiting on her. Then she married my daddy and found out it wasn't to be.

I'd been taking care of her since Daddy went off to war. Now I knew what I'd missed.

I recognized it instantly in Maude's broad face, calm manner, and busybody ways. She let me give Mama the medicine in the doses written on the bottles in Uncle Valentine's hand. I told Mama the medicine came from Herold. She never would have taken it if she knew her brother had sent it over. I told her Maude was a friend of Mrs. Surratt's.

Maude never sat down for a second but that she took up her knitting needles. She could knit without looking at what she was doing. All through the war she'd knitted things for the wounded soldiers and taken them to the hospitals.

"Who will you knit for when the war is over?" I asked. Mama was sleeping. We spoke in whispers.

"There are plenty of young men in the hospitals who still need attention. Your uncle still tends them at Douglas Hospital. Of course, let's hope they'll all soon be going home."

"I wonder what we'll all do when the war is over," I said. "I wonder what we'll blame our misfortune on."

She smiled at me. "That's an awfully astute thing to say."

I was thinking of Mama. That would make anybody astute. I shrugged. "People make lots of their own problems. Then they blame them on the war."

"Most girls your age are so tainted with their own concerns, they scarce notice a thing." The knitting needles clicked. "We had a young man staying at our house for a while who was one of the wounded from Fredericksburg. Your uncle tended him in Douglas Hospital, found out his father was a country doctor and the young man wanted to be a doctor, and brought him home to recover. He's attending the university now, and all your uncle's classes. His name is Robert deGraaf. He's a lovely young man but very much alone in the city. You should come to our house sometime and meet him."

"I have no time for socializing," I said.

"Not now, of course. But you will in the future."

I had no future; didn't she know that? But the way she said it, with a presumed knowledge about me, set my teeth on edge. Still, I was grateful to her. She settled right in. She cooked, she tended Mama, she received the reverend when he came. She sent me on meaningless errands to get me out of the house. To market for food. To post a letter.

On Sunday the ninth, General Lee surrendered to General Grant and the long war that had worn us all down, turned us against each other, and taken away every bit of graciousness from our lives, ended. Outside our windows Washington City went wild.

Inside, Mama was dying. She seemed to dip in and out of consciousness. Yet she held on. It was eerie, as if she were holding on for a reason, waiting for something to happen before she would die.

"What's all the shouting in the streets?" she asked early on Sunday morning.

"People are saying Lee is likely to surrender today," I told her.

"Oh, good," she said. "I'll just wait a bit and find out. Then I can tell your father."

The woman who always wanted to be a Southern belle was waiting to hear that the rebels were whipped, that her husband hadn't died for nothing, before she went to join him.

Around dusk the shouting got louder. Firecrackers started going off. They lit up the distant sky. People were coming out of their houses and gathering in the street, hugging each other, jumping up and down, screaming.

"Why don't you go out and see?" Maude suggested. "Maybe buy a paper."

"The papers won't have it yet."

"We have telegraphs."

I went. I didn't want to, because I knew that once Mama found out Lee surrendered, she would up and die. But I couldn't tell Maude that. She would think I was nervous or hysterical. Nervous and hysterical were the worst things a young girl could be. You had to be careful. Once they accused you of such, they watched you like hawks.... Maude would have told Uncle Valentine. She was devoted to him. And even though she was married, I thought she lived for him alone. Then Uncle Valentine would have had a claim on me, and I'd never have gotten to live with the Surratts. He did have a certain amount of power, after all. He was my blood uncle. I had no doubt that he could make me come and live with him if he had sufficient reason.

It was strange to be out on the street and not worried about attending Mama. It was dusk and mild. The air smelled of spring. Palm Sunday.

People were screaming, yelling, dancing in the streets now, setting off firecrackers on every corner. They were stringing bunting and colored lights from lamppost to lamppost. Young children ran unattended, rattling sticks on iron fences, throwing stones. One group of boys had a herd of goats they were pushing along. Goats, pigs, even cows were not unusual on Washington's streets, but these goats had red, white, and blue streamers around their necks. I remembered Mama telling me once that President Lincoln's little boys had had goats as pets in the White House. Before Willie died.

Groups of college boys were jostling each other and blowing paper horns. Some militiamen were shooting off muskets a block away. A man was hawking American flags. In the distance I heard cannon boom. Then church bells started. The college boys had put down their paper horns and were pulling up the plank sidewalks and starting bonfires. A horse-drawn carriage came along; the horse shied at the sight of the fire, then bolted, dragging the carriage. A policeman came along and started shouting.

At the corner of H Street I found a newsboy. "Read all about the meetings with Grant and Lee!" he was yelling.

I purchased a paper. "Is it over?" I asked him.

"Yes, miss. Word came to the White House coupla hours ago. Lee surrendered earlier today. The *Intelligencer* will have it all tomorrow."

I saw a crowd of revelers coming from around a corner and ran home.

Upstairs I gave the paper to Maude and told her the news. Mama was sleeping. But with the rattling of the newspaper, her eyes flew open.

"Tell me," she said.

"The surrender happened earlier today," I said. "At Appomattox."

"Good," Mama said.

Then she closed her eyes and slept.

In a little while, she died.

She just stopped breathing in her sleep. It was very peaceful. And I was taken with the fact that she didn't have to *do* anything to die. It took no effort. That was the shock of it for me. Seeing someone die for the first time, it came to me: You don't have to do anything to die. You just have to stop doing all the things you've been doing all along. In Mama's case, this was not coughing anymore. Not breathing.

I saw it at the same time as Maude. "Mama!" I yelled.

But Maude took hold of my wrist. "It's all right, she's gone."

"All right? All right? How can it be all right? I never wanted to go and get that stupid newspaper. I knew the minute she found the war was over, she would die on me. But you had to have it, didn't you? You had to let her know!"

Maude went over to the bed and closed Mama's eyes. Then she came back and put her arms around me. I pushed her off. I flailed at her with my arms. I had to hit somebody, didn't I? Still, she held me. "Go ahead," she said, "hit me if you want to. It's all right."

I told her I didn't want to hit her. I wanted her to send for the reverend. She made me a cup of tea. I drank it, and then I collapsed.

I slept for fourteen hours. I think Maude had dosed the tea with laudanum. I opened my eyes at eight the next morning and couldn't figure where I was. I thought I was back in my bedroom in our house in Surrattsville. I smelled coffee. Mama was making breakfast. Today I would go to the store, because Johnny was coming home.

And then I remembered. I was in Washington. Mama had died. Johnny was gone and would likely never come home again.

I got up and sat on the edge of the bed.

If I were home in Surrattsville now, I wouldn't have to move from the edge of this bed, I thought. *Our one remaining servant would come to my room and help me dress, take me out onto the front porch, where I would receive neighbors. They would bring food and let me sit there so I could mull my fate properly, the way it is supposed to be mulled.*

Here I had no such luxury. I had to do for myself.

I heard voices downstairs. One was Uncle Valentine's. I stumbled about my room. Uncle Valentine must not see me sloppy. He must not think I was an orphan, needing him. I put on a fresh cotton frock. I didn't have a black one. It was dark blue, with some white on the collar and cuffs.

I went downstairs. When I got to the bottom, some men came in the front door with a lead coffin, the one Mama had so insisted upon. *Why lead?* I wondered. *What was Mama afraid of?* It looked like one of the ironclads the North had on the Potomac River.

The reverend had come, was directing the men into the parlor, where Mama had been taken. "Everything is going according to plan," he said. He seemed immensely pleased with himself.

What plan? I wondered. Mama and I hadn't had a plan since we came here to Washington. Did we have one now?

"The undertakers are here," he explained. "Everything will be all right now."

I supposed that in the mind of reverends, everything got to be all right when the undertakers came. Well, that was their business.

"Doctors Brown and Alexander. They are the same ones who worked such miracles on Mr. Lincoln's little boy, Willie, when he died three years ago. They'll take your mama away for just a while and bring her back this afternoon. Don't worry. All her wishes are being honored."

I nodded my thanks. "What about clothing for Mama?"

"Maude selected it. I hope you don't mind. The brown silk with the lace collar."

Dimly, in back of my aching head, I wondered what the men would do about the hoops. They wouldn't fit in a coffin. But I was sure Doctors Brown and Alexander, who had worked such miracles on Willie Lincoln, would know what to do about a little thing like hoops.

"Fine." Tears dimmed my eyes. From outside on the street I heard noise, shouts, gunshots, cheering. "Are they still taking on about the surrender?" I asked.

"Isn't it wonderful?" He smiled as if he had arranged that, too. "General Grant never asked Lee to hand over his sword."

What could you expect? I thought. General Grant was like my daddy. He wouldn't have asked for it, either. I would have, all right. It was the least Lee could have done, hand over his sword, considering all the trouble he'd caused.

"We'll have to have a brief service in the parlor. The churches are all crowded with people giving thanks. As they should be. Then your mother will be interred at the parish cemetery of Christ Church tomorrow at one. Go have some breakfast."

I moved woodenly toward the kitchen. There I found Uncle Valentine, Maude, and a strange young man who reminded me of Johnny. My heart lurched. He wasn't Johnny, of course, but I didn't need anybody reminding me of him now. So I resented the young man on the spot.

"A million Northern men can now come home," he was saying to Maude. "That's what it means, this surrender."

Uncle Valentine hugged me, long and hard. "Are you all right?"

"Yes." I blushed under his concern. But it was good to be hugged.

"I don't like those circles under your eyes. Maude says you've slept. What is it, headache? You need to eat. And have some coffee. Then I'll give you something for the head." He pulled out a chair for me, and I sat down. The young man had gotten to his feet.

"Robert," Uncle Valentine said, "this is my niece, Emily Bransby Pigbush."

I saw that the mouth was fuller than Johnny's, the nose longer. But there was something of Johnny in the high cheekbones, the determined thrust of jaw.

"Please accept my condolences for your loss," he said. His eyes were very brown. And they had a look about them. Confused, and yet knowing. Like he'd just gotten up from the battlefield after being hit by a mortar shell.

37

"My name is Emily Pigbush," I told him. Might as well get that cleared up right off. "Uncle Valentine likes to add Bransby to fancy it up. Because Pigbush is so silly sounding." I was rambling, and I didn't know how to stop. "Everyone's teased me about my name ever since I can remember. Back in Surrattsville, in school, I finally got used to it. It doesn't plague me anymore. There was a girl in school there who had a worse name than mine. It was Fealegood. It's spelled F-e-a-l-e, but you can imagine the jokes the boys made."

"I can, yes," he said.

"I'd rather be a Pigbush than a Fealegood." I didn't tell him that my father used to call me Miss Muffet. That was my secret, not to be shared.

I stopped. They were all staring at me. I wanted to run and hide, but my head was pounding and I needed some coffee.

Robert poured some for me. Then he got up and went about the table heaping a plate of food. I noticed, right off, how he half dragged, half limped with his right leg. "When I was in school in Pennsylvania I had a friend named Goatarm," he said. He handed the plate to me.

I took it and started eating ravenously. Only then did I pay mind to the white tablecloth, Mama's good dishes, the display of food. Fresh-baked biscuits, ham, fish, and eggs, fresh fruit, fruit preserves, coffee. I was dazed. I wondered how these people had come to be sitting at our breakfast table, talking so amiably, when my mama had just died and the undertakers who had worked miracles on little Willie Lincoln were taking her away to do unspeakable things to her.

"Where did all this food come from?" I asked.

"There's more in the larder," Maude said. "From your

neighbors, the women your mama worked with, and your uncle. Eat."

"My head hurts."

Uncle Valentine made a movement toward a bag on the floor, took something out, and set it down by my plate. A powder. Robert gave me a glass of water.

I took it and swallowed the powder.

They started talking again. "A group of wounded soldiers were surrounded by crowds on E Street this morning," Robert said, "and made to recount their war experiences. Then the people hugged them and stuffed their pockets full of greenbacks. And I saw three effigies of Jeff Davis hanging from lampposts on my way here this morning."

"Fireworks popped all night," Maude said. "The whole city needs headache powders."

They compared notes about the revelry. I had the feeling they were talking just to fill in the spaces, talking around what needed to be said.

They were. "Come and live with me, Emily," Uncle Valentine said finally.

Maude and Robert looked uncomfortable. *So they know,* I thought. "I've already promised the Surratts."

"Valentine isn't a bad person to live with," Robert said. "He coughs a lot, mornings, and comes in all hours of the night. He goes to the theater and bets on baseball games. But he isn't a bad person to live with."

"You should be with family," Uncle Valentine continued. "Isn't that right, Robert?"

"Absolutely. Everyone should be with family," Robert agreed.

"I don't think you should do this to me now, Uncle Valentine," I told him. "It isn't fair."

"You're right. The decision must be yours." He stood up. "I have appointments. But first I'll stop by Alexander and Brown, however, and make sure they are doing justice to your mother."

"No!" I said it sharply. My cup clattered in my saucer. "No, please, don't go there. Leave it be. The reverend is handling everything. Just leave her be. Don't touch her."

He was taken aback. So was everyone else. "She is my sister, Emily."

His voice. He could do things with it, enunciate the words so carefully, make them carry so much weight, aim them so accurately. I felt ashamed.

"I'm sorry, Uncle Valentine," I said. "Those are Mama's wishes. I must honor them."

"I understand," he said. But I could see he was hurt. He gripped the back of the chair, his knuckles very white. "I shall not touch her, Emily," he said. Then he looked at Robert. "Are you coming with me?"

"I'll be along later. I'll walk back," Robert told him.

Uncle Valentine's eyes went to Robert's leg. "With that limp you'll be telling stories about Fredericksburg all morning and come home with pockets stuffed with greenbacks."

"I'll fend them off," Robert said.

There was something between these two; I saw it then. Uncle Valentine had a fondness for Robert. I felt jealous. He hadn't used that indulgent tone with me. Likely Robert adored him. All Uncle Valentine's students did. They would march into hell itself for him, Mama had once told me.

And then she'd said something odd. "Some have," she'd said. I never asked what she'd meant. But there was something about Robert, something in the eyes that made you know he had been in hell. And if it was Fredericksburg or some other hell he'd marched into for Uncle Valentine, I didn't know. It didn't matter. He'd been there.

Uncle Valentine was leaving. There was something I should say to him, and I didn't know what it was. The powder was just taking effect and I felt woozy. Maude got up to clear the table, saying something about putting up more coffee, that people would be stopping in.

Robert was staring at me. "You've hurt him," he said. "He's a good man. He doesn't deserve to be hurt. He saved my life and my leg, do you know that?"

"I heard tell."

"They wanted to cut my leg off, were just about to, when he came along and said no, he could save it. The doctor who wanted to cut my leg off had been on his feet for thirty-six hours and didn't care. He just wanted to get me over and done with. He was waving his saw and screaming at Uncle Valentine. They near came to blows."

"I'm glad you have your leg," I said, "but I've made my plans."

"You're making a mistake. A big one." He got up and stood looking down at me. "He is a decent, dedicated man. Do you know how many times he's gone to the Sixth Street wharves when the boats docked bringing in the wounded after a battle?"

"No, but I suspect you're about to tell me."

"That's where I first saw him. Standing there with the hospital workers and other doctors, when they brought me in after Fredericksburg. It was nighttime. The members of the Sanitary Commission were holding torches. The horse-drawn ambulances were waiting. It was like a scene from a

nightmare. But to us wounded, on deck, they were like an-
gels, standing there in all the confusion, with boat whistles
blowing and men groaning all around."

I let him talk. He had to.

"He tagged me immediately for Douglas Hospital. Then
he took me into his house to recover. When I did, I accompanied him many times to the Sixth Street wharves to receive
wounded. And he's saved more legs than mine, I can tell
you."

"I'm glad," I said.

"I know what families can do to each other. I joined the
army because my mother and father were always fighting. He
was a country doctor. She accused him of carrying on with
his woman patients if he came home late. It got so bad he
stopped coming home at all. He'd sleep in his carriage in the
woods. Her mind was poisoned against him. Like your mother's was against her brother. Wars end, Emily. But families
keep on fighting all the time."

Well, he had that much right, anyway.

He smiled at me. *God*, I thought, *he reminds me so much
of Johnny, I want to cry.* And then he stopped reminding me
of Johnny and reminded me of somebody different. And
exciting.

Himself. Only, how could he be exciting? A medical student with a gimpy leg?

"I'm very glad to have met you." He stepped away from
the table, ran a hand through his thick dark hair, and gave a
little bow. Then he kissed my hand.

Dear God, I thought, *he should have fought with the
Confederacy. All that chivalry.*

"I hope to meet you again, Miss Pigbush," he said.

"Did you really go to school with a fellow named Goatarm?" I asked.

"Yes. He was a childhood friend of mine."

"What happened to him? Did he ever live down the name?"

"No. He died. Killed at Gettysburg."

He went down the hall. I stood watching by the kitchen door. He made a little dragging sound with his leg. I thought, *His school friend was killed at Gettysburg. He almost lost his leg at Fredericksburg. And here I am sassing him. While crowds out on the street are crowding around wounded soldiers, making them retell their battle stories.*

"Don't take too many greenbacks," I called after him.

He turned and smiled, and it was better than Johnny's. Then he went out the door.

THE MILLER'S DAUGHTER

Annie Surratt was counting candles. She had dozens of them on the table in front of her.

I'd gone over as soon as Robert left. I needed to see Annie. She was the only one who could ever understand what I was feeling. And explain it to me.

I felt no real grief that Mama was dead. Only relief that it was over. For weeks I had been caring for her, missing school, confining myself to the house, watching her suffer, listening to her ravings about Daddy and unable to defend him.

Annie jumped up when she saw me. She hugged me. No words. She didn't have to say any. Her hug was enough.

"I've come to say I'll accept your mama's invitation to stay here."

"Oh, I'm so happy!" She hugged me tighter. "Come on, sit down. Do you want some tea?"

"No, I've been drinking enough coffee to sink an ironclad."

We sat together on the tufted sofa in the front parlor. In the corner was her mother's piano. Mrs. Mary played all the time. Their parlor was a gathering place for guests and boarders. There was lively conversation, friendly discourse, and good food all the time in this house. How could Uncle Valentine say the Surratts were trouble? How could Mrs. Keckley say a serpent had taken up residence here?

"I was thinking I could do chores around the house and earn my keep. Your mother always needs help with the boarders." I didn't want to tell anybody about Johnny's gold pieces. Not even Annie.

"You don't worry about that," she said.

I looked around the room, to the hand-carved paneling on the doors, the astral lamps, the rich draperies. I felt close to Johnny here. "Where is your mother?"

"Gone to mass. To pray for yours. I'm furious that she didn't get over to see your mama before she died. I kept after her. 'What good are prayers now?' I asked her this morning. But you know how Mama is with her religion. If I ever get that way, will you do something for me, Emily?"

"What?"

"Shoot me."

Annie's mother had sent her to convent school, and she had hated it. Not like Johnny, who'd wanted to be a priest. For most of the time I had known her family in Maryland, she was away at school. When she came home, she went wild, riding Johnny's horses astride, climbing trees, reading French

45

novels, and disappearing for hours at a time. In Maryland I had not been close to her. She was all blond curls, all dimples and girlish curves. She was disdainful of the pretty dresses her mother made her wear, dresses I would have killed for.

She was disdainful of everything. I would have killed to be able to be like that, too. I envied her because she seemed fearless of things all young girls were taught to fear. Things I feared.

When the family came to Washington last fall, she became my friend. She was sixteen to my fourteen. (She turned seventeen in January.) She was out of the hated convent school. Our paths crossed and we decided we were both fatherless, our mothers were impossible, and we both adored Johnny and hated being in Washington. It was enough for us to become fast friends.

We went everywhere together, to Gautier's for confections, to the triangle below Pennsylvania Avenue where General Hooker had concentrated the fancy women in their own colony. We gaped at them in their outlandish gowns. We went to the Smithsonian to see the stuffed orangutan in a glass case, and to hops at Willard's.

I was the first one she'd confided in about Alex, a young captain in the Northern army. The Surratts were Secesh. But Annie didn't care about politics. She cared about Alex Bailey. She and her mother fought constantly about Alex. There was something strange about the family. For instance, Annie's real name was Elizabeth Susanna. One day she just changed it to Annie. This was the kind of thing I loved about her. I knew that if her last name was Pigbush she'd change that, too.

"Shoot you?" We looked at each other and laughed. And then I leaned against her and cried. I couldn't help it.

She held me. "It's all right."

"No, it isn't," I said. "I'm not crying for Mama. I'm crying for myself. Annie, only you can understand this. I feel no grief for Mama. All I feel is glad it's over."

"Don't plague yourself with guilt. I can't stand guilt. It's what the nuns tried to put on me for years. You've lost both parents and now you have to figure out how you're going to live. And you're angry, too, aren't you? At both of them for leaving you."

"You're wonderful, Annie. You understand so much."

"I'm not wonderful. I'm truthful, something most people aren't. Most people are hypocrites. I can't stand hypocrites. Look at my mother. She goes to mass, hides in the church. But do you know what she's about these days? She's in love with Booth."

My eyes went wide. "She isn't."

"It's true. She's smitten with him. He's near twenty years younger than she is, and my brother's friend. And she chides me because I love Alex and he's fighting for the Union."

I did not know what to say.

"Booth's here all the time. Mama pets him, fawns over him, makes him special things to eat. It's disgusting." She went back to the table and picked up some of the candles. "It's why I'm going to put all these candles in the windows. Tonight. It's illumination night. All over Washington, every home will be ablaze with candles. Booth will be by. He'll hate it. So will Mama. 'How can you celebrate the defeat of the South?' they'll say. Well, I can and I will. I don't care about this old war anymore. All I care about is that Alex will soon be home."

She sat back down on the sofa next to me. "I know you can't take part in the illumination, what with your mama just dying. But would you like one candle to put in the window tonight? Your daddy died fighting."

"Yes," I said. "I'll take two candles. One for each front window in the parlor. Now I have to go home and pack, Annie. And work on finishing Mrs. Lincoln's dress."

She gave me two candles and walked me to the door. "I'll be by in a while and sit with you when people come. We'll have a grand time when you come here, Emily."

"Yes, grand," I said.

This house had its share of sadness, too. I was foolish to think there was any place that didn't....What with Mrs. Mary worrying about Johnny, the undercurrents between Annie and her mother, and now this thing with Booth, I was beginning to worry.

Was I doing the wrong thing coming here? Was Uncle Valentine right?

Then, in the next instant, Annie brightened. "Who was that handsome young man who came calling this morning with your Uncle Valentine?" she asked as I went out the back door.

"Handsome? Oh, that was a student of his, Robert deGraaf. They wanted to cut his leg off. Uncle Valentine saved it."

"How romantic."

"How can he be romantic? He limps."

"He has two legs," she said simply. "Many who will be coming home will have one. Some will have one arm or one eye." She gripped my arm as I went out. "I fear for my Alex. I haven't heard from him. He's been down-country with Sherman in Georgia."

"I'm sure Alex will be fine," I said.

"Promise me we'll always be friends, Emily. I need a friend like you."

I said yes, we would always be friends, and went home.

All afternoon people came, dozens of them. They brought chicken and biscuits, cake and corn pudding, oysters in cream sauce, and sugared ham, more cake, and long faces. They brought tears and gossip. I recognized a few women who worked with Mama, and some of Mrs. Mary's boarders. But Mrs. Mary didn't come. Annie did. She came and stood and sat with me. Others wandered in and out and said how lovely Mama looked in her lead coffin, and wasn't it God's blessing that she was at peace now?

They called me "dear." They clucked over me. They patted my head. I wondered where they all had been these last few weeks, when I'd sat here alone except for Ella May, in the rain, listening to Mama's coughing, wondering where I would get a chicken to put in the pot.

The wake took on a life of its own. It gathered momentum. And soon it had nothing to do with Mama.

"Who are these people?" I asked Maude.

"Some of them are professional funeralgoers."

"How do you know them?"

"Oh, I've been known to go to an occasional funeral myself. There are people who have no mourners, you know. It helps when some of us show up to pay respects." She smiled and handed me a cup of tea. When I'd just about drained the cup there was a taste to it that was different, a faint bitterness about it.

By the time the reverend arrived I was ready to agree with everyone that Mama looked beautiful. I think Maude had put something in my tea.

"Is my Uncle Valentine coming?" I asked Maude.

"No. You hurt his feelings. He felt it best he stay away. But he sent all the flowers."

Hurt his feelings? Yes, I supposed I had. I would have to make it up to him somehow. I looked at the flowers. The room was awash with them. But something was wrong.

"If he paid for the flowers he was cheated," I told Maude. "They look wilted already. They aren't blooming."

"They will be tonight."

"Tonight?"

"Yes." She smiled at me. "Over your mother's grave, in the dark. They are nightflowers. My husband delivered them earlier. They are from your uncle's garden."

Was she serious? Or was I muddleheaded from the tea? No matter, the reverend was starting prayers. I closed my eyes and sank back in the chair. Next thing I knew the reverend was saying good words about my mother, speaking about her in glowing terms. It didn't sound like my mother he was talking about, but like a stranger.

Before we left for the cemetery Annie took me into the kitchen and gave me a glass of cold lemonade. "Who is that funny little man who came in just before prayers?" she asked.

"I don't know. I didn't see him. I don't know half the people here, Annie."

"He looks like a dwarf. Like he should be in a circus. And he's all done up in tweed and a cape, like it's midwinter. He's spent most of his time near the coffin."

"My head seems fuzzy. I think Maude put something in the tea. Everything's soft around the edges."

"It'll be hard around the edges soon enough," she said.

They took the ironclad coffin outside. People went to the

waiting carriages. Annie and Maude went upstairs to freshen up. I was alone with the funny little man in the parlor.

"I don't believe I know you, sir."

He couldn't have been more than four feet tall. Yet he reminded me of somebody. He bowed, a sweeping gesture. "Miss Emily, is it?"

"Yes."

"Guess, guess, you will never guess my name," he said. His eyes twinkled.

Guess? I stared at him.

Then he sobered. "Please let me tender my condolences. Your mama was a lovely woman. Lovely. A great loss."

"You knew my mama?"

"I knew her indirectly. I am husband to Maude."

Husband to Maude? He was under five feet. Maude was *enormous* in comparison.

His eyes twinkled. "I am small of stature but big of heart," he said. "And I know your Uncle Valentine well. He could not make it today. I come as his emissary."

"What do you do for Uncle Valentine?"

"I am a man of all trades, Miss Emily. And because of my size I am looked upon fondly. All dwarves are these days. Ever since Tom Thumb and his wife were received by the Lincolns in the White House . . . I make deliveries for your uncle. Receive shipments. Facilitate things."

It was a vague answer. He looked like a gnome from my childhood fairy tales.

"The nature of your uncle's work is such that certain shipments must be delivered on time or they will spoil."

I understood then. "You bring the flowers!" I said. "The nightflowers! Like you brought them here today!"

"Ah, you put it so nicely. Yes, I bring the nightflowers. You have spoken a lovely sentiment there. Lovely. Nightflowers. Why didn't I think of it?"

But he had! Was the man mad? Before I could study on it, Maude came down the stairs, followed by Annie. "Merry, you aren't tiring this child with your gibberish, are you?"

"Maudee, Maudee, are my words gibberish?"

Merry? What kind of name was that for a man? He should change it.

He stamped his foot. "Now you've done it. You've gone and given away my name to this child. And she was supposed to guess it."

It was then that I knew who he reminded me of.

Rumpelstiltskin, the gnome in the fairy tale. From the Brothers Grimm. I could still hear my father's voice reading it. And telling me the lesson of it. "Don't ever enter into difficult arrangements just to save the moment, Miss Muffet," he'd said.

When the miller's daughter was put in the tower by the greedy king, to spin the flax into gold as her father had boasted she could do, Rumpelstiltskin had come to help, because she could not make good on her father's boast and was crying. If she did not spin the gold for the king, he would have her head cut off in the morning. Twice Rumpelstiltskin helped her, spinning the flax into gold. But she had to give him jewelry first. Then she ran out of jewelry and he demanded her firstborn child. She promised it. What did she care? She would never marry and have a child.

But she did marry. She married the king. Why anyone would want to marry a man who had threatened to have her head cut off, I never could understand. Even if he was a king.

Then they had a child. And Rumpelstiltskin came to claim her firstborn.

But she cried so, that Rumpelstiltskin gave her three chances to guess his name. So she sent scouts throughout the kingdom. One saw Rumpelstiltskin dancing in the forest, chanting his name, and told the miller's daughter, who was now the queen. And when the little gnome came back to claim the child, she guessed his name. Then he got contentious. He stamped his foot through the floor and was killed.

When Merry Andrews stamped his foot, I'd seen Rumpelstiltskin.

But then, who was Maude? Some scheming matron in a Grimm fairy tale, with her calming ways and bitter tea that set my head to reeling? I saw it now. Perhaps I wouldn't have if my head had been clear. But when I looked up at them standing in front of me, she towering over him with her arm around his shoulder, him smiling, it came to me that these two were not what they seemed.

She goes to funerals, I thought. *He delivers shipments on time, so they won't spoil. Why do I think he is speaking of something other than flowers?*

"Come along now, Emily." Maude put her arm around me. "Don't pay mind to him. He loves to spin tales. Don't believe anything he's told you."

"But he hasn't told me anything," I said. Or had he?

I had the feeling he had. And that I had been too doltish to understand. Oh, I wished my head were clear.

The cemetery was deserted and cool. The grave had been dug, the flowers were in place, the reverend said the words about ashes and dust, which I never will understand. How can we return to dust when we are supposed to be made in God's image? From about a block away came the strains of "Dixie" being played by a brass band. It was Abraham Lincoln's favorite song.

Someone handed me a single flower. Its head was bowed, its petals drooped. I set it on top of Mama's coffin. Then I looked up. There was Mrs. Mary standing across the grave from me. *In love with John Wilkes Booth*, I thought. Well, she'd gone to that fancy girls' school with Mama. Like Uncle Valentine said, it had given them notions.

Everyone was leaving the cemetery. The funeral was over. I felt spent. From the street it seemed as if the revelry were getting louder. Dusk was falling. Tonight all of Washington would be illuminated in honor of the end of the war.

Annie came up to me. "Booth took Mama to Surrattsville this morning. He's coming tonight, too. I can't wait until he sees my candles in the windows. And I'm not moving them. I don't care what anyone says. Do you want me to come home with you?"

"I'll take care of her," Maude said. "She's my responsibility until she moves in with you people, if that's what she insists upon doing."

Maude and I went home, and I put Annie's candles in the two front windows of the parlor.

"Now, why do you want to do that when you've had a death in your family and can be excused?" Maude asked.

"I don't want to be excused." The candles looked lovely. The windows were open and the sweet spring air drifted in. "My daddy fought in the war. And this may be the only war I'll ever be able to celebrate the end of."

"Well, I certainly hope so." Then she turned and went

back into the kitchen. "Come have your supper. There's plenty of food left over."

I followed her into the kitchen and sat down at the table.

"I went to the hospitals so many times with your uncle to attend the wounded. That's when you learn that suffering has no uniform," she told me. "Many times we met Mrs. Lincoln in the hospitals. She would bring flowers from the White House, candies, cakes, liquors, chickens, turkeys. Nobody knows this about her. She didn't want people to know. But we met her many times in the hospitals."

"What is she like?"

"A small, modest woman. Nothing like they write about her. She never wanted to be noticed. But I did speak to her on one occasion. It was right after they lost Willie. Do you know what she said to me?"

"What?"

" 'We must let them go and get on with the business of living. The only way to let them go is to mourn them. We must work at it, the same as we must work at being happy.' . . . I noticed you didn't cry today at your mother's funeral."

I fell silent. "I'm going upstairs," I said, "to finish Mrs. Lincoln's dress."

I don't know how long I worked on Mrs. Lincoln's dress. Perhaps an hour. Outside I could hear the sound of rockets going off, bands playing in the distance, music, and the shouts of people enjoying themselves.

Grief is hard work. We must work at it, the same as we must work at being happy.

Who would have thought that you had to work at grieving? Was it a chore you had to apply yourself to? Was that why Mrs. Lincoln had gone visiting the hospitals?

I had not worked at grieving for Mama. I had not even tried.

An especially bright rocket went off down the block, but it was as if it was in my own mind. I set the black silk dress with the white flowers on it aside and went downstairs, meaning to slip out the back door.

"Where are you going?" Maude was there, watching me.

"Out. I'm going out."

"Where, at this hour of the night, with the streets full of unsavory characters?"

"It's only eight o'clock. I'm going to the cemetery."

"What for? Lunatics go to the cemeteries at night."

"I'm going to work out my grief. Like Mrs. Lincoln. I'm going to cry for my mother."

She took off her apron. "You can't go alone. Take someone with you."

Not her. Please, God, I prayed, *don't let her want to come with me.*

"I'll send for a hack," she said. "Why don't you go and ask your friend Annie to go with you? She offered to keep you company tonight, didn't she? Go and ask her to come back here and wait for the hack."

I looked into her eyes to see if she was scheming. They were bland, innocent. *If she offers to make me tea, I won't take it,* I decided. *Because she'll put something in it again. Likely she'll knock me out this time.* But she was putting on her cloak and bonnet to fetch a hack. "All right," I said. I went out the door to cross the backyards to the Surratt house to fetch Annie.

$\mathcal{T}$HE MOLE AND THE SPOON

I waited outside the back door while Annie got her shawl. She slammed out of the house.

"Booth is making me crazy. I told you he'd make a fuss over the candles in the window, didn't I? I swear, he's a madman. Denouncing the people who are celebrating the war's end. Saying he hopes Washington burns down from all the candles in the windows. I'm so glad Johnny's gone away so Booth can't influence him anymore. Oh, the night is delicious!" She raised her arms to the crescent moon and smattering of stars overhead, and we tramped through the underbrush of the backyards. "Oh, what I would give to be with Alex on a night like this," she said.

"I'm glad you could come."

"I'm glad you asked. No, I'm honored. I think it's a

wonderful idea to go to the cemetery. It was so crowded this afternoon."

Maude was back from ordering the hack. It had cost her ten dollars. "You'd think prices would start going down now that the war is over," she complained. "But I was glad to pay it. It'll make me feel better, knowing you'll be safe. It will be here in an hour."

"An hour!" Annie and I both said it at the same time. "But we want to go now!" I told Maude. There was something devious in this, I was sure of it. "What will we do for an hour?"

"You can work on your sewing, for one thing," she suggested. "You said that dress for Mrs. Lincoln had to be finished tonight, didn't you?"

She was right, as usual. She took up her knitting. I ran upstairs and got down Mrs. Lincoln's dress, and Annie took up a needle and helped me finish the hem. The hour went quickly. The hack came, and as we went out the door I was laughing.

"What is it?" Annie asked. "Tell me."

"She didn't offer to make us tea," I said. And I told her how if Maude had offered, I would have known she was up to one of her tricks. "And I wouldn't have gone if she'd made tea, ten dollars or no ten dollars for the hack," I said. "I swear it."

Christ Church looked different at night, looming overhead with its stone architecture. It looked like something from the Brothers Grimm. Eerie candlelight flickered in the windows.

"They're still using part of it as a hospital," I told Annie. "I know your church doesn't do that, but ours does."

"The Protestants live their faith," she said. "We Catholics talk it."

Just then a cart pulled away from the church. We stood watching. The driver waved to us and we waved back.

"Dead soldiers," I told Annie. "They always take them away in the middle of the night, so people can't see. He's taking them to Arlington, the new national cemetery. It's on Robert E. Lee's front lawn, across the Potomac. How would you like to come home from the war and find your front lawn turned into a cemetery?"

"After what Alex told me about Gettysburg, I would think that man's mind is a cemetery," she said.

Annie's astuteness amazed me. I was always learning from her. We went around the corner and in the side gate of the cemetery. What with the candlelight from the church windows and the gas lamps on the street, the cemetery was not dark. Each tombstone stood out, though shadows played about in the slight evening breeze.

Mama had no tombstone yet. But it was light enough to see two people by Mama's grave. They were surrounded by tools, and they were using shaded lanterns.

And they were digging.

I grabbed Annie's arm. "Who could they be?" I whispered.

"Grave robbers," she said.

My heart lurched. I'd heard of grave robbers. At school the girls joked about them. All the girls in school boasted that they knew of someone whose relative's body had been robbed from the grave. But I never believed it. I thought it all talk. "Here?" I croaked. "In Washington?"

Annie gave me a look. "Especially here in Washington," she whispered. "Because of the war. Doctors have just come to realize how much they don't know about the human body."

I nodded, and Annie pulled me behind a tombstone that had an avenging angel on top of it.

"We have to do something," I told her. "We can't let them take my mother!"

"Wait." She got down on the ground and crawled around the tombstone to get a bit closer. I watched and waited. I was trembling, more from anger than fright. I could hear the soft but distinct digging sound coming from Mama's fresh grave, the *plop-plopp*ing of soft earth.

They were trying to dig up my mother!

I gulped back a sob.

"Hush!" Annie ordered fiercely.

I hushed. She was a distance from me now. Then, having satisfied herself that she'd seen enough, she crawled back.

"They look like children," she said. "They can't be grown-ups. They're too small. They must be children out on a lark."

"Children? A lark? What children do such a thing?"

"I don't know, but Washington has changed with the war. Come on, we're going to stop them."

"How?"

She had a plan. I would circle around to the left of them and she to the right. "We'll scare them off," she said. "We'll make them sorry they ever drew breath."

We parted.

No sooner had I taken my first step, with shaking limbs, than a sound pierced the night.

"Whooooo! Whooo! I'm a-coming, Lord, I'm a-coming."

It was a lonely, soul-searing sound, half-animal and half-human. At first I thought Annie had made it. But in the next instant she was back beside me, clutching me so close I thought I'd die.

"Annie, what is it?" Fear ran through me, a cold river of fear, the kind that settles in your lungs and drowns you.

Annie pointed. "Look."

Did I dare? I did, and fair trembled at the sight.

There, in a far corner of Christ Church cemetery, rising above a large granite cross of a tombstone, there was a white figure—rising, rising, from behind the cross.

"Whooo! I'm a-coming, Lord, I'm a-coming." And it did come, out from behind the giant granite cross, with arms, *or whatever they were*, upraised.

"Annie," I whimpered, "it's a ghost."

I must give Annie credit. To my everlasting shame, I really believed it was a spirit unloosed on the world. Annie didn't. She was too practical, too unbelieving, too disdainful of everything to hold with spirits, unloosed or otherwise.

"Ghost, my father's nightshirt," she said. And her voice was so edged with distrust, with anger, that I clung to the wonderful sanity of it.

"What is it, then?"

"Someone who's outflanked us." Annie sometimes talked army talk. She got that from Alex. Usually she annoyed me with it, but now I thought it most reassuring.

Still, we clung together and watched as the "ghost" made its way around the headstones, *whoo*ing and calling upon the Lord for all it was worth, going right toward the grave robbers. Or children. Or whatever they were.

There was a sudden clattering as they dropped their tools, a screaming and a scrambling as they ran through the cemetery toward the gate, leaping over headstones, running around them, tripping and recovering themselves, the ghost in pursuit.

Annie laughed. Then I did. My laughter was more with relief than anything, I don't mind saying.

"That'll teach the little varlets," she said. "Oh, how I wish I'd thought of it."

At the cemetery gate the "ghost" had taken off its sheet and was waving long arms at the intruders. Its whole angular body agitated as it waved the sheet that had covered it.

"You, Spoon, you, Mole, go elsewhere for your subjects! I'll have you hauled off to county jail if you put in an appearance here again. Go to Potter's Field! Go to Harmony Cemetery. Let decent people rest in peace!"

The voice had familiar clear rich tones.

Uncle Valentine!

"Annie, it's my uncle," I said.

"I know." She sounded less than enamored.

"What do you suppose he's doing here? How did he know those two would be robbing Mama's grave? And who are they?"

"The Spoon and the Mole, didn't you hear him? Grave robbers."

"Children?"

"No," Annie said, "dwarves."

I said my proper good-bye to Mama.

Without a word to either of us, Uncle Valentine took up the long-handled shovel the grave robbers had left and replaced the earth neatly. Then he rearranged the flowers, which, as Maude had promised, were full blooming now in the dark, their lovely white petals giving off pleasant fragrances. I stared at them. I had never seen flowers blooming at night before.

He said a brief silent prayer and gestured to me that I should do what I had come to do. He and Annie walked away.

I knelt. But I could not form my thoughts. They raced through my mind, tumbled together, pulled apart, and ran away, only to scamper back into my mind, a mixture of fear, joy, and confusion, like the light and shadows around me caught up in the night breeze.

I couldn't concentrate. I thought of Merry Andrews asking me to guess his name, of Maude giving me that cup of tea, of Annie telling me her mother was in love with John Wilkes Booth, of the man in the cart hauling his grisly cargo of bodies to Robert E. Lee's front lawn for burial, of stitching Mrs. Lincoln's gown, of the dwarves digging around Mama's grave.

I thought of the way Mama had begged me not to let Uncle Valentine touch her once she died. And how vigilant he had been about chasing away the grave robbers, how respectful and tender. He had replaced the earth around her like one tucking in the blankets of a child, rearranging the flowers like you would for someone in a sickroom.

Had Mama been wrong about him? Why had her mind and her heart been so turned against him?

From the corner of my eye, I saw Annie and Uncle Valentine waiting for me at the cemetery gate. So I gathered my thoughts in like errant children and spoke to Mama.

"You should have seen him chase them, Mama," I told her. "Oh, it would have done your heart good. I don't know who they are, but I'm going to tell the reverend all about them. Oh, Mama, I'm so sorry I didn't cry today at your funeral. But I'm going to grieve, properlike, I promise you.

Just like Mrs. Lincoln said we have to do. And, oh yes, I finished her dress tonight. Annie helped me. I'm sending it over to Mrs. Keckley's place first thing in the morning. And tomorrow I'm going to pack my things and move in with the Surratts. And everything will be fine with me, Mama, you'll see."

I stayed a few minutes longer. I said some prayers. But it was no good. I still didn't feel as if I were grieving properly. I still couldn't cry. So I promised Mama I'd be back soon. I couldn't keep Annie and Uncle Valentine waiting any longer.

The driver of the hack Maude had paid ten dollars for had left. We got into Uncle Valentine's chaise.

"What would you have done if I hadn't come along?" Uncle Valentine scolded gently.

"Walked home and been accosted by every vagrant on the streets," I said.

"We most appreciate your coming," Annie told him. "But how ever did you know those two would be here doing their vile work?"

"I'm going to hire guards to watch over your mother," was all he said.

"I'm beholden to you, Uncle Valentine," I told him as his chaise drew up in front of our house.

"Are you?"

"Yes. And I missed you at the funeral."

"I wanted to come, but I didn't want to upset you."

"Oh, Uncle Valentine, I'm so sorry I hurt you."

"Then perhaps we can have a new start," he said. "Perhaps you will do me the honor of coming to my house for a luncheon tomorrow."

I looked up into his warm brown eyes. They were so earnest. They even twinkled. "Yes," I said. It felt good saying it. I was my own person now, making my own decisions. Mama was gone. I had to think for myself. I felt a certain freedom, doing so.

"I'll be there," I said.

$\mathcal{T}$HE HOUSE ON J STREET

UNCLE VALENTINE sent a hack for me the next day. I knew what Mama would have said. "It's a grandiose gesture. It has no substance." But I was grateful for it.

I took Mrs. Lincoln's gown with me and asked the driver to stop at Mrs. Keckley's, where I dropped it off. She was out. I was disappointed. I knew she'd just returned from a trip on the James River with the Lincolns. The president had met with his generals to discuss the war's end. The gown was needed, her assistant said. The Lincolns were going to Ford's Theater tonight.

I went on to Uncle Valentine's house. When I stepped out of the hack at 128 J Street, my spirits lifted. It was Good Friday, a marvelous spring day. I stood looking up at the three-story stone structure. Each floor had its own tower jutting out from the right-hand side. The windows in those towers seemed to sparkle like jewels in the sun. *Why,* I thought, *that top tower could be where the miller's daughter is sitting, crying because she cannot spin her flax into gold.*

It reminded me of the Brothers Grimm. Some kind of vine crawled up the wall of the house on the side of the garden. In the middle of the garden I could see a small pond, and behind it a stone shed, which in itself looked like a fairy-tale cottage. The whole place was enclosed by a tall black wrought-iron fence. Brass lanterns on either side of the double-glass front doors gleamed. There was something solid and permanent, yet something forbidding, about it, too.

Mama had always hated the house. "It's the putting on of gold and costly apparel," she'd said. She always went after Uncle Valentine with quotes from the Bible. But I didn't think that described the house. Or Uncle Valentine.

The door opened. A young girl stood there holding a cut-glass bowl of candy, and I thought her the most beautiful and delicate thing I had ever seen. She was wearing gray bombazine with a white apron and a lace collar. Her hair was tucked under a white kerchief, but wisps of it peeked out. It was a burnished brown.

"Come in, do. We're so glad to have you. Let me take your wrap."

I handed over my light shawl. From the back reaches of the house came the sound of children shrieking and laughing. "Is this the right house?"

She laughed. "They're from the Ebenezer Free School. I'm their teacher. We're pulling taffy today." She held out the bowl of candy. "Have one?"

I took one. They were nougats. Then she thrust out a slender hand. "I'm Marietta."

Her grip was cool, firm. "Your uncle isn't here yet. He's been detained. Come, let me show you the house."

"Are you kin to Uncle Valentine?"

She laughed again, a light, musical sound. "Kin? Hardly. Until last week I lived here. On the third floor. In the tower room."

The miller's daughter, I thought.

"No, my father wasn't a miller. He owned a plantation below Richmond."

I hadn't said it aloud, I was sure of it. Oh, I must watch myself.

She raised delicate eyebrows, indicating the floors above. "Someone else lives in that room now."

"How did you come to know my uncle?"

"He saved my life."

I stared at her. *Not another one*, I thought. But how? She was no more than twenty and in charge of herself. "How does someone like you need your life saved?" I asked.

"Come, I'll show you the house." She smiled at me. "I tried to drown myself," she said as she led me through the wide hall. The floors were highly polished, the place smelled of beeswax. There was a grouping of more strange-looking flowers in a bowl on a gateleg table. "Yuccas," she said. "All day the flowers hang down like bells at rest. At dusk they turn up to the evening sky to bloom all night."

"Nightflowers," I said.

"I have a whole garden in back. I'll show you later."

"Why did you try to drown yourself?" I asked.

"I jumped off the Navy Yard Bridge." We were paused in front of the parlor door. "I'm one-eighth Negro. I come from below Richmond. I was a slave. My master was my father. But he had three other white daughters, my half-sisters. When their beaux came around they'd always ask, 'Who is that pretty girl?' My half-sisters weren't so pretty. It was a curse that I was. So I had to be sold off. The girls demanded it. I was sold on the block in Richmond. My own half-brother bought me. He was running off to join the Union army. He was so against slavery. He'd fought with Father about it and purchased me as an act of rebellion. He brought me north with him, to Washington, and said, 'Now you're free. And now, so am I. You don't have to go home again and neither do I.' He left me some money, and I lived for a while in a small roominghouse. He went off with the army. He was killed in the Shenandoah Valley last August."

Her calm recitation gave me the chills.

"I ran out of money and had no place to go. I had no way to make a living. I had a choice: Become a fancy woman or drown myself. So I jumped off the bridge. The water was so cold. It was first light. All grayness and mist. No one about, or so I thought. Next thing I knew these two little dwarves were swimming beside me, pulling me out."

I blinked. "Dwarves?"

"I thought I was dreaming. They worked on me. Got the water out of my lungs, then one of them ran off and came back in a little while with your uncle Valentine. He brought me here and Maude took care of me. He gave me a home, got me a tutor, and now I'm instructing the little freedman children at the Ebenezer Free School."

She smiled. "School is out because of the end of the war, and their parents are working. So I brought some here today. He lets me do that, your uncle Valentine. This is the parlor."

All I could see was this girl standing on the block, being auctioned off. *One-eighth Negro.* She did not look Negro. How had she looked up there on the block? I'd heard about slave auctions. Annie had told me of them. *They pick up a girl's dress and show buyers what they're getting.* That's what Annie had told me. *And sold by her own father!*

I made myself look at the parlor. It was elegant. In the circular area that formed the bottom tower was a piano. The windows overlooked a side garden and were graced with yellow satin curtains that dripped like tears. The floors were highly polished and there were one or two Persian rugs. There was a cherry highboy, a desk, a gathering of chairs around a round table.

"You like it. You are drawn to it," Marietta said, again reading my thoughts.

I stared at her. *One-eighth Negro. Some of them have powers.* Did she? *I must be careful.*

"It's peaceful," I allowed.

"Dr. Bransby likes it that way. Come on upstairs, I want to show you something."

I followed her up the wide, uncarpeted stairs and gasped when she opened the door to a room that was the second-story tower. There was a cushioned window seat in the tower. In the middle of the room was a Sheraton four-poster draped in blue. Again, there was an elegant plainness about it. There was a small ladies' desk, a dressing table with a gilt-framed mirror, a chiffonier, a shelf filled with books. Lying across the blue-and-white bedspread was a blue velvet dressing gown.

"This is your room," she said.

I drew back, angry. "I'm not moving in."

"You don't have to. It's your room when you want to visit. He had it redecorated in blue and white because he knows blue is your color. Go and look at the books in the case. Go on."

Gingerly I stepped into the room and went to the book-case.

Sir Walter Scott; *The Adventures of Roderick Random* by Smollett; the plays of Shakespeare; John Ruffini's *Lavinia*—all three volumes; *Jane Eyre* by Charlotte Brontë; and so many others! I ran my fingers over the books, then backed away.

"Come downstairs now. Meet my charges."

Downstairs in the large kitchen in back of the house, Maude was at the stove, and six brown children, all under the age of ten, were pulling sticky candy. The girls wore pinafores, the boys large aprons. They were paired off into three sets, and they stood across the table from each other, the gooey caramel-colored candy stretched out between them. Their faces were splotched with flour. They were having a grand time of it, and when Marietta and I came into the room, they didn't stop. She had to clap her hands and silence them to introduce me.

"All right, all right, now you all will have to finish soon. Dr. Bransby will be back for lunch, and I told him we'd be finished."

"Help us, help us, Marietta," they begged. They gathered around her, sticky hands and all.

She handed me an apron. "We'll both help and get the job done."

I hadn't made candy like this since I was a child. And soon Marietta and I were both helping. Then the candy "set" and we got the children washed and helped Maude pack lunches for them—apples, cheese, biscuits. Six checkered napkins full. Maude made a pitcher of lemonade. They clutched the napkins close, and Marietta had them file out the back door.

Never had I seen a garden like this. "Is that a grape arbor?" I asked.

The children were gathering around the arbor, under the vine, and starting to eat their lunches.

"Not grape," Marietta said. "It's a chocolate vine. See how the branches are covered with small purple-brown flowers? Likely you thought they were grapes. As the afternoon warms, it will produce a sweet-spicy scent. It gets stronger at night. That other vine, growing on the side of the house, is a serpent gourd. The white flowers open late afternoon and bloom all night."

I nodded and walked across a stone path to the shed.

"Don't go there," she said. "Nobody goes there. It's Dr. Bransby's laboratory. With some specimens in it."

"What kind of specimens?"

"He does experiments on animals. Don't worry. They're all dead." She met my eyes.

I shivered in the warm sun. "I just wanted to see the rest of the flowers," I said.

"All right, then, I'll show you. Here. These by the shed wall are mouse plants. Don't they look like mice?"

They did, all clustered in a bunch like that. The flowers had dark brown tops and white bottoms, and a long tail wound out of each one. "Why are they blooming now?" I asked.

"I couldn't resist planting them." She beamed. "They aren't nightflowers, but they just look so dear. Like mice having a meeting."

"What is *that*?"

"Devil's tongue." She sighed. "I had such trouble growing it. I had to start it in a pot in your uncle's laboratory at the college. Under a skylight. And look how the flies are drawn to it. But it has a certain beauty. Sometimes it grows six inches a day. When it gets to eight feet a long liver-colored tongue will grow out of that green spike. And it will smell of decayed fish."

Was she mad? "Why do you want to grow something like that?"

"It has its own beauty. Everything does. Don't you think there is a reason for everything that exists in this world? And everything that happens? Even the bad?"

"No."

"I do. Or I wouldn't be standing here talking to you like this now. So much bad has happened to me. I look at it like fertilizer in a garden. It has helped my soul to grow."

"Well, I've had fertilizer in my life, too, then. But my soul could have done without it."

"You don't know that yet, do you?"

Now, what did she mean by that?

"This," she said, leading me over to a flower with willow-like leaves, "is an evening primrose. It will be yellow at dusk and gives off a lemony scent. This is a night-blooming cereus. The petals that bloom tonight will be white with dark yellow spikes surrounding them. Sometimes I cut one off and bring it into the house. By midnight it will be perfect."

"Those are the ones Uncle Valentine sent for my mother's wake."

"Yes. We often send some when a patient dies. It comforts him to do so."

"Why do you plant only flowers that bloom at night?"

"It intrigues me to know that certain things can only happen at night," she said. "It's a little sad, I think. Thoreau said that moonlight is a light we have had all day but have not appreciated, and proves how remarkable a lesser light can be when a greater light has departed."

We walked back to the pond. She showed me the water flower, spider lily, the turtleheaded flower, the maiden grass at the pond's edge. "The people from the Smithsonian have tried to get in here and see my flowers," she said, "but I won't allow them in."

"Why?"

"I want to keep this private. Your uncle enjoys it. I want it to be my gift to him for saving my life. And taking care of it gives me an excuse to keep coming and seeing him."

"If my uncle treated you so well, why did you move out?"

"Because it was time to be on my own. And because then he could give the room to someone else who needed it."

"Who's in there now? Someone else whose life he saved?"

"Someone whose life he's trying to save," she said soberly. "Her name is Addie Bassett. She's an old Negro woman. Don't go near her, ever."

"You needn't worry," I said. "I won't be coming back after today."

She was peeling apples for the children. They had crowded around her. "You'll be back," she said. She had the graciousness to flush and lower her gaze. "Sometimes I just know things," she said. "I can't help it and I don't like it, but sometimes I just do."

"And you think you know that I'm going to come and live here?"

"Yes."

"Well, you're wrong."

She sighed. "You'd best go inside and clean up. You've got flour on your face. . . . He'll be here soon. He likes his guests

74

to be on time. He's a good man. He gives money to the Ebenezer Free School. He cares for the health of my students free of charge. Christmas Day there is a constant stream of visitors here, people bringing him gifts because he helped them somehow. Here." She bent to cut a night-blooming cereus. "Wrap it in a wet cloth, then put it in water. Spanish servants in the sixteenth century dipped the branches in oil and burned them as torches at night."

I turned and went back into the house. Maude was bustling around as if President Lincoln himself were coming for lunch. She wrapped the flower in wet paper for me.

"Who is she?" I asked about Marietta.

She wiped the flour off my face. "Someone very special."

"I don't like her."

"Your uncle does. Very much. So be careful what you say about her."

It was just the two of us at the long, polished dining room table. Maude served. For the honor, she had changed into gray moiré with a white pinafore apron. The dress rustled as she moved about the room. She had made something called felet de beef. The windows were open and the mild April air ruffled the curtains. From outside could be heard the *pop-pop-popp*ing of some firecrackers a block or so away.

When she left the room, I waited to speak. I did not know what the purpose of this luncheon was; I would find out before I went mouthing off about anything.

"On the way here I saw a group of hoodlums attacking a Negro," he said. "I had to send for a policeman. I'm afraid that prejudice is becoming stronger against the Negro." He paused to take a sip of wine. His table manners were impeccable, I noticed, just like everything about his person. He was clean-shaven and his hands were long, the nails trimmed and clean. His shirt was the whitest, his cravat of good silk. And he gave off some spicy scent. Was it tobacco? Soap? I didn't know. But he fascinated me.

"Washington has lived through all kinds of threats. That of a Confederate takeover. Betrayal, physical hardship, and loss of spirit. Now some of our best Southern families here and elsewhere will suffer dishonor and poverty. I wrote asking your aunt Susan to come and live with me. A widow. What will she do in Richmond? It's all but destroyed. But no, she's as stubborn as your mother. 'This is my home,' she says. 'Here I will stay. Richmond will rebuild.'" He shook his head. "I just never will understand women."

Aunt Susie was the youngest in their family. Before I could reply, he gave the conversation a new turn. "Have you ever heard of Alexander Shepherd?"

"No, sir."

"In 1861 he was a gas fitter's assistant. He is now one of four owners of the *Evening Star* newspaper. Family and heritage no longer matter. The war has made instant millionaires. People for whom money is the only reward." He shook his head and spooned his felet de beef into his mouth.

"Mrs. McQuade, my teacher, says the next thirty years will make many millionaires," I told him.

"She's a good woman. Very smart. I have been to visit her at the school. She says you are getting the highest marks in French, English literature, composition, and drama."

"You visited my school?"

"I wanted Mrs. McQuade to know you are not without family. She asked when you are coming back."

I was dumbstruck. In all the time we'd lived in Washington, Mama had never set foot in my school.

"All the girls there have family paying close mind to their progress," he said.

I thought of Myra Mott, Stephanie Wilson, Melanie Hawkes. Family? They had more than family. They had kinfolk that went back to the original settlers of Maryland and Virginia. The girls lived in houses that would make this look like a shack on Murder Bay. Before the war they had summered in Saratoga and their mothers had taken shopping trips to New York. Their fathers had business dealings in Lexington, New Orleans, connections in Boston. They banked in London, were on familiar terms with Du Ponts in Delaware.

"Mrs. McQuade knows your mother did not have time to attend theatricals you were in. Or your piano recitals. Because she had to work for a living. I would be most happy to attend. If my presence does not offend you."

He was being so kind. It made me ashamed for giving him an uneven time of it.

"There are no strings attached. I assure you. By the way, did you know that Mrs. McQuade's maiden name is Desrayaux? That her parents were guillotined in the French Revolution?"

"No."

"Yes. She was brought to this country as an infant in 1794. To French Azilum, in the Pennsylvania farmland. It was a log-cabin community built for emigrés fleeing the terror of the Revolution. They built a great-house for Marie-Antoinette. And settled in to await her arrival. And that of Louis-Charles, her son, the dauphin."

I was stunned. "She never told us."

He shrugged. "People confide in me. Did you meet Marietta?"

"Yes."

"A fine girl. A wonderful girl."

"She's got powers," I told him.

"We all have powers, if we choose to recognize them. Hers are exceptional. And that garden of hers is really beautiful, isn't it?"

"Did you save her life?"

"Others found her and brought me to her...I was hoping you two could be friends."

He talked some more about Louis-Charles. "Over a dozen men came forth over the years claiming to be the dauphin, but their claims were never proven. Imagine that he may be in this country somewhere, perhaps living as a back-woodsman."

"The girls at school say he is the owner of Gautier's, the sweetshop."

He raised his wineglass to me. "Then the next time you go for ice cream, think of who made it. We never know who people really are, Emily. Remember that, always."

It seemed to be the point of the story, the whole point he was trying to make.

When the meal was over I made a pretty little speech. "I appreciate your having this luncheon for me, Uncle Valentine," I said. "I'm beholden to you for what you did at the cemetery and for posting a guard at Mama's grave. And for going to my school. And I'm sure we can be friends."

He walked me out to the hack in front. "You are welcome here, Emily," he said. "Anytime." He kissed me. "I hate to think of you going back to that empty house tonight."

"I'll be fine. It's only for one night."

"Lock your doors. And remember, I am here if you need me."

I thanked him again. He seemed distracted, as if his mind was somewhere else.

It was. He told me just before I left that he was going to Ford's Theater that night with a doctor friend. He was looking forward to seeing the Lincolns.

8

$\mathcal{H}$OME ALONE

UNCLE VALENTINE had been right. Home was dreary and dismal. My footsteps echoed in the deserted rooms. The landlord had come in my absence and taken up the rugs for cleaning. All my things were in boxes. The dust made me sneeze. I went into the kitchen and put the night-blooming cereus in a vase of water. I would put it in my bedroom. On my way upstairs I avoided the parlor, where they had laid Mama out. I would have avoided her bedroom, too, but I was missing a good shawl. I stopped in the doorway, saw the bed where she'd lain for the last six weeks, the imprint of her head on the pillow—and fled. Forget the shawl. But there were still some boxes of her things to go through. So I took them into my room.

One box held old love letters to her from my daddy. I read

them all on the floor of my room, with the dust motes floating in the late-afternoon sunbeams and the night-blooming cereus in a vase on the floor beside me. I devoured them. When I looked up finally, it was dusk, shadows everywhere. I was starved for food. That's what the love letters had done to me.

But downstairs I couldn't find matches or candles. Finally I discovered some matches on the mantel in the dining room. Then I remembered the candles Annie had given me. I crept into the parlor. The mirrors were still covered and the cloth draping them was ghostly white. I fetched the two candles and took them into the kitchen. The parlor was not to be borne.

The fire in the stove had gone out. There was some kindling but no paper. I searched and searched. Now what to do? No fire, no tea. I fetched the box of love letters, put them in the stove, piled the kindling on top, and watched them burn. They made a good fire. Mama would have cried, I thought, but my daddy would have said, "Good girl, that world's all over with, and you must go on." I set some water to boil, searched in the larder to see what was to be had to eat. Not much. Some cold ham and leftover hard biscuits. No milk, no butter. Hadn't there been a pot of strawberry jam this morning?

The place was wiped clean. Maude had taken everything. Why? Because she wanted me to be miserable when I came back here. So I would flee back to Uncle Valentine's. Well, I would settle for cold ham, hard biscuits, and tea without milk. I sat down and waited for the water to boil.

The house was so silent. I wished I had a cat or a bird. I'd had both back in Surrattsville, but Mama wouldn't let me bring them here. Annie took care of them for me. The cat had been old and died. Annie had let the bird go free. I'd always wanted to, but Mama had said no.

Mama again. Would I never stop thinking of her? Even in anger?

Mama was gone! The fact of it closed in on me. How could she be gone? For my whole life she had been moving about in the background, telling me what to do, complaining, plaguing me for the most part, but *there*.

Now she was gone. The quiet mocked me. I was worn down—there's the truth of it—from the last six weeks of nursing her. I was glad the drudgery was over. No more cleaning up bloodstained handkerchiefs or sheets. No more changing the bedding because she'd wet herself. No more hearing her hacking cough in the middle of the night. That's why I was unable to cry. Because I was glad it was over.

By her own admission, she had been a selfish person. "My daddy spoiled me so." She was proud of it.

Mama, Uncle Valentine, and Aunt Susie had grown up in a two-story frame house in Richmond. It had upstairs and downstairs galleries, and outbuildings for servants. Mama said her father was collector of the port, but I think he must have owned the port for all the money they had. Her family had eight slaves just to keep that house in Richmond. Her father also owned a country seat in Roanoke.

My daddy never deceived her. He was not wealthy. But he had gone to West Point. He was still in the army when she met him. It was 1848 and he had just returned from the Mexican War, dashing and full of the Devil's own merriment, as Aunt Susie once told me.

Uncle Valentine was back from Edinburgh, Scotland, a doctor already. "He has no money, Mary Louise," he told Mama. "And you need money to live."

"Don't marry him," Aunt Susie begged her, "you'll kill each other." Aunt Susie was sixteen and had already toured Europe, where she had learned, apparently, how some men and women who are in love can kill each other.

Mama married him. She did not think she needed money to live. She thought that what she needed was culture, gallantry, protection, tradition. Daddy had all those things. I remember her saying that Uncle Valentine was crude and cruel, Aunt Susie jealous.

The water started to boil. I got up and made tea. I found an old pot of honey that had eluded Maude. I poured it into my tea, lots of it, and sat sipping the hot sweetness. I put some honey on the dried biscuits.

Daddy stayed in the army for two years after they married. When he was sent to other posts Mama lived in Richmond with her family. That's when he wrote her all those love letters. Then in 1851 I was born; Daddy left the army and bought the place in Surrattsville from Johnny's daddy.

He made it into a lovely little farm. He was a success. The only failure was in Mama's eyes because it was just a farm. She had wanted a country seat.

And then, too, Daddy would not buy slaves. He and Mama argued constantly over it. She said a woman bred to gentility and culture had slaves. Daddy hired her one housemaid. All the other hired help was for the fields. Then came the panic of 1857. I don't know what a panic really is. It seems I've been in a panic all my life. But when it has to do with the failure of trust companies, shipping lines, and cotton crops, everybody loses money. Mama's parents, who have both died since, were wiped out. They lost near everything, or I think Mama would have taken me and gone home. We muddled on for four more years. That's a long time to muddle. When the war broke out, Daddy said he was duty bound to re-enlist.

"The Confederate Army will honor your commission," Mama told him.

"Most likely," Daddy answered, "but I prefer to get my old commission back in the army of the United States."

This was the argument over slaves, with a new twist. Mama could not abide it. All our neighbors were going off to fight for the Confederacy. Daddy left for war a sad man, thinking he'd failed my mother. She let him think it.

I have never forgiven her for that alone.

She let the hired help go, let the fields go fallow. She and I lived on what we could grow in the kitchen garden. That's when she took up the occupation of the needle. Aunt Susie, who had married a wealthy planter, introduced her to some rich ladies in Richmond. Mama sewed for them. I think when Daddy was killed and Johnny's uncle foreclosed on the farm, she was glad to come to Washington.

I had no right to miss her now. But I did. I missed her so bad I wanted to die. You don't have to love somebody to miss them. You get used to having them around, like a cat or a bird. I finished my tea and went to bed. I had to be up early in the morning so I could move in with the Surratts.

During the night I heard it. A sound outside my windows like a great cry, as if a wild beast had been loosed in the night. I roused myself and sat up.

The first thing I saw was that flower on the nightstand, blooming for all it was worth. I made my way to the window. In the distance there were torchlights. Then I heard a drum and the sound of many pairs of feet marching, double time.

Next came shouts. A man dashed by on horseback. A door

opened in a house across the street. Another cry. "Shot, shot, I tell you!"

So far no one had been shot in the revelry that reigned on Washington's streets. Now, finally someone had been. Likely some drunk. I went back to bed.

Then, just as I was dozing off again, I heard it distinctly. Two short staccato raps on the wooden sidewalk, repeated three times. The danger signal of the Union League, a secret loyalist society. Annie had told me about it.

I heard doors slamming. Again I went to the window. People were throwing on clothes as they poured out into the streets. They were huddling in bunches, lighting torches.

Something had happened. What? Were the Confederates coming to attack though the war was over? Well, there was nothing I could do but wait until morning and then go over, as soon as I could, to the Surratts'. I lay awake for a while staring at the flower that fairly glowed in the room, listening to the commotion in the street, grateful for the safety the Surratt house would offer. Then the noise outside died down. I fell asleep. When I woke up it was to another noise.

A pounding on a door, insistent, angry. I heard yelling.

"Let us in! Police!"

I sat bolt upright. Was it my door? I got up and knelt on the floor to look out the window. It was coming from down the street. I heard a door open, saw some light cast out onto the wooden sidewalk, but could not see whose door it was. Likely the drunk had lived on our street and the police were coming to inform his family. But who?

I got back into bed. Annie would know. She knew all the gossip. She'd tell me in the morning.

Again I dozed. And woke to more door pounding.

This time it was my door.

"Emily, Emily, are you home?" A hoarse voice, a voice filled with ominous urgency. *Uncle Valentine's voice.* I leaped out of bed, grabbed a robe, and went stumbling down the stairs. Thoughts raced through my mind like scurrying mice, tripping over one another. Someone had robbed Mama's grave! Aunt Susie was dead in Richmond! Johnny had been killed and the police had been pounding at the Surratts' door last night to tell his mother. Oh, God, not Johnny!

But then why would Uncle Valentine be here? Why not Annie?

"I'm coming!" I said, racing through the front hall. I opened the door. As I did the hall clock struck nine. Nine! Had I slept so late, then? I was supposed to be at the Surratts' for breakfast.

"Thank God I caught up with you before you went to the Surratts'. You must come with me to my house, Emily. Now." Uncle Valentine stood there, without his cape or shawl or tall hat. He was unshaven and bleary-eyed.

My distress turned into anger. "Uncle Valentine, I told you, I am not coming to live with you. And to wake me up and frighten me like this! Well, I think it's selfish and mean!"

"There is need to be frightened, child." He had pushed his way into the hall. It was raining out and he was wet. "I never should have allowed you to come back here last night. Thank God you're safe. I have failed in my duty toward you. No girl your age should be without a protector. And I intend to be that, starting now. Where are your things? Are you packed?"

Something was very wrong. "What's happened? You look terrible."

"I've been up all night. I was in attendance at Peterson's lodginghouse with some other doctors."

"Then go home and sleep."

"I was the first doctor to respond when they called for physicians from the audience last night. But we could do nothing, Dr. Leale and I. Nothing. Leale tried to breathe air into his lungs, pour a little brandy down his throat. Laura Keane, the actress, held his head in her lap. Nothing."

A cold chill came over me. "Uncle Valentine, tell me who it was you could do nothing for."

He looked at me. I saw such pain in his eyes I knew that whatever had happened could never be fixed. Never.

"You haven't heard, then. Oh, child. The president. The president's been shot." He sank down on a bench, rested his elbows on his knees, put his head in his hands, and wept.

I did not know what to do. A grown man weeping. The sound of it was unnatural and echoed through the empty rooms. I leaned against the wall. It couldn't be true. Was Uncle Valentine deranged? The president? Shot?

"How can this be?" I asked weakly.

"Oh, child, forgive me." He wiped his face. He took out a handkerchief and blew his nose. He spoke. "I saw him at the theater last night. He and Mrs. Lincoln came in a little after eight. The play was started already, but the dialogue stopped, the crowd roared, and the orchestra played 'Hail to the Chief.' The play went on. Then, in the third act, it happened."

"What happened?"

"The noise. The shot. A man leaped from the president's box onto the stage. Confusion, screaming, cries for help came from that box. Then calls for physicians. People yelling,

'Catch that man!' It was terrible. And when I got to the box, there he lay, his head on Laura Keane's lap. A head wound. Shot in the head. What could we do? Oh, I must study head wounds. I must do heads."

"Uncle Valentine."

"We know nothing about heads. We know nothing at all yet. And people criticize our work. The do-gooders would stop us. If we knew about heads we could have saved him!"

My voice was hoarse. "Is he dead, then?"

"Leale, I, and another doctor carried him out of the theater, through the crowds, and into Peterson's. Up the stairs, down a hall, to a room with a bed in it. The bed was too small for him. He was so tall. We had to put him diagonally across it. Mrs. Lincoln said that's how he slept at home in Springfield."

"Mrs. Lincoln was there?"

"Yes. And many others. Doctors, all over the place. Members of the cabinet.... The room was small. They sent for Robert, his oldest son. And Mrs. Keckley. No one could do anything. He had one more strike coming to him. I always said it. And now it's happened. He died this morning."

"Did they catch the man who did it?"

He looked up at me. "No. And that's why you must come home with me now, Emily. That's what I've been trying to tell you."

"What have you been trying to tell me?" I felt something coming, something awful. And it seemed, when it came, that I always knew it would.

"They are saying John Wilkes Booth shot him. And the police are looking for Booth. And for Johnny Surratt. I know one of the detectives. McDevitt, his name is. I saw him this morning. He said they searched the Surratt house in the middle of the night. They are looking for Johnny Surratt. And Booth."

I ran.

That's all I remember. I ran through the hall, into the kitchen. In my bare feet and robe I ran out the kitchen door and down the back steps and out into the rain. It was raining hard now, but I didn't care. All I knew was that I must run from Uncle Valentine's words.

They are looking for Johnny Surratt. And Booth.

I ran through the next-door yard, through the damp grass and flowers and stones. I felt a sharp pain in my right foot and kept on running. Uncle Valentine was calling after me. "Emily, come back! No, don't go there, please! Come back!"

I ran into the yard of the Surratts' house. My nightdress and thin robe were wet through already, but I didn't care. I ran up the back steps and then pounded on their door. Behind me Uncle Valentine was following.

Mrs. Mary answered the door. Annie stood right behind her. They were still in their nightdresses. They did not invite me in.

"Yes, we know, child," Mrs. Mary said when I told her the president had been shot. "We know. They came here last night, the police, asking entrance, searching, demanding answers. They said I was hiding culprits. My boarders were in a terror. None of us got any sleep." She was more annoyed than upset.

"Are they looking for Johnny?"

"Yes. But I was able to tell them he's in Canada. And that I just had a letter from him Friday. I read it to my boarders at the table Friday night."

"It's Booth," Annie said from behind her mother. "It's

Booth, Mama—I told you he's trouble. And yesterday afternoon you went on that errand for him to Surrattsville."

"Hush, Annie."

"And he was here last evening." Annie would not hush. "He came about eight o'clock."

"He stayed only five minutes," Mrs. Mary said. "He didn't bother anyone, Annie."

"Didn't bother anyone!" Annie was aghast. "He came here, Mama. Right before he killed the president. What does that say about him? He implicated us."

"I am not implicated," Mrs. Mary told her daughter sadly. "Nor are you, nor anyone in this house. Even though my boarders are fleeing as if this house is a sinking ship."

"Emily!" Uncle Valentine was calling to me in a hoarse whisper from the far edges of the Surratts' garden. "Emily, come away, now."

"Who is that?" Mrs. Mary asked.

"My uncle. Don't pay mind to him."

"Your uncle, the doctor? Is that Mary Louise's brother, Valentine? What does he want? Why is he here? Has he come to gawk at us?"

"No, Mrs. Mary. He wants me to come and live with him."

"Well, you should go with him, then, child."

"No!" I said sharply. "I'm coming to live with you. And Annie. As we planned."

"But you can't do that now, child. Don't you see? Everything's changed. This house is a sad place. Terrible suspicion has fallen on us. The detectives are even now watching us. I strongly advise against your coming here."

"Emily!" Uncle Valentine called again.

I felt ready to cry. I felt a great heaving in my chest. "Annie?" I said. "Is that true? I can't come here now?"

Annie pushed past her mother then and came out onto the steps. She held my arm and guided me down the steps. I limped. "Your foot is bleeding," she said.

"It doesn't matter."

She walked me down the path into the garden. Uncle Valentine was still waiting. He had his arms out in a gesture of appeal. I felt torn, confused, destroyed. I didn't know what was happening. I still didn't believe that President Lincoln was dead. It was all some kind of a bad dream and I would wake up soon in my little bed in my room and get up and dress and come here to have breakfast.

"Go with your uncle for now," Annie said.

"Annie, no. We had plans. You promised."

"Well, I can't keep my promise. Go with your uncle. Until we see how all this turns out." She was begging me, in the rain.

"You mean the president isn't dead?"

"No, he's dead, Emily. We know that. They showed us his bloody shirt—those detectives, when they came here last night."

"Oh, how awful."

"Yes. It's a nightmare. Nightmares don't only happen when you sleep, Emily. Most of them happen when you're awake. I know that now. And I know we've been living in one, only I was too stupid to recognize it. And now we've got to pay."

"I'll stay here and help you."

"No, you must go. Please, Emily. I need to handle things. And I can't with you around. Please, I need time. Go with your uncle and we'll straighten this all out in a few days. Then you can come with us. Here or wherever we go."

I felt hope. I believed her. "Truly, Annie?"

"Yes. I need you for a friend, Emily. I need a friend now. I'll be in touch. I promise."

So I went limping to Uncle Valentine, who was right once again about things. And who stood there, his coat open, his cravat askew, his shirt and hair dripping, and held his arms out to me, looking as if he wished he had never been right about anything at all in his life.

He hurried me inside, through our house, and toward the front door.

"I'm not dressed," I said.

"Not important," he answered.

"My foot is cut and bleeding. It hurts."

"I'll carry you." And he did. He picked me up, opened the door, and carried me down our front steps in the rain. He put me in the carriage.

"My things! I'm not going without my things!"

"I'll send back for them."

"No!" I started to get out of the carriage.

"All right," he said, "all right. Where are they?"

I told him and he was like a man crazed, running in and out of the house for my portmanteaus and boxes. I sat there telling him where they were and what to get. My foot was bleeding. He just kept running, back and forth from the carriage to the house, mumbling something about doing heads. His last trip in the house I begged him to go into my room and reach under my pillow to where I kept a small velvet sack. And bring it.

He brought it. He never asked what was in it, even though it jingled. It held Johnny's twenty gold pieces. Soon all my things were loaded in the carriage. We drove off, and I left the house, forever. And the night-blooming cereus, which had likely already drooped its head because it could not stand the light of day.

We drove off down Washington's maddened streets. The rain was steady and cold. But people were gathering on corners like the sun was out. They were standing there staring at nothing in disbelief. Negroes stood in the middle of the avenues weeping. Soldiers had turned out with drawn bayonets.

Squads of infantrymen were mustering; people were ripping down the red, white, and blue buntings and putting up black crepe. Others were running by, screaming. Some galloped past us on horses. Newsboys were crying as they yelled the news.

Uncle Valentine used his whip on his horse and we raced through the streets to his house. He didn't stop out front but drove in through the wrought-iron gates.

Merry Andrews stood at the gates. And closed them behind us. They made a clinking, solid sound. Uncle Valentine wiped his brow. "Thank God, we're home," he said.

Maude came to meet us. "They say Secretary of State Seward had his throat cut by an assassin as he lay in his sickbed. And Grant is dead, too."

"Don't believe rumors," Uncle Valentine said. He jumped down from the carriage seat, came around, and helped me out. "Come inside and I'll bind up your foot," he said. "Merry, get her things."

"What's the matter?" Maude said, gaping at the blood on my foot. "Did you get attacked in the street?"

"No, we're all right," Uncle Valentine assured her. "But Washington has gone mad. We are launched upon the maddest hour of our history."

And with that he scooped me up and carried me into the house, yelling for Merry and Maude to lock all the doors and windows.

I looked up. There she was, in the tower room of the second story. My room. Marietta. I saw her clear as day, standing there looking down on us, pushing the draperies aside and watching.

9

OLD ADDIE

UNCLE VALENTINE took me into his office and attended to my foot. But first he did a strange thing. He washed his hands with warm water and soap that Maude brought in.

"I've been in correspondence with a man named Lister, who is a professor of surgery in Glasgow," he said. "He believes that the air and dirt on the hands causes putrefaction. I've fought with officials in this city to clean the offal off the streets."

I looked around. I saw instruments, terrible things; vials, jars, books. One was *Observations on the Gastric Juice and Physiology of Digestion.* Another, *The Injuries of Nerves and Their Consequences.*

Uncle Valentine washed and cleansed my wound. I had never seen him do doctor things before, and I decided he was very good at it. Marietta held my hand. She had come downstairs. Why was she here, I wondered? And not teaching? She handed him things. "Are you a nurse?" I asked her.

We'd all heard about Florence Nightingale, nurse during the Crimean War. And our own Clara Barton, who'd followed the army in our war.

"No," Marietta answered. "But if I could, I'd be a doctor."

"Women can't be doctors," I said.

"Yes, they can," Uncle Valentine told me. "And they are. Dr. Mary Walker was an assistant surgeon during the war. She was taken prisoner by the Rebels, exchanged for a soldier, and given a medal. She visits and lectures here in Washington frequently."

What with all the talk, my foot was soon finished, stitched up and all. But it hurt. Uncle Valentine gave me a powder and told Marietta to take me to my room.

My room. I hobbled upstairs. Marietta brought along my things. When she wasn't looking I fished the velvet sack with the twenty gold pieces out of my pocket and hid it under the pillows on the bed. I'd find a better place for it later.

"You'd best get in that bed," she advised. "That powder is going to start to work soon." She was unpacking my clothing and putting it into the chiffonier.

"Why are you here?" I asked.

"Lincoln," she said. "It's so terrible. They closed the schools. Nobody knows what's really happened yet. They're saying it's a Confederate plot. There are thirty thousand Confederate soldiers in town on parole after Lee's surrender. I came in case any of them were attacked. Your uncle might need me."

"Is it true about women being doctors?"

"Yes." She was hanging my dresses.

"Then why don't you become one if you want to? Uncle Valentine could help you."

"I'm part Negro. It's difficult enough for white women who want to become doctors."

"You look white."

"There is always someone who would find out. I don't wish to put myself through that. So I teach. And I help your uncle in his laboratory, though it's not supposed to be known."

"Why?"

"Dr. Walker is the exception, not the rule. Women don't help in laboratories in this country. We're very behind Europe. Oh yes, your uncle has been summoned to the White House."

"The White House?"

"Yes. The authorities want his advice. Likely about what to inject in Lincoln's body so it holds up for the funeral. He knows about that. And he wants to see the head wound. He's very interested in head wounds."

"He says he knows nothing about them."

"Not enough yet, no. But he will learn. He is doing some very important work in medicine. If you are going to live here, don't pry."

"I didn't say I was going to live here."

She gave my pillow a final pat. "You will."

The powder was starting to work. Rain was pouring down outside. Even through the closed windows we could hear the shouts of the people in the streets. "Kill the damn Rebels! Kill the traitors!"

"I fear for Annie and Mrs. Mary," I allowed.

"And what of this Johnny of yours?" She arched her brows at me.

97

"He isn't mine," I said sadly. "He never was mine. And he's in Canada."

"Change your clothing. I'll bring some hot tea."

I took off my wet clothing, toweled myself dry, and put on the dressing gown. It felt soft and comforting. My head was spinning from the powder.

Marietta brought up the tea. It was darkening now, so she lighted the gaslight. Then the bells started to ring, what seemed like dozens of them, from all over; deep and solemn, they rang, some from distances far across the city.

"The death bells for Lincoln," she said, "and it's about time, too. Your uncle said Secretary Stanton ordered them hours ago. Oh, that reminds me, if you hear anything, don't be frightened."

"Like what?"

"Sometimes Addie Bassett gets out of her room at night. She's locked in days, because the medicine makes her woozy. Nights she's allowed to walk around, though the rest of the house is locked. She's harmless, so don't worry."

"She's locked in days?"

"It's for her own good."

Of course, I thought. *Like my being here is for my own good.*

Marietta's smile deepened. "It *is* for your own good," she said. And before I could reply she was gone.

I drank my tea. I read a bit. I heard some noise outside and went to look out. Uncle Valentine's carriage was just going out the gate. Merry Andrews secured the gate behind it, then leaped back up inside and they drove off. Would Uncle Valentine take Merry into the White House with him? A dwarf? Why not? Tom Thumb and his wife had been received by the Lincolns. Oh, the world had gone mad.

It was raining in gusts. I was glad for the warm fire in the grate, for the rain had chilled the room. I leaned back in the chair and listened to the steady tolling of the death bells. I must have closed my eyes and dozed.

Images flashed through my mind. Uncle Valentine telling me they were looking for Surratt and Booth. Johnny handing me that handkerchief with SUNDAY written on it. Uncle Valentine carrying me out of the house. Mrs. Mary saying how the police were asking entrance, searching, demanding answers. Me running through the backyards in my bare feet in the rain. The Negroes weeping in the street. Annie promising she'd stay in touch. Marietta saying "Don't pry." Inside me my feelings were all crossed, like cavalry sabers clashing. I struggled to wake from this sleep, which was more disturbed than restful. But I could not rouse myself.

Then something else roused me. "Little missy." It was a whisper. "Little missy."

I opened my eyes. An old hag of a nigra woman was bending over me. Her hair hung about her, gray and disheveled. She had two teeth missing in front. Her breath smelled like that of a hedgehog. I screamed.

She touched my arm lightly. "Hush, little missy. Please." I froze more than I hushed.

"My, you're a pretty one. Did they just bring you in?"

"I just came, yes."

"What ails you? The Wasting Disease? Like me? Oh no, I see the bandage on your foot. Do it hurt?"

"Yes, but I've taken a powder. It dulls the pain."

"You cain't be a prisoner. They doan keep prisoners here but on the third floor."

"I'm visiting." This must be Addie, then. I looked at her. Her clothing was clean, though her breathing seemed to be a difficult business. She took great breaths between sentences.

Of course, that could be from her weight. She was very fat. And she smelled of some kind of medicine. "My uncle Valentine doesn't keep prisoners," I told her.

"Your uncle, is he? He be a good man. But I needs to get away. They keep me prisoner here. Locks me in my room days. And locks the house up nights. Would you help me get away?"

"You're Addie Bassett."

She took my measure with eyes so old they made me shiver. "What did they tell you of me, then?"

"That you're sick, and he's taking care of you."

"Hmmph," she said. Then she nodded. "Yes. He's takin' care o' me. Like my old master's son would care for birds with broken wings he catched. Those birds always wanna get away even if just to die free in the woods. I'm gonna die anyways. So I wanna die free." Then she cocked her head and listened. "What are the bells for? Why are people yelling in the streets?"

"The president has died."

"Linkum?"

"Yes."

A great cry of dismay escaped her throat. And she raised her arms to heaven. Tears rolled down her face like on the Negroes' in the streets. She wiped her eyes with the corner of her apron. "Linkum, my Lord, Linkum." Then she said something strange. "My fault," she said.

"Your fault?"

She nodded. "He set me free. Gave me my freedom. A gift. Then I went an' lost it. He musta heard 'bout that. Addie Bassett lost the gift he give her. Musta killed him, poor man."

"No," I said, "you didn't kill him. Someone else did. He was shot. They're looking, now, for the person who did it."

"I did it. Me, an' all my kind who take this gift from this man and wander in the streets an' doan work an' earn our keep. But wait fer the white man to lead us. I did it." She sobbed and walked away from me, across the floorboards that creaked under her heavy weight. She stood looking out the window, wiping her eyes and quieting herself. Her great bulk cast a shadow across the room. "What do that mean? My freedom gone now?"

"No, your freedom isn't gone. President Lincoln gave it to you for always."

"I still gots it?"

"Yes."

She turned, unbelieving. She held out her hands to me. "Then it's more 'portant that I get outta here. Help me get outta here, please. I gotta use my freedom right."

I shook my head, no. "I can't do that. You're sick."

"I'se better now. As better as I ever be. Gonna die anyways. I jus' wants a chance to do somethin' wif this freedom Mr. Linkum give me, before I die. Please. I kin do things. I jus' had a spell o' bad luck. I wanna go out there an' help my people."

"How?"

"I was workin' fer the Relief Society. I got sick. They found me in the streets and brought me here."

"But you said you weren't working and that's why you killed President Lincoln."

She bowed her head. "I wuz workin', but I wuz drinkin', too. I doan drink no more. Tha's one good thing that come o' my bein' here. Please help me—please."

"I can't," I said again. "I'm sorry."

She walked back across the room to lean over me. "Missy, you know what he does? Do you?"

I backed away. "No."

"Well, you gonna be livin' here, you gonna find out. An' when you do, you'll help old Addie. Yes, you will. *Un-hun!*" She gave the last words deep emphasis.

"What does he do?" I croaked.

"That ain't fer me to tell, missy. No, sir, no." She shook her head. Her white hair stuck out every which way. "It's fer you to find out yourself."

I thought of all the terrible things Mama had hinted about Uncle Valentine. "Is it bad?" I whispered.

"Ain't fer me to tell, no, sir," she said again. "Old Addie got only so many words left in her. An' she ain't 'bout to waste 'em talkin' 'bout things she cain't do nuthin' 'bout. You'll find out, sure 'nuf. An' when you does, you'll help old Addie leave." Then she waddled out of the room.

"Wait!" I begged. But she was gone. A gust of rain beat against the windows. The candles flickered. The room was silent except for the distant tolling of the death bells for Lincoln. And the rain pattering against the windows. I looked around.

Had I dreamed her? I rubbed my eyes. What was Uncle Valentine doing in this house that she would not tell me? Why had Marietta warned me not to pry? Oh, I wished I were home in the narrow little house on H Street. I wished Mama had not died. I wished Johnny would come knocking at the door. Or Annie. What was happening to Annie and her mother?

I took another powder. My foot was starting to hurt. Then I decided to just get in bed and lie back and rest for a while. I fell asleep. And I never woke until the sun's rays were pouring in my window the next morning.

10

BLACK SUNDAY

THE NEXT DAY started out innocently enough. Which should have given me warning. I hadn't had an innocent day in months. I woke feeling refreshed, but when I got up, my foot was throbbing again. I hobbled around the room, dressed, and went down the stairs.

Some people were still yelling in the streets. And the death bells were still tolling. But the sun was shining and the birds were singing and I was starved.

Uncle Valentine was at breakfast, waiting for me.

He looked tired. "Good morning, Emily. Did you sleep well?"

"Yes."

"I see you're limping. How is the foot?"

"It hurts a little."

"I'll change the dressing later. You must eat now. Fix yourself a plate. Everything is there on the sideboard."

Maude had an array of good things set out. Fish and ham and eggs; biscuits, grits, coffee. I looked around. The table was set with four places, good china and sterling. "Who's coming?"

"I never know who. Sometimes a colleague will drop by. Sometimes Marietta. Or one of my students. I'm always grateful for company. But now that you're here, I won't have to worry about eating alone anymore, will I?"

I filled my plate and sat down to eat.

He was reading his newspaper. "For years people called Lincoln a clown and a gorilla, or a Negro-lover. And now they are making him a saint," he said. "His portrait is hanging out front of so many houses. Mobs wanted to burn down Ford's Theater last night. They still might do it."

"Did you go to the White House?"

"Yes." He set down his cup and shuddered. "Poor man. He never had a chance. Oh, there is so much for us yet to learn in the medical profession, Emily. So much. This is a terrible thing, terrible. I hear authorities have raided Booth's room at the National Hotel and seized his papers. The War Department has offered fifty thousand dollars' reward for Booth. And twenty-five thousand for each of his accomplices."

I wondered if that meant Johnny. Was Johnny an accomplice?

It was then that the front-door bell rang and Maude went to answer it. She came into the dining room. "A letter. For Emily."

"Well, give it to her," Uncle Valentine said.

I trembled, taking it. Was it from Johnny? It was from Annie: "Meet me today at the cemetery. Say you're going to visit your mother's grave. Three o'clock." Nothing more. I stuffed it in my pocket and said nothing.

"They are advising homeowners to drape their houses in black bunting," Uncle Valentine was reading. "Mobs are attacking any houses not so decorated. Maude?" He called out.

She came running. "Yes, Dr. Bransby?"

"Do we have any black bunting?"

"Now, why would we have such?"

"Every house should have black bunting, Maude. Every house should be prepared."

"For what? The assassination of a president? There has not been one in my lifetime, Dr. Bransby. And I certainly hope I shall never see one again."

"It says here," and he continued reading, "that if there is no bunting available, old black dresses should be torn up and made into bunting."

"I have no old black dresses, Dr. Bransby. And I'll not give any of my good ones."

"You could dye paper with ink and hang that," I offered.

They looked at me as if I had uncommon powers. "Wonderful idea!" Uncle Valentine said. "Where did you get it?"

"We do it at school sometimes. When we cut silhouettes."

Uncle Valentine asked Maude if we had enough paper, then. "I'll see, Dr. Bransby," she said. And she went to see.

"Would you be so good as to help Maude make the black decorations this afternoon, Emily?" he asked me. "I don't want to be perceived as a Southern sympathizer and have my house attacked."

"I'm going out this afternoon."

"Out? Where out?"

"To visit my mother's grave. With my friend Annie." The moment I mentioned her name I knew I shouldn't have.

He scowled. "Not today, please," he said. "I can't permit you to go out today."

Permit? I stared at him.

He shook his head. "First, you must keep off that foot, or the stitches won't hold. It could become infected. Second, the city has gone mad. People still think it's a conspiracy. No one is sure who was involved. Everyone is under suspicion."

"I won't be under suspicion, Uncle Valentine. I'm only going to visit my mother's grave."

"To meet Annie Surratt," he said, "brother of Johnny. Daughter of the woman whose house the detectives visited the other night, waving Lincoln's bloody shirt. No, Emily, you are not going."

"I must go. Annie needs me."

"No," he said again. "I'm sorry, but I must forbid it."

Forbid? "You have no right to forbid it."

He looked at me for a long moment. His eyes were very brown and sad. Then he sighed and got up without saying a word, went out of the room and across the hall to his office.

I sat waiting. I may have been only fourteen, but I knew by then that whenever someone says they are sorry about having to do something, they are not a bit sorry. And they have just been waiting for the right opportunity to do it.

He was back in a few minutes. Without saying a word he put a paper down gently on the table beside me.

Apparently he had gone to court—or wherever one goes to get such a paper—and had it drawn up. He had friends in high places. He knew how to get such things done.

The paper said I was underage. It had a lot of *heretofores* and *whereases* that I didn't understand. But what it said that I did understand was that I was under his jurisdiction.

Oh, it couched the message in fancy feathers. It said things about my happiness, well-being, and security. It said I needed a protector. There was even a phrase bringing Southern honor into it.

"What does this mean?" I asked him.

"That I am responsible for you." He was stirring his coffee.

"I don't need anybody to be responsible for me."

"You're only fourteen. A minor child. You need a protector."

"I can take care of myself."

"If I didn't do this, Emily, you would be in the Washington Orphan Asylum. Or St. Vincent's. Or St. Ann's Home for Foundlings. The Guardian Society in this town is very dedicated. Orphanages enlist more interest than any other charity. Do you want that? Do you want to go to an orphanage?"

I was trapped. "No," I said weakly. I sank back in my chair. I was an orphan. And it was something you weren't allowed to be. I supposed I should be grateful to him, but I wasn't. I reached into the wellspring of strength that had carried me through the last six weeks. I found it dry. I had no more strength. I felt like the miller's daughter—no, I decided, I was like Addie now.

"Come now, Emily," he was saying. "I'm not that bad, am I?"

I scowled across the table at him. "We have to have some understanding," I said to him.

He nodded. "I agree."

"I can't have you ordering me around like I'm a child. I took care of Mama all that time. Since Daddy was killed."

"You did a wonderful job," he said. "And you are more mature than most girls your age. But you still need a protector, Emily. And I intend to act in that role until you are of age. I do not intend to order you around like a child. I haven't

107

the time for it. I respect your ability to make intelligent decisions and I expect you to respect mine."

"Then why can't I go out and meet Annie today?"

"Because it is not an intelligent decision. Mobs are attacking people in the streets out there. People are running around with knives and guns. They are calling it Black Sunday, for heavens' sakes! People are frightened and angry. To say nothing of your injured foot."

I fell silent. I could see how he had always bested Mama. Why she was always angry with him. Because he was probably always right.

"So I'm like Addie, then," I said dismally. I knew I was being petulant, but I didn't care.

"Addie?"

"Yes. I met her last night."

"She can be a nuisance. Don't listen to her."

"She says she's a prisoner."

"She is not a prisoner, she is a patient. I keep her door locked, days, because she is on special medicine, and it makes her addled. She must rest. And you are not a prisoner. It is my duty to care for you. If you are angry over that, then you do not have the intelligence I have credited you with."

There was anger in his voice. It brought tears to my eyes. "What's wrong with Addie?" I asked.

"She has the Wasting Disease. Same as your mama and my wife. I'm giving Addie treatments."

"Why isn't she in a hospital?"

"Negroes don't have a very good time of it in our hospitals."

"She says you do bad things here, Uncle Valentine. And that if I live here, I'll find out."

"I do experiments, Emily. In my shed out back. And I see

some patients here. In my office in front. I'm writing a paper on the diaphragm, a protector of the heart and cardiac vessels, and its influence on the organs of circulation. All this is frightening to Addie. Progress in medicine is frightening to many. They cling to the old ways. Marietta, for instance, is as bright a girl as you'll ever meet. She helps me in my lab. But when she takes sick, she won't have my medicines. Has her own supply of herbs that she grows in her own garden."

I had no answer for that. I was embarrassed. He was so forthright.

"Now, promise me you'll stay in today. And rest that foot. You can make the black paper for the front of the house. And tomorrow I'll have Robert take you to see Annie.... It's Black Sunday out there. Please, child, we're in the throes of one of the worst times we've ever had in this country."

I promised him I'd stay in. I have always known when I am bested—there's one good thing about me. I ought to know. I've been bested often enough in my life. Black Sunday.... Well, they'd named it right, anyway.

$\mathcal{T}$HE MAN FROM
THE MARBLE VAULT

Oh, Johnny, Johnny, where are you? Why did you run away? How could you leave me here like this? And what about your mother and Annie? Oh, Johnny, you don't know what's going on here. You wouldn't have run away if you'd known what was going to happen. You're not a coward.

Robert was asking me something. I had to pull myself out of my reverie. "I beg your pardon?"

"I think we ought not to drive up directly in front of the house. I think we ought to park a little away down the street. Don't you?"

"Are you afraid?"

His handsome face that still sometimes reminded me of Johnny stiffened. His voice grew sad. "Why do you taunt me, Miss Pigbush?"

"Call me Emily."

"All right, then, Emily. Why do you taunt me? I've been nice to you. I like you. And I think, deep down, you have esteem for me. If I've done something to offend you, please tell me. But since I came to your uncle's house this day you've been taunting me."

"I'm sorry," I said. "But I suppose that's why. You're begging me to tell you what you did wrong. Johnny never would have begged."

"Johnny, is it?"

"Yes."

He drew the horse to a stop a little down the street from the Surratt house. "Well, your precious Johnny may be begging for more than the understanding of a fourteen-year-old girl before this whole thing is through." He was angry now, but he did a good job of controlling that anger.

There was one other thing that made him different from Johnny: He still had that old military bearing about him. The way he walked, despite the limp; the way he never gave away what he was thinking; the guarded yet polite way he spoke to people; even the way he held his head.

"I apologize for not being Johnny," he said.

"And I apologize for being only fourteen."

We sat looking at each other on the front seat of the carriage. There was a challenge in the brown eyes. The moment held, with each of us staring the other down. Then, of a sudden, I smiled. And he did, too. Then we both laughed. And the tension broke.

"To answer your question, yes. I am afraid of pulling right up in front of the Surratt house this morning," he said. "I've been through a few battles, Emily. I know when to be afraid and when not to be. And I'm not ashamed of it. And I tell you now that I'd rather face a charge by Stuart's cavalry than go into that house right now."

"You don't have to go in with me. I'll go alone." I started to get down from the carriage.

He held my arm. "Discretion is the better part of valor," he said.

"What?"

"Shakespeare. *Henry IV*. I had a lieutenant who quoted that to us all the time. He saved lots of lives. You see those four men at the end of the street?"

I looked in the direction he indicated. "Yes."

"They're detectives."

"How do you know?"

"I just do. Wait. Watch them a moment."

It only took a moment of watching before the four men walked across the street to the Surratt house.

"If that isn't an advance at the double," Robert said, "nothing is."

The detectives went up the front steps of the Surratt house and knocked on the door.

"Oh, what do they want?" I whispered to Robert.

"Just what your uncle hoped to have you avoid. I'm beginning to think you should have met Annie in the cemetery, as you originally planned. If you had to meet with her at all."

"She's my *friend*, Robert. A person doesn't desert a friend in time of need."

"All right. All right. Just be quiet. And as calm as possible. No matter what happens. Those detectives aren't here to take Annie for a stroll in the park," he mumbled.

We could see the Surratt door open. The men went in. We waited. Robert unfolded his newspaper and started to read it. The front page was full of a proclamation by Secretary of War Stanton:

ONE HUNDRED THOUSAND DOLLARS' REWARD!

THE MURDERER OF OUR LATE BELOVED PRESIDENT, ABRAHAM LINCOLN, IS STILL AT LARGE!

Fifty Thousand Dollars will be paid by this Department
for his Apprehension!

Twenty-Five Thousand Dollars' Reward
for A. Atzerodt, sometimes called "Port Tobacco"!

Twenty-Five Thousand Dollars' Reward
for David E. Herold!

All persons harboring or secreting the said persons, or
either of them, or aiding or assisting their concealment
or escape will be treated as accomplices, subject to a trial
before a military commission, and the punishment
of death!

LET THE STAIN OF INNOCENT BLOOD BE REMOVED FROM THE LAND!

At least they aren't offering a reward for Johnny, I thought. That means they can't prove he had anything to do with it.

"Robert," I said finally, "maybe Annie needs my help. I can't sit here like this."

"You must. I can't have you charging in there. I promised your uncle I would look out for you today."

"I should have come this morning, like I wanted to." I moaned.

"I couldn't make it this morning. You know I worked last night."

"Why do you have to work at night? You're a medical student."

"I stay late at the lab. Sometimes it's the only time I can get any work done on my experiments. . . . Now, just be patient a few moments longer. Nobody in their right mind would go charging in there now."

Just then a man came tearing down the street, right past our carriage. He paused for a moment in front of it, eyes riveted on the Surratt house, completely unaware of us.

"I know that man," Robert said.

I looked. I knew him, too. I gasped. He was wearing a gray coat, black pants, and an old cap. His name was Powell. He'd been to the Surratt house when Johnny was home. And he'd stopped with Booth at the president's box at Ford's Theater the night Johnny took me there.

It came over me then like a cold sweat. *Booth had stopped to visit us in the president's box at Ford's Theater! Where he would come, almost a month later, to shoot the president!*

Why had Johnny taken us there that night? Was it to meet Booth? So Booth could familiarize himself with the president's box? *No, no, I must stop going down that road,* I told myself. *Down that road lies madness.*

"He was hiding in the Congressional Cemetery last night," Robert said of Powell. "I saw him climbing out of a marble vault. Just lifted the slab off and got right out. Pretty as you please. Like he was getting out of bed in the morning."

"I thought you were working in the laboratory last night."

"I had to go to a late funeral."

I had the feeling he was lying to me. But I had other things to think of now.

Together we watched as Powell crossed the street right in front of us, walked to the Surratt house, went swiftly up the steps, and knocked on the door. It opened. He was admitted.

"That's the same man," Robert said with certainty. "He was up to no good then, and he's up to no good now."

Powell's clothing had looked disheveled, as if he'd been hiding somewhere. I said nothing. Why would Powell go rushing into the Surratt house now? Apparently he did not know detectives were inside. We waited some more. After a while a carriage pulled up in front of the Surratts' house and two more men went inside. Then they came out the front door: four detectives, Annie, Mrs. Mary, and Powell.

Their hands were manacled behind their backs. Even Annie's.

"No!" Again I started to get down from my seat.

Again Robert stopped me. "Don't be a fool!"

"A fool? To care about my friend? They're taking her away!"

"They have to. Likely to question her. If she and her mother are innocent, they'll let them go. What do you think you can do, anyway? Besides involving yourself?"

He was right. I could do nothing but watch as two detectives got into the carriage with Annie, Mrs. Mary, and Powell, and the other two walked back across the street to where their own carriage was parked. The two carriages, one following the other, drove right by us, going the other way.

I saw the detectives, grim faced, staring ahead. I saw Annie. She seemed to be struggling with her hands so manacled. She looked right at me as their carriage passed by.

"Robert!" I moaned.

"She'll be all right," he insisted. "If she's innocent, she'll be all right."

"You believe that? Didn't you just read that proclamation by Stanton in the paper? He's out for blood!"

"Damn," he said. "I knew that man Powell was up to no good, climbing out of a vault in the cemetery at midnight. Somehow he's connected with all this! Why didn't I stop him when I had the chance?"

"Midnight?" I looked at him. "They hold funerals at midnight now?"

"Sometimes they do," he said.

"You and Uncle Valentine seem to go to more funerals."

"Doctors do, when their patients die. And the time isn't always convenient. Don't split hairs, Emily."

"Don't you sit there all superiorlike and tell me not to split hairs. You just lied to me, Robert deGraaf, telling me you were working last night in the lab. And now it turns out you were in the cemetery at midnight, seeing a man climb out of a marble vault!"

"I wasn't aware that I had to account to you for my actions. *You* lied to *me*. You knew that man. You'd seen him before. Likely at the Surratts'."

"I think you're despicable to hold me to everything I say when I've just watched my best friend being taken away by the police! You don't know how that feels!"

"My best friend was killed at Gettysburg. So don't tell me I don't know, Emily, please."

"Well, this is different."

"It sure is." He picked up the reins and clicked to the horse.

"Where are we going?"

"Home."

"No, we can't, please. We must go in the house."

"The *house*! What for?"

"The cat," I said. "Annie has a cat."

His stare got colder and colder. "Go on."

"Well, there's no telling how long the police will keep Annie. And Puss-in-Boots has to be fed, doesn't she?"

"Puss-in-Boots?"

"The cat. Annie took care of my cat and my bird when we had to leave Surrattsville and couldn't bring them here to Washington. I can't do any less for her, can I?"

He agreed that I couldn't. But he didn't like it. Reluctantly, he guided the horse up in front of our old house. "Now what?" he asked.

"The detectives are all gone. And I know how to get in the back door. Please."

He relented. But only if he could come with me. So we went through the yard of my old house, then through the yard next door and into the Surratts' yard. The last time I'd been here was when Uncle Valentine came to fetch me in the rain. It seemed like years ago, instead of days.

No one was home in the house next door. Or if they were, they were minding their own business. "I'm indulging you," Robert kept saying as he followed me up the back steps and I fetched the key from under a flower pot on the back porch. "I know I'm going to be sorry for this."

"Here, kitty-kitty," I called.

We went in through the kitchen. I kept calling for Puss-in-Boots. Then I heard her meowing. "She's upstairs," I told Robert.

He gestured that I should go and he would follow. We found Puss-in-Boots in Mrs. Mary's room, on the bed. She blinked at us. I gathered her up, stroked her black fur. "Isn't she pretty?" I asked Robert. "Look. She has white feet and a white vest."

"Feed her," he growled, "and let's get out of here."

"I'm not going to feed her. I'm taking her with me. To Uncle Valentine's."

"You can't."

"Why can't I?"

"Because— Look around. This place has been searched. Everything here is evidence."

"Not Puss-in-Boots, Robert. She isn't evidence. I'm taking her."

He sighed. He ran his hand through his hair in distraction. We looked around. He was right. Mrs. Mary's room was a shambles. Pictures had been taken from the walls. The desk in the corner, where she kept her accounts, was in disarray. "One picture had the arms of the state of Virginia," I told Robert. "And it said, *'Sic Semper Tyrannis.'*"

"Wonderful," Robert said dryly, "that's what Booth is supposed to have said when he fled across the stage after shooting Lincoln. Let's get out of here, for God's sake."

He hurried me downstairs. I clutched Puss-in-Boots in my arms. Robert locked the back door and put the key back under the flower pot, and we went back across the two yards and out into the street to the carriage.

Only when we were driving off did it all come together for me in my head. "Robert," I said, "if Uncle Valentine had let me come yesterday as I wanted, I would have been able to see Annie. Now she's gone."

He did not answer.

"I'm never going to forgive him for that. I may never see her again."

"You'll see her again."

I stroked the cat in my lap. "And I'm not going to stay with him," I went on as if Robert hadn't spoken. "I just won't.

I'm going to find a way to go and live with Aunt Susie in Richmond."

"Well, that would be going from the frying pan into the fire. Richmond is the only place in America probably in a worse state than Washington right now."

"I don't care. I'm not staying with him." *Nothing could be worse than Washington right now*, I thought. The president was dead. The whole town was in an uproar. People were running through the streets, forming mobs. Detectives were arresting anybody who looked suspicious. Cavalrymen were riding in groups with drawn swords. My best friend had been taken by the police. And Robert had just told me he'd been in the cemetery at midnight and seen a man I knew, a man who'd been a guest at the Surratts', climbing out of a marble vault.

"I thought you told me a person doesn't desert a friend in time of need? What about Annie?" he asked. "You going to run to Richmond when she needs you now?"

"That's why I hate you, Robert," I said.

He sighed. "I know, because I'm not Johnny."

"No," I said, "because you're always right."

"Well, I hope I'm not right about this."

"What?"

"I'm not so sure your uncle is going to let you keep that cat."

MISS WINEFRED MARTIN'S
YOUNG LADIES

UNCLE VALENTINE let me keep the cat.

But he made me go back to school. And so it was that I stood in the large carpeted hall outside my classroom in Miss Winefred Martin's School for Young Ladies the very next day, knowing that I had seen too much in these last two weeks to ever feel like one of Miss Winefred Martin's young ladies again.

Mrs. McQuade smiled at me. Her large blue eyes, usually so open to the possibilities of the world around her, looked bleary this day. Black did not become her. She usually wore lavender or yellow. Clothing was her one passion. "Life can be a costume party or a wake, girls," she'd once told us. "I prefer to think of it as a costume party."

"I am so glad you are back, Emily," she whispered. "The girls are very unsettled, what with the assassination. And I must confess, I am myself. This is a most dreadful thing, most dreadful. I never expected to find such chaos in America."

The last four years have been chaos, I thought. *Haven't you noticed? Of course, nobody is cutting off anybody's head and the blood isn't running in the streets like it did in France during your revolution. Leastways not in any way you can see yet.* In all the time I had known her, Mrs. McQuade had refused to let anything shock her out of the ordered certainty of her existence.

Now this had. The assassination. She was plainly shaken.

"We are having our Wednesday Morning Discussion Group," she said. "Your calming influence is needed."

I had always thought of myself as the hand-wringer type. I muddled through, trying to get things right, while everyone else knew what they were doing. "It's Tuesday," I reminded her.

"I know it's Tuesday. But I thought the girls needed it this morning."

"I don't know, Mrs. McQuade. I don't know if I can even go in there. I just know they're all whispering about me because my mother died."

"Mr. Lincoln's dying is all that's on their minds. I am afraid they have quite forgotten your mother's passing, Emily. I shall remind them."

"Don't, please. If I have to come back to school, I'd just as soon slip in and take a seat and have nothing said of the matter."

"'If'?" She scowled. "Certainly you aren't thinking of leaving school, Emily."

"It isn't school, Mrs. McQuade. It's that I just don't know if I can come back and be one of Miss Winefred Martin's girls again after all that's happened."

And then there was Myra Mott, my archenemy. I just knew she'd have something vengeful to say to me. She never let me forget that I did not have the social standing of the other girls. I did not think I could abide Myra Mott this morning, but I didn't say it. Mrs. McQuade did not allow rivalries in her classroom.

"You never were one of them, child," she whispered now. "You always had a bucketful of common sense that the others don't have."

"Thank you. But sometimes I wish I didn't. And now I feel so old. And all they do is talk about parties and boys."

"Not this morning. So come right on in. I'm sure you can contribute something, can't you?"

In the Wednesday Morning Discussion Group everyone was expected to have an opinion. Sometimes the discussion would be about food prices, especially with all the inflation with the war. Sometimes it was the freedmen problem. Sometimes it was fashions. We were graded on our comments. Mrs. McQuade did not hold with the notion that women should speak of nothing but children and matters of the home. New times were coming, and we must be ready for them.

I went into the bright, sunny classroom and slipped into my seat. The discussion was already in progress.

"The newspaper says his body is in the East Room of the White House," Lydia Rath was whispering, "and that he's wearing the suit he wore at the inauguration, just five weeks ago!"

"The doors of the White House are to be thrown open

today!" Carol Johnson put in. "And the public is going to be allowed to file by and see him!"

"Remember, girls"—Mrs. McQuade rapped the desk with her pencil—"this discussion must remain on an intelligent level. Where should Mr. Lincoln be buried? Here in Washington? Or back in Springfield? And are the fortunes of the Republican Party, and not the needs of the people, on Mr. Stanton's mind?"

"I think he should be buried right here in Washington," Lucy Cameron said firmly, "under the Capitol's dome, the space originally made for George Washington." Lucy wore glasses and always made intelligent comments.

"Do you consider Mr. Lincoln on a par, as president, with Washington, then?" Mrs. McQuade probed.

Everyone agreed he was.

"I think the funeral should be long," Lydia Rath said wistfully, "and stately. I think all the cities that want to see him should be allowed to see him."

"Well, I'll tell you what I think," Marcia Wilson put in, "I don't think all those Southern relatives of Mrs. Lincoln's should be allowed in the White House. Not until they find out if this was a Southern conspiracy or not."

Everyone murmured their approval.

"My daddy said that the Todds are already here." Myra Mott knew they regarded her as someone to be reckoned with. Her father was a reporter for the *Intelligencer*. And she always knew more than anybody. She smirked. "My daddy tells the story that Mr. Lincoln once said the Todds spell their name with two *d*'s. And one *d* is enough for God."

"Gossip," Mrs. McQuade said. "We do not want gossip, Myra. We want to speak of issues."

Myra flushed, then recovered. "All right then, issues. For

everybody's information, it's all true about a man named Powell stabbing Secretary of State Seward. He broke into Seward's house the night Lincoln was shot. And tried to stab him in the throat. Only thing that saved Seward was a steel brace he was wearing to hold his broken jaw in place."

"Thank you for that information, Myra," Mrs. McQuade said.

"And, I'm going to the White House to see Mr. Lincoln's remains this afternoon with my father," she said imperiously. "He said it's an historic moment, and I mustn't miss it."

The others oohed and aahed.

"Is she getting out of school early, then?" Lucy Cameron asked.

"You all are," Mrs. McQuade said. "But I advise you not to go near the White House. The crowds will be crushing. The papers say that tomorrow there will be a grand procession along Pennsylvania Avenue. Certainly you can catch a glimpse of the hearse there. We'll be going together as a class."

"People are charging twenty-five cents to sit in a window along Pennsylvania Avenue," little Elizabeth Townsend piped in. "Isn't that exploitation, Mrs. McQuade?"

"It is. But I imagine we'll be seeing a lot of that, human nature being what it is. What other signs of exploitation do we see in all this ceremony, girls?"

"I think dragging poor Mr. Lincoln's body around for fourteen days is exploitation," Elizabeth said. "How can a dead body last fourteen days?"

That's when I spoke and shouldn't have. "My uncle Valentine was called to the White House yesterday," I said.

They all stared at me. And of a sudden, I wanted to get up and run out of the room.

"Emily is living with her uncle, Dr. Bransby, now, girls," Mrs. McQuade said softly. "Since her mother's untimely death. Tell us, Emily, why was your uncle called to the White House?"

Myra was glaring at me. I had no real friends in my class, though I got along with everyone after a fashion. The girls respected me, though outside school we did not mix. But with Myra Mott my relationship was clearly defined.

She considered me something that had been sneaked in the back door. Someone not worthy of my place in the school. And I had the nerve to get better marks than she did, too.

Her marks were respectable; she was prettier and popular. Her mother had social standing. But the enmity had come to a head when I won the midwinter essay contest, hands-down, over her. The prize had been a copy of *Uncle Tom's Cabin*, signed by the author, Harriet Beecher Stowe. Mrs. McQuade knew her.

I'd written about how it felt to have your father killed in the war. Myra had written a high-minded examination of Sherman's morals in his March to the Sea. It almost killed her that I won. She could not stand to be bested at anything.

"I don't know exactly why my uncle was invited," I replied to Mrs. McQuade's question. "He doesn't discuss his doctor business with me. But he was in Ford's Theater the night the president was shot. He helped attend him."

The girls' eyes were wide. They wore the terrible fascination with the whole business. I saw it sitting there, like a buzzard, on the shoulders of every girl in the room. Then everyone spoke at once, speculating on what it must have been like at the theater. The horror of it went through the room like a brushfire.

Mrs. McQuade rapped her desk again. "Girls, girls, I think we should get back to our regular work now. You all will be dismissed at one instead of four. We have much to do."

Everyone settled down. But Myra kept glancing over at me the whole morning. And her eyes glittered with malice.

When it came time to be dismissed, she lingered in the cloakroom. "I know why your uncle was summoned to the White House," she said.

She never spoke to me voluntarily. She would never lower herself to do so.

"Then you know more than I," I told her.

She came to stand beside me. "It's because he knows about dead bodies."

I met her steady gaze. Inside me I was trembling, but I would not let her see this. "He's a doctor, after all," I said.

"Most doctors deal in live bodies."

"Uncle Valentine teaches anatomy." I tried to sound bored. I turned to go.

She put a hand on my arm to restrain me. "I feel I should tell you. He is under investigation."

I felt weak in the legs. I wanted to run. I did not want to hear her words, delivered in her clear, mocking girlish voice. For I knew they would render me senseless. I knew something bad was coming. "By whom?" I asked lightly.

"The *Intelligencer*."

The newspaper her father wrote for. "Well, go on, Myra. I can tell you're just dying to tell me something. Say it plain and get it over with."

"All right, I will. My father is doing the investigating. Your uncle is under suspicion of being a body snatcher."

"No wonder Mrs. Lincoln always refers to the newspapers as the vampire press," I said. But I wasn't as flippant as I sounded. "Well, for your information, Myra, the night of my mother's funeral, when I went back to the cemetery with a friend, my uncle was there, watching for grave robbers. And he chased some. And posted a guard around Mama's grave. So if he is one, how do you explain that?"

Her smile was slow and knowing. "It's an excellent cover. Especially since he knew you were coming to live with him."

I hated it when she spoke like a news reporter. "He didn't know I was coming to live with him," I said. "That was decided a few days later. Saturday, likely. Only Sunday did he show me the paper that said he was assuming legal responsibility for me."

She smiled. "Do lawyers work on Saturday now?"

"What?"

"What is the date on that paper?"

"I don't know. What does it matter?"

"Why don't you look? I'll bet he knew you were coming to live with him. I'll bet that business at the cemetery was all a little farce. So you would never dream he was involved in body snatching."

"My uncle is a respected doctor, Myra," I said. "He doesn't rob graves. The very idea!"

She shrugged. "We'll find out, won't we?"

" 'We'?"

"When my father finishes his investigation. It's against the law, you know. Such culprits have been convicted and sent to jail!"

She tossed her head and started out. "I just thought I'd warn you, Emily Pigbush. I'm doing you a favor."

I couldn't think. I felt my face go white. What right did she have to accuse Uncle Valentine of such? How dare she? Oh, I'd known there was good reason why I hated her. "You varlet!" I yelled. But by the time I got the words out of my mouth, she was gone. I dashed out into the hall after her and stood there, my lips trembling, tears coming down my face.

All the way home Myra's words swirled around and around in my head.

Uncle Valentine a body snatcher! The business at the cemetery a farce! An excellent cover-up! *Especially since he knew you were coming to live with him. . . . Do lawyers work on Saturday now? . . . What is the date on that paper?*

I ran the rest of the way home. *What is the date on that paper?* I would look. I knew where Uncle Valentine kept it. In his office, under the paperweight statue of Hippocrates. I'd seen him put it there. I'd prove Myra wrong. The she-wolf! She made me ashamed of my own sex.

13

SAVING THE MOMENTS

DADDY HAD TOLD ME a story once about a beautiful princess who had three men courting her. She couldn't make up her mind which to wed. But she'd always been told she had wonderful eyes. So she decided to ask each man what color her eyes were. "Brown," said the first. "Blue," said the second. For, though they had known her since childhood, they had never paid mind to the color of her eyes. "Green," said the third, who always noticed eyes and teeth and every other thing of importance in the workings of the kingdom. So the princess married the third.

Was that the Brothers Grimm again? I didn't know. I thought sometimes my daddy made stories up as he went along. I knew now what he'd been trying to tell me with this story. *Always notice things that are important in the workings of the kingdom*. I hadn't noticed the date on that paper of Uncle Valentine's. And because I hadn't, Myra had been able to get the upper hand with me.

When I got home I would storm into Uncle Valentine's office and find that paper.

But nobody was home. It makes no sense to storm if nobody is there to see it. So I went quietly to the office. The paper was where I expected to find it, under the paperweight statue of Hippocrates. I looked at the date.

It was April 12, in the year of our Lord 1865. The day *before* my mother's funeral.

I sank down in Uncle Valentine's chair. My head was spinning. Had he set up that scene in the graveyard, then, to make me think he was against grave robbing, because he already knew I was coming to live with him?

Was Myra right?

Why had he allowed me to go home to an empty house, thinking I would be living with the Surratts? Why? Why, if he had the paper already? Worse yet, how had he known I'd be there in the cemetery that night? Then I groaned, realizing how. Maude. When I'd told her I was going, she'd stopped me, suggested I go with Annie, gotten a hack. It took an hour for the hack to come. She'd sent word to Uncle Valentine.

Oh, I was so confused! Well, I would just end the confusion, that was all. I would confront him with the matter. As soon as he came in the door.

And then I heard talking outside the windows. I looked out.

It was Uncle Valentine coming up the walk. *With Annie!* What was he doing with Annie? I ran through the center hall and flung the front door open. "Annie!"

"Emily!" She ran to me.

I almost killed myself going down the steps. We embraced, right in the front yard.

In the center hall we appraised each other. "What happened? I came by your house! I saw them take you away! Oh, Annie, are you all right?"

"I'm fine," she said. But she looked wan. There were dark circles under her eyes. "They still have Mama. They let me go after a day of questioning. Oh, Emily, it was terrible! They came and searched the house again. They said that yesterday they arrested Samuel Arnold and he made a clean breast of everything. He said he was in on a conspiracy to kidnap the president. And that Booth, O'Laughlin, Atzerodt, Herold, Powell, and my brother Johnny were involved in it."

"Oh, how could he?"

"And they keep questioning Mama. They have her in Carroll Prison. And we need a lawyer. And don't have one."

"I told you I'd take care of that, Annie," Uncle Valentine said.

I had forgotten him. We'd wandered into the front parlor and sat down. I looked up now to see him standing there in the middle of the room.

"Oh, I couldn't, Dr. Bransby. I couldn't allow it," Annie protested.

"You can and you shall," he told her. "I loved President Lincoln, Annie. And this tragedy is of the utmost proportions for all of us. But I do not think it right that someone accused of taking part in it should not have proper legal counsel. That is after all what Lincoln himself would say. He was, first and foremost, a lawyer, remember."

Annie nodded yes. "I met your uncle on the way here,"

she told me. "We started talking. And I'm afraid I blurted it all out. Your uncle is so good, Emily. You are so lucky to have him."

What could I say to that? "Annie, I've got Puss-in-Boots." That's what I said.

"Oh, I'm so glad! I thought she'd run off! Can you keep her for now? I just don't know what's going to happen."

I said I would. She and Uncle Valentine drew chairs up close to each other and were soon deep in conversation. I went to make tea.

I dreamed about my father that night. He was going off to war, wearing his wonderful blue coat with the double row of brass buttons and the cape collar lined with red. He wore his brace of pistols and his saber. Manfred, his horse, neighed in impatience as Daddy gave last minute orders to Elihu, his hired manager. Daddy's hunting dogs lay around his feet.

I awoke from the dream with a start, as if someone had put a hand on my shoulder.

Someone had. Addie. "You wanna come see?" she said.

I shook the dream off. I was thinking of Daddy's dogs. The day after Daddy left, Mama had had them sold off. I never knew it until I came home from school and found them gone.

"See what, Addie?"

"You jus' come," she said.

I picked up Puss-in-Boots, who slept with me now, and went with Addie. I was annoyed that she'd interrupted my dream. Daddy's presence had been very strong in it.

"There," she said, pointing out a window that overlooked the garden.

I looked. It was a moon-flooded night and I could see that Marietta's flowers were all in bloom. I also saw two lanterns, a horse drawing a carriage, and three figures inside the carriage.

Uncle Valentine, Robert, and Marietta.

The neigh I'd heard in my dream was from the horse pulling the carriage into the yard. It came to a halt in front of Uncle Valentine's stone shed.

"There," Addie was saying, "I tol' you."

"Told me what? What are they doing?"

She snorted. "Tha's for me to know," she said. "An' for you to find out."

"How am I supposed to find out?"

"You go inna that shed and look. That's how! They never home inna afternoon. Always out on biz-ness. If'n I could do it, me a half-drunk, no-'count, slave woman, so could you."

"You've been in the shed?"

"Why you thinks he locks me up days? 'Cause I went outside coupla times. Wanted one o' them flowers that girl grows. All day long they hang down like bells at rest. At dusk they turn right up to the sky."

"The yucca flower," I said.

She nodded. "S'all I wanted. It wuz near the shed. I looked inna window. An' saw."

"Saw what?"

"You make it your biz-ness to find out, girl. And when you do, you let old Addie go. Like you promised."

I peered out the window. Uncle Valentine and Robert were unloading the wagon, taking some barrels out, lifting them down from the wagon, then rolling them into the shed. Marietta held the lantern. "Barrels," I whispered. I felt relieved. Not coffins. Barrels. "He does experiments."

"If'n that's what you wanna call it."

We watched in silence for a few more moments. Then I

turned around, but Addie was gone. I picked up Puss-in-Boots and went back to bed, wondering if this was part of my dream. And wondering at the same time how I could make it my *biz-ness* to find out what was in the shed.

The next day was the nineteenth. The day of Washington's own funeral services for President Lincoln before his body started on that fourteen-day and sixteen-hundred-mile trip so they could finally lay him to rest in Springfield, Illinois.

A day of marking the ends of things. And the beginnings of others. I decided to ask Uncle Valentine about the paper.

At breakfast when I told him Mrs. McQuade was taking her girls to see the funeral, he nodded. "Stay with your teacher. It's going to be a circus out there today. I worry about you, you know that, Emily."

I saw my opening. "Can I ask you something, Uncle Valentine?"

"Of course."

"You had that paper of yours saying you were responsible for me when you invited me to lunch with you here on Good Friday, didn't you?"

"Yes," he said.

"Then why didn't you tell me about it? Why did you let me go home from here thinking I was moving in with the Surratts? And come and get me only after Lincoln was shot?"

He folded his paper and put it aside. He looked shame-faced. "Vanity," he said.

"Vanity?"

"I was trying to prove something to myself. That even after all your mother said against me, you would come to me of your own choice. And not because I had a legal paper in hand. I was wrong, child. I'm sorry."

I nodded, humbled by this admission from him. I could see how difficult it was for him to make it.

"But there is something else you should know."

"What?"

"I wasn't doing anything your father didn't want. He asked my help to get you into Miss Martin's. He wrote to me when he was away at war. He sent me the money for your education and asked that if anything happened to him I'd bring you to Washington and put you in that school."

"Mama said she put me there. That all he did was leave the money for my education."

"Your father wanted it, Emily. And if you and your mother hadn't moved here after he was killed, I would have brought you here anyway. Your mother couldn't have done a thing about it. It was his wish, stated in his letter."

My daddy. I felt a warmth wash over me. And a rush of gratitude toward Uncle Valentine. How could I ask him about that night in the cemetery now?

He was looking at me with those warm brown eyes. "Is there anything else, Emily?" He used his voice like a surgical instrument. He could cut you with it or heal you with it. I had felt both, and I much preferred to be healed. Now that voice was indulgent, with a hint of amusement and a touch of caution.

"Did you get the lawyer for Annie?"

"I got two, Frederick Aiken and John W. Clampitt. They are the best."

I nodded and picked up my schoolbooks.

"Well, Emily," he said as I took my leave of the room, "what about it? Don't you think you would have come to live with me by choice?"

I let him think it. It was a small price to pay for Mr. Aiken and Mr. Clampitt. *Another difficult arrangement entered into,* I thought. *Another moment saved.* How many times now had I gone against Daddy's instructions? How many moments had I saved? And what would I do with them?

Uncle Valentine was right. It was a circus out on the streets.

"Quiet, girls. And stay together," Mrs. McQuade told us. "Abraham Lincoln's trip into American folklore is beginning."

She was right, too. We stood across the street from the White House in the press of people who were straining to catch a glimpse of the coffin as it was brought out the front doors by the pallbearers. All the church bells of Washington were tolling. Guns began to boom from the many fortresses that had sprung up around the city during the war. For as far as my eye could see, all up and down Pennsylvania Avenue, there was an ocean of people.

Young men were climbing trees. Young boys who had somehow staked a claim on those trees were selling places in them for twenty-five cents. A man up front was hawking places on the curb for ten dollars.

Above us, the rooftops were crowded with people. On Pennsylvania Avenue itself, policemen on horseback were trying desperately to organize the hook-and-ladder companies, men from lodges, clubs, churches, and military regiments, into some kind of procession to follow the hearse. I saw a whole contingent of Negro soldiers ready to march.

Mrs. McQuade wore a bright red bonnet. Most people around us wore black. There were several remarks about her bonnet being unseemly, but she didn't care.

"Look for my bonnet above the heads, girls," she'd told us,

"if you lose sight of me. I will be there, like a beacon in the night."

"More like one of General Hooker's ladies," Myra hissed. Myra was angry because six hundred tickets had been given out for people to file past the catafalque in the White House and she was supposed to go with her father. But at the last minute, his editor had asked him to give the ticket to a reporter from France. To assuage that unhappiness, she kept us informed about what she knew.

"General Grant is to be at the head of the catafalque. He is supposed to be wearing a white sash across his breast to show he's the head pallbearer. Well, he'll be dressed properly, for a change—not like Appomattox, when he had to borrow a clean shirt to attend the surrender."

She spoke in a very loud voice. Several people around our small group were listening. So Myra took on an air of importance.

"Robert Lincoln is to be right up there with Grant, too, of course. Likely he'll be wearing his army captain's uniform. And with him will be the only other remaining Lincoln son, Tad, who's only twelve."

"What are they doing now?" a young man asked Myra. He was done up in showy attire. Annie would have called him a hustler. Or worse.

Myra preened. "It looks like they're putting the coffin in the glass hearse."

"How come you know so much, little missy?" The hustler grinned. His two young friends nudged each other and winked and raked their eyes over Myra, whose black silk dress emanated anything but mourning.

"My father's a reporter for the *Intelligencer*."

"Is he, now? And you're out here alone? Couldn't you use an escort? And perhaps, at the same time, educate us as to what's going on? My friends and I are from Baltimore."

"I could do that," Myra said.

"Myra," Carol Johnson whispered, "don't be silly. We don't know them!"

"Mind your own affairs," Myra retorted.

Was a tattletale the worst thing one could be? I thought not. There were worse things, far worse, although I couldn't think what at the moment. I ran to Mrs. McQuade and told her that Myra was about to go off with three young men from Maryland.

Myra was already well started on going off with them. Mrs. McQuade had to run and push her way through the crowd. "Hold on there, Myra, you're going in the wrong direction," she said.

Myra turned around, a sneer on her face. "I can take care of myself."

"Not while I am commissioned to do it," Mrs. McQuade answered.

I stood directly behind her to offer what support I could. Myra glared at me. "You'll pay for this," she threatened.

"If anyone is to pay for anything," Mrs. McQuade said, "it is you, Myra. For disobeying. I told you I did not want my girls talking to strangers. Is there some problem, gentlemen?" She looked at the young men.

"We thought the young lady was alone and were looking to assist her."

"She does not need assistance. She is with my class. I am her teacher." Mrs. McQuade grabbed her arm and started to pull her away.

Myra tried to jerk free but couldn't. "I'm only telling

people what I know, Mrs. McQuade. What's the sense in knowing things if you can't tell?"

"You can tell all you want tomorrow, back in the schoolroom. You may write an essay for me. Five hundred words on today's doings. Then perhaps next time I take my class out in public you will mind my words." Mrs. McQuade pulled her along.

"The funeral train is to be eight coaches long," Myra called over her shoulder, "draped in black. And they're taking the coffin of little Willie Lincoln along with that of his father's. They dug it up. Can you imagine that? It's going back to Illinois."

"A thousand words!" Mrs. McQuade said. She grabbed Myra by the ear. It did my heart good to see it. As we walked away, I heard the three young men laughing. Myra looked at me and saw me smirking. "You'll pay for this," she said again.

Somehow I knew I would.

OUR ENEMIES
MAKE US STRONG

I LIFTED THE KETTLE of hot water off the small stove in Mrs. McQuade's office and poured it into the basin at her feet, to warm up her foot bath water.

"Don't burn yourself, child. You shouldn't be doing this. You'll scald yourself."

"I did a lot more for Mama." I set the kettle back on the stove. "Can I pour you more tea?"

"No, thank you. Get your things together now. Your ride should be here shortly."

Robert was fetching me. Mrs. McQuade would not let any of her girls walk home alone this day.

The funeral procession was over. It was four o'clock. All that could be heard on Washington's debris-laden streets was some muted talk as crowds of people walked by the front of our school on their way home from the proceedings.

The day had been sunny but now was clouded over. It was starting to drizzle. I stood back and eyed Mrs. McQuade as she soaked her feet in the basin of water.

"Such a day! I'd have forgone it if not for the honor," my teacher said. It was humor. She'd told us this was what a man once said when he'd been tarred and feathered and ridden on a rail out of town in the American Revolution.

"Mrs. McQuade, can I ask you a question?"

"Ask away. As long as it hasn't anything to do with Abraham Lincoln. I loved the man as much as anyone, but if I hear any more conjecture about the number of coaches on the funeral train or why a Negro regiment was allowed to take the lead in the funeral procession, I shall die."

"It isn't about Lincoln."

"Good."

"It's about body snatching."

She had been fanning her face with a handkerchief. She stopped fanning. "Body snatching. A good subject. An excellent subject. Worthy of consideration."

"Is it against the law?"

"Of course."

"Why do people do it?"

"To make money. They sell the bodies to medical schools, where they are used for experimentation."

"But why do the medical schools need to buy bodies from such people?"

She smiled. "Excellent question. I am so glad when my girls ask thought-provoking questions. For one simple reason: Not enough states have passed laws saying that the bodies of criminals sentenced to death should be delivered to surgeons for study."

I felt a shudder pass through me. "Have any states done this?"

"I believe some have. But too few. And anyway, even with such laws there are not enough cadavers for medical schools. So we have body snatching. But why such a question, Emily? What brought it about?"

I shrugged. "Today when Myra told that man how they dug up the body of Willie Lincoln to take back to Illinois some of the girls started talking about body snatching," I lied.

"What they did with Willie Lincoln isn't the same thing."

"I know."

"Perhaps we should have a discussion on it in our Wednesday-morning group. What do you think?"

"No," I said quickly. "I think that with the president's funeral enough of a pall has been cast over us. Some of the girls are getting morbid. I think we need something happier for a discussion."

"I suppose you are right," she said. But she was giving me that quizzical sidelong glance, like she did when she knew a girl wasn't being entirely truthful. "Don't be affected by things Myra says, Emily," she told me. "The girl likes to hear herself talk."

"Yes, ma'am." I gathered up my things. "I hear a carriage out front. I must go."

"Perhaps you would like to do a paper of your own on the subject of body snatching, since your curiosity has been aroused. I will give you extra marks for it."

"No, ma'am." I shook my head.

"Very well, the decision is yours. Go along now. And lock the door on the way out."

It was a long walk to the front of the house, past empty classrooms, parlors, the library. My footsteps echoed. Then I came to the front foyer.

"Hello, Emily."

I near jumped out of my skin. "Myra, what are you doing here?" She was in the shadows of the foyer.

Her smile was knowing. "Waiting for my father. Why didn't you tell her how the question of body snatching came up? And why you don't want it in a Wednesday Discussion Group? And why you don't wish to do a paper for extra marks?"

"It isn't nice to eavesdrop."

"It's less nice to lie. I could suggest, in front of the whole class, that we do body snatching as a subject for the Wednesday Discussion Group. The other girls would love it. You'd be outnumbered. Shall I?"

I recognized a threat when I heard one. "What do you want of me, Myra?"

"It's very simple. Get me in to see what's in that shed your uncle has behind his house."

I couldn't believe it. "What?"

"You heard me. My father has been looking his place over. He says if only he could get into that shed he would have a story. Only he can't trespass. And he hasn't enough evidence on your uncle to warrant going in on his own."

"I'm sorry for your father, then."

"I'm sorrier for you if you don't. Because I shall bring up the discussion of body snatching to Mrs. McQuade, then. And tell her, and the whole class, the reason why."

"She wouldn't stand for such."

"No, but they'd all know my father is investigating your uncle. Do you want that?"

"No, but neither do I want you poking about my uncle's shed."

"Am I to take that as an admission that he is engaged in body snatching, then?"

I was trapped. "He isn't engaged in body snatching," I said.

"Then why not do as I wish?"

"Because I can't just ask my uncle to let you in there. He has his laboratory in there. Important things."

"I'm not asking him to let me in. He'd clear out any evidence first."

"What are you asking, then?"

"Sneak me in."

"So you can spy for your father."

"I'll not be spying if there's nothing to spy on."

Was there no way out of this dreadful dilemma? Would this hateful girl never get out of my life? Why hadn't I let her run off earlier today with those three men from Baltimore? Maybe then her father would have been so busy investigating her disappearance he'd have had no time to investigate Uncle Valentine. What would be worse? To call her bluff? And let her tell the class of her father's investigation? She could prove nothing.

But it would cast suspicion on my uncle. And he had given me a home. I didn't need the girls in my class gossiping about my uncle. You have to defend the honor of your kin, don't you?

Then I heard my daddy's voice. "Don't enter into difficult arrangements to save the moment, Miss Muffet," he'd said. "Remember the miller's daughter."

But what if they're going to cut your head off in the morning? I thought. *What if all you want to do is live through the next day without losing your head?*

Surely with one more day in your favor you can figure out what to do. And for the first time, standing there, I understood why the miller's daughter had given in to Rumpelstiltskin. With one more day to bargain, you could think of something, surely.

"All right," I said. "Give me a day or two to figure out how I can do it."

She hesitated. "How do I know you won't go to him? And give him a chance to get rid of any evidence?"

We had been whispering. Now I whispered savagely. "Do you think I could go to my uncle and ask him to let you in there? He's a busy and important man. I've never been in there. I don't even know how to get in. And I have to figure it out. That will just have to do for you, Myra. Or you can tell the class about your father's investigation."

"You think I won't?"

"I know you would," I said wearily. "But somehow I think what you want more right now is to get into that shed. To please your daddy."

I pushed past her and went to the front door. I was stalling for time.

What if there is evidence of body snatching in that shed? I asked myself, going down the front steps. *What will I do then?* I was comfortable in Uncle Valentine's house. For the first time in a long time I didn't have to worry about where my next meal was coming from. Or even cook it. I could go to school without any worries. I could study and dream of the future without wondering if I'd have a home next month.

Didn't I have a right to feel such? I was only fourteen.

But I knew better. I wasn't my father's daughter for nothing. I had become too comfortable. I had put my luxury before right and wrong.

I hadn't wanted to face the nagging doubts and suspicions in my mind. And they'd been there all along. Hadn't Addie hinted to me? I had to get into that shed. For my own sanity. It was something I'd known all along I'd have to do if I wanted to live in peace with myself. Myra was just pushing me to do it a little sooner, that was all.

It all got back to something my daddy had once told me. "Our enemies make us strong, Miss Muffet, not our friends. Our friends will lie to us, tell us what we need to hear. Forgive us. We must keep a few good enemies on hand, always, to keep us sharp and teach us never to do anything that needs forgiveness."

Well, I'd gotten that right, anyway. I had Myra Mott. She qualified as a few good enemies all on her own.

"Hello," Robert said. He was waiting for me with the carriage. "I thought you'd never come out. We're late. I was about to turn into a pumpkin."

I looked at him. Somehow the reference to the fairy tale made me look on him kindly. "What are we late for?"

"Your uncle is having company for supper. He wants you there on time."

"Who?"

"Me." He grinned insolently. "And then he has an appointment for the theater. I'm afraid you're stuck with me for the rest of the evening."

"Why?"

"He is expecting a shipment, and I'm to be there to receive it."

My head started to swim with the wonderfulness of it. *So,* I thought, *my fairy godmother has not deserted me.*

"I'm afraid the evening will be long and dreary with this rain," Robert was saying. "Do you play chess?"

"A little."

"Well, how was the funeral procession? Gory enough for you young ladies?"

"Yes. Speaking of which, Robert, I need a favor."

"Ah, I knew you were being nice for a reason. What's your pleasure?"

"I'm doing a paper for extra grades at school. I want to surprise Uncle Valentine with an A-plus in science. It would help, ever so much, if I could get into his shed in back, so I could see his laboratory and write all about the equipment a doctor uses."

He gave me a down-turned smile. "Why don't you ask your uncle to let you in?"

"I told you. I want it to be a surprise. Do you think that after we play chess this evening, you could take me in there?"

He was thoughtful for a moment. "A paper, you say?"

"Yes. Mrs. McQuade said she wants to see more initiative on the part of her girls. She says that science is all around us, if we open our eyes and pay attention. She suggested we try our backyards and come up with a topic." I was warming to it, proud of my lying. "Well, I looked in my backyard and I saw Uncle Valentine's shed. And so that's when it came to me. Of course, I might not understand everything he's got out there. But you could explain it to me. If you would, I mean. Would you, Robert?"

I'm starting to sound like a Southern belle, I thought, *the one thing Daddy wanted me never to be.* But it was for a good cause. Wasn't it?

"I don't see any harm in it," Robert said. He said it casually, not realizing what he'd done for me.

I could breathe again. There was no evidence in the shed. If there were, Robert wouldn't have agreed. Not unless he was planning on slipping away from me sometime this night to remove the evidence. But he'd not be able to. I'd watch him tonight, every minute. I wouldn't let him out of my sight. Then at some future date, I'd slip Miss Sly Boots into the shed. And watch her disappointment. She'd have to go to her father and tell him he was wrong.

She'd be so angry, she'd stamp her foot and go right through the floor like Rumpelstiltskin.

15

$\mathcal{T}$HE INSIDE OF THE SHED

SO FAR I HAD managed to do very well. Robert hadn't been out of my sight once and we were at dinner. I watched Maude take away the soup dishes, wondering if I could manage as well for the rest of the evening.

"Do you like the fish, Emily?" Uncle Valentine asked.

"Yes. I love the stuffing Maude made. But I'm afraid I ate too much turtle soup."

"Eat the fish. Fish is good for you. It's brain food," Uncle Valentine said.

Robert winked at me. "Eat the fish and you can swim better," he said. "Do you swim, Emily?"

"Yes."

"Where did you learn?"

"In Maryland. We had a creek."

"Who taught you?"

"Johnny Surratt," I said.

"Oh." Robert scowled. I knew what he was thinking. Did everything in my life go full circle and get back to Johnny Surratt? "I hear he's still in Canada. There's a twenty-five-thousand-dollar price on his head."

I picked nervously at the fish. I hadn't thought about Johnny all day. I felt disloyal to him. All I could think of was if I'd really get into the shed this night.

The table was set beautifully. Night-blooming cereus, their white petals down because it wasn't dark yet, were in a bowl as the centerpiece. Candles glowed. Even though the house was equipped with gaslight, Uncle Valentine preferred candles. There was, in addition to the fish, roasted potatoes, green beans, pickled preserves, cheddar and Gloucester cheeses, a chicken pie. And a whipped syllabub.

Where Mrs. McQuade had her Wednesday Morning Discussion Group, Uncle Valentine had his Thursday Evening Dinners. I hadn't lived with him long enough to experience the range of guests, but I had lived with him long enough to know he hated eating alone. Tonight it was just Robert. What with the Lincoln funeral, everyone was exhausted.

"I heard that Booth was arrested in Toronto," Robert said.

Toronto? I looked up quickly. If they'd caught Booth in Toronto, did that mean they'd also catch Johnny? Then I realized Robert was joking.

"I heard he was arrested in Massachusetts. And Pennsylvania. And Chicago," Uncle Valentine said.

"How can you make sport about it?" I asked him.

"It's becoming quite the thing to come up with new and

absurd stories about where John Wilkes Booth was last seen," Robert said.

"It's no joke to any handsome man with a black mustache," Uncle Valentine said. "The paper said today that dozens of them have been seized and rushed off to jail." He sighed. "The funeral is over here in Washington, but I don't think the country will ever recover from this blow. Ever. In the North, mobs are attacking anyone who has the hint of being a Southern sympathizer, tarring and feathering them, beating them. I'm not sure it was a good idea allowing the funeral train to go on this long journey through so many states."

"The people would have it no other way," Robert reminded him. "I heard they are lining the tracks, thousands of them, all the way to Baltimore. Singing."

Just then came the sound of a wagon coming in the gate. Uncle Valentine and Robert exchanged glances. "Too early," Uncle Valentine said. "The fool."

Robert got up and went to the window. "It's only the ice wagon," he said.

Another shipment of ice? I thought. Maude had ordered enough ice all week to make an igloo. Then Uncle Valentine started talking again. He said he'd heard that John Wilkes Booth had been seen on a train wearing women's clothing, with burnt cork on his face to make him appear as a Negro.

The ice wagon rumbled into the yard. I heard Maude go out the kitchen door to greet the driver. Uncle Valentine offered me some of Maude's fresh beaten biscuits. I did like beaten biscuits. And Maude's were lighter than any I'd ever eaten. But if Robert went outside to greet the iceman, I was going with him. I didn't know what excuse I'd give, but I'd find one.

As it turned out, I did not have to. Robert stayed at the table all through dinner. After Uncle Valentine left for the theater, we went out to the shed.

I watched as he lifted a stone out of the side wall of the shed, secured a key, and ingeniously replaced the stone. As he did so, another wagon appeared at the gate.

Robert set down the shaded lantern. It was still raining lightly, a fine rain that did not deter Marietta's nightflowers from blooming but seemed to make them glisten. From somewhere in the distance a clock in a church steeple chimed. Nine woeful bells.

"I'll take this shipment first, then show you inside," Robert promised.

I stepped aside. I was shivering. The horse-drawn wagon came in through the gate and stopped just short of the shed. The driver jumped down.

"Mr. Christian?" Robert asked.

"The same," the man said.

"How many casks did you bring?"

"Three." The man was well built, with black hair and beard. He was also well dressed, though a bit wet. "Who is this?" he asked, gesturing to me.

"Niece of the doctor."

"One of us?"

"She's still in school," Robert said. "Are the contents of merchantable quality?" He peered at the casks in the wagon. They said PICKLES.

"Yes."

"Not from out of state, I hope. The doctor wants no out-of-state pickles."

"Local," Christian said. "Fresh picked from a nearby farm."

"How much a cask?"

"Forty dollars. And seven dollars each for shipping."

"Seven? That's outrageous!" Robert sounded angry.

The man shrugged. "The contents are packed in the right solution."

"Rum, arsenic, and corrosive sublimate?"

"Yes."

Robert grunted. "The formula works wonders. Very well, but you've made a tidy profit. If the merchandise isn't fresh, you'll hear from us." He reached inside his coat, took out his wallet, and counted out the cash.

"I was chased by three roughs," the man complained. "Pickles are in short supply these days."

They struggled getting the casks out of the wagon. *Awfully heavy for pickles,* I thought. They rolled the casks on the ground. Robert opened the shed door and they went inside. I waited out in the fine misty rain. Then Mr. Christian came out. "Tell the doctor if he wants any more pickles, I can get them fresh. Always." He climbed into his wagon, clucked to the horses, and the wagon rumbled off.

I looked at Robert. "Pickles?" I asked.

He smiled. "You must know everything, mustn't you? It's the solution the pickles are packed in that we're after. It's used to preserve specimens and is in great demand."

"Why did he ask if I was one of you?"

"He meant working for the doctor. Now, do you want to come in and see the shed or not?"

We went down four steps once inside the door. The first thing I noticed was the cold.

"Be careful," Robert said. "Sometimes there is water on the floor."

"Why is it so cold?"

"To keep the specimens preserved." He went about lighting lamps.

The place came to life. The back wall was lined with heavy draperies. "Window," Robert said. "When your uncle works in here he opens the draperies to let sunlight in. Nobody lives back there, so he has privacy."

The walls were painted white. And lined with wooden shelves. Some of the shelves had large jars filled with floating things. I saw the head of a pig in one jar. A frog in another. Even a snake. From a far corner a human skeleton glared at me. I gasped.

In still another jar a human finger floated in some solution.

Robert smiled. "It was saved by your uncle when it was found on the floor of one of the army hospitals. I see you brought pad and pencil. Aren't you going to take notes?"

"Yes."

Robert showed me around. He showed me syringes, stones taken from a gallbladder, a human skull. I saw no bodies. But I was fascinated just the same.

He showed me some carbolic acid, used as a disinfectant. He held up a jar with some dark liquid. "This is iodine," he said. "It was first used in a field hospital in Jonesboro, Georgia, during the war, where it was sprayed into the air as an antiseptic. But we here in America are way behind Europe in our medical progress. Here, for instance, is a clinical thermometer. It is hundreds of years old. Yet during the war there were not more than twenty in the whole Union Army."

I wrote.

"This is a hypodermic syringe. It is still only used by some surgeons. Most still prefer to dust morphine into wounds or give opium pills. This is an ophthalmoscope. A doctor can examine the inside of the eye with it. It was invented in 1851. But then years after its invention few doctors in our army could yet use it."

"Why?"

"Because the army had too many incompetent medical men. And because before the war most medical schools did not have the advanced knowledge of the day. The war opened up those opportunities for us. It gave us the chance to do things, out of sheer necessity, that were not even allowed or taught in medical schools."

"So there was some good to the war," I said.

"Yes. War always brings us technological advances."

"My daddy died of a stomach wound."

"So many did. The son of Dr. Bowditch of Boston, for instance. Young Bowditch was wounded on the battlefield. No ambulance was sent out to him. He was brought off on a horse and died. Bowditch fought the War Department for a trained ambulance corps."

"Did he get one?"

"Yes. Where did your father die?"

"Chancellorsville."

"May of '63. By then we had an ambulance corps. But it was a Confederate win. The ambulance corps brought about eight thousand of our men into the division hospitals, but twelve hundred were left on the field when our army retreated. They were treated well enough when captured, but in the ten days before the prisoner exchange there was a real shortage of supplies."

I nodded. My mouth was dry. "I know what that is." I pointed. "A stethoscope."

"Yes. Invented in 1838. And Harvard Medical School still

doesn't have one. Its catalogs still don't mention many of these instruments."

"Why?"

He shrugged. "Too many medical schools are just diploma mills. What we've learned from the war still hasn't gotten to them. It's why the work your uncle is doing is so important. He is directly teaching what he learned in the war. And he is one of the most qualified teachers of anatomy around today."

"You mean he works on dead bodies."

"All medical schools use them, yes. Anatomy courses are the reason for the establishment of medical schools. Before that students learned as apprentices, following doctors around."

"Where do you get the bodies?"

"They are bequeathed to us. Or they are those of executed criminals." His gaze was warm and direct. Was he lying? No, I decided. His answers were too easy. I wrote some more.

"And finally, this is an achromatic microscope," Robert said. "The headquarters of the Army Medical Department didn't have one until 1863. Well, does that satisfy your curiosity?"

"Yes. Thank you, Robert."

He extinguished the lamps. As we walked past the casks, it occurred to me that the label, PICKLES, on each one was ludicrous, in light of all this scientific equipment. I followed Robert out the door. Not for one moment did I believe there were pickles in those barrels. What, then? I did not know. But I was sure whatever was in them was for the good of mankind. Perhaps some new discovery. Who was I to question it?

"What are these flowers?" Myra stood on the stone path, her eyes wide. "I've never seen such flowers."

"Never mind the flowers. They're an experiment for the good of mankind," I told her. That shut her mouth for a while and added just the right touch so that when I asked her to turn her back while I got the key to the shed, she obeyed without a fuss.

"This is a hypodermic syringe," I said inside the shed. I picked it up. "It is still only used by some surgeons. Most still prefer to dust morphine into wounds or give opium pills."

She stared, openmouthed. "It's an ugly thing. Put it down."

"Perhaps you would prefer to see this. It's an ophthal-moscope."

She shivered. "What's it for?"

"To examine the inside of the eye."

"The *inside*?"

"Yes. It was invented way back in 1851. And few doctors yet use it."

She ran her tongue along her lips. "Thank heaven for that."

"And this is called an achromatic microscope. The head-quarters of the Army Medical Department didn't have one until 1863." I had memorized my notes well, so I was able to repeat, word for word, what Robert had told me.

It was late afternoon, two days after my visit to the shed. Maude, Uncle Valentine, and Robert were all out, as I'd known they would be. Myra and I had skipped out of school to do this. Well, not exactly. We'd told Mrs. McQuade we were going on a field trip to discover nature in our sur-roundings.

I had decided to bluff it out with Myra. To give her the full treatment, hoping the sight of all this would terrify her.

It did. She did not know where to look first. Her eyes slid from one object to another, staring in horrified fascination and moving on. She moved gingerly around in the damp cold of the shed, bumping up against things. She moved now.

"Look out for that skeleton," I said.

She had bumped against it. The skeleton, in cooperation, rattled. Myra screamed and moved away.

I picked up the jar of solution with the human finger in it. "This was found on the floor in one of the hospitals my uncle worked in during the war."

She covered her hands with her mouth.

"You aren't taking notes, Myra. You'll have to report back to Mrs. McQuade."

"Horrid stuff. I won't write about it. What's *that*?"

"What?" I looked in the direction of her finger. "Oh, it's a pig's head. And, of course, that other jar holds a frog and the third a snake. On that shelf directly behind you are stones from a gallbladder. Now, see this dark stuff?" I held it up. "Iodine. Used in a field hospital in Jonesboro, Georgia, during the war. As an antiseptic. Sprayed in the air."

She nodded numbly. "Where are the bodies?"

"No bodies, Myra."

"You've hidden them."

"There were none here when Robert first showed me around, and there are none here now. The only bodies are in the college lab. And they were bequeathed. Or they are bodies of executed criminals."

"My father says medical schools have nowhere near enough bodies. And that's why they have to steal them."

How could I scare her off if she was going to use logic? "There are no bodies here," I said again.

"How do I know you didn't get this Robert person to get the bodies out before I came?"

I sighed. "I got in here on a pretense with Robert. Do you think I'd tell him why I wanted to see the place? They trust me. And he had no time to remove anything. From the time I asked him to bring me in here to the time he opened that door, I was with him the whole evening."

She had no answer for that. She was running out of answers. But not questions. "What's in those casks?"

"They're empty now. They held pickles—don't you see the labels?"

"Pickles?"

"Yes. The solution from them is used to preserve specimens. It is very much in demand." I opened the lid. I'd known it was empty because I'd seen the lid unsealed. It hadn't been the other night.

She peered inside. "Smells of whiskey."

"They were packed in rum, arsenic, and corrosive sublimate to preserve them. Well, now you've seen everything. What have you got to say?"

"Let's get out of here." She shuddered. "I'll never eat pickles again."

Uncle Valentine was picking at the food on his plate. It wasn't his way. He had a hearty appetite. It was dinner on Saturday, the twenty-second.

He had invited Marietta. The windows were open, and from outside came the sounds of carriages on the street, children playing. It was dusk. Candles flickered. For most of the meal Marietta had kept us entertained with the clever sayings of her students and talked about their progress. Now she fell silent, and I sensed something was wrong.

Marietta sipped her wine and twirled the stem of her glass with her slender hand. "He'll be all right," she said in her low, well-modulated voice. "I promise you, Valentine."

They exchanged glances and I knew that she was "just knowing things" for him now, as she had described her special gift to me.

"Things will be difficult for him for a while," she said. "He may go on trial, even to prison for a while, but eventually he'll be released. People will understand that he did the right thing."

My uncle sighed. Then he turned to me. "We're being rude," he said. "You should know that my friend Dr. Mudd was arrested at his place in Maryland yesterday. And named in the conspiracy to murder Lincoln."

I gasped. "I don't understand," I said.

"Neither do I," Uncle Valentine muttered. "I saw him today. He's here in Washington in prison. It seems Booth and Herold came to Mudd's farm on the fifteenth after riding all night and day. Booth had a broken bone in his leg. Mudd fixed the leg. On the eighteenth, soldiers came to Mudd's place. Mudd lied. Said a man had come with a broken leg, but he didn't know who he was. The soldiers left and came back yesterday. And Mudd admitted he'd previously known Booth and known whose leg he had set."

He looked at Marietta. "He shouldn't have lied. That will implicate him. Otherwise he could just claim he was doing his duty as a doctor."

"He was," Marietta said simply.

He scowled. "Is a doctor to be persecuted, then, for doing

what he thinks is right? Does he not have a duty to mankind?"

He brooded on the matter through dinner, in spite of Marietta's reassurances. And I began to wonder if he was asking the question about Dr. Mudd or about himself.

WISH YOU WERE HERE

I BECAME ACCUSTOMED to the rhythms of Uncle Valentine's house. In the mornings, before I was out of bed, I'd hear him down the hall in his water closet, blowing his nose and making all the sounds men make upon rising. I recognized those sounds from my daddy and they were, in their own way, comforting.

Uncle Valentine was afflicted by what he called "the curse of the goldenrod." My daddy had had it, too. Only he'd come by his distress in August. Here it was only April 27, and Uncle Valentine was sneezing all over the place and there was no goldenrod in sight.

"Would that I could find a cure for this wretched sneezing and eye itching," he'd say.

For half an hour each morning he coughed up phlegm.

"Maude," he'd call, "two grains of quinine, an ounce of whiskey, and a mug of hot coffee." I'd hear Maude climbing the stairs.

On her way back down she'd knock at my door. "Are you awake?"

How could I not be, with all that noise?

Uncle Valentine then shaved. He did not sport a beard, like so many men of the day. And he wanted all his students clean-shaven, too. Robert was.

I'd lie in bed for a while in my second-story tower room, in my Sheraton four-poster that was draped in blue. I had never had such a lovely room. I'd feel like a princess. Until I remembered that towers also held prisoners. Like the miller's daughter. And though I liked it and everyone was nice to me, I hadn't decided yet which I was.

I'd scratch Puss-in-Boots around the ears. She slept with me every night. But I knew I must get up and get dressed. I was expected at the table for breakfast.

While dressing I'd hear Maude coming up the steps again. And I'd know it was with a tray of food for Addie. Before he went down for breakfast, Uncle Valentine would go up to the third floor to visit Addie. I'd hear Addie complaining, Uncle Valentine saying the same thing every morning. "Well now, how do you feel today, Addie? Is that medicine working?"

Every morning, Uncle Valentine ate a hearty breakfast of fresh fish, biscuits, eggs, and coffee. I couldn't bear so much food in the morning. So I'd have hot cooked oats with brown sugar. Was that what Miss Muffet ate sitting on her tuffet? I'd always wondered what curds and whey were.

Uncle Valentine would read his paper while eating. Maude would come in and out softly, setting down more food. I'd hear her talking to deliverymen at the back door—the man

163

who brought the milk, another with fish. Then to her husband, Merry, who stopped by for breakfast. Maude and Merry lived a few streets over. And she went home each night.

Merry popped his head in the door of the dining room every morning. "No shipments last night, boss," he'd say.

"All right, Merry. You better go home and get some sleep," Uncle Valentine would answer.

Merry worked nights.

Or else Merry would tell Uncle Valentine about a shipment that had come. "A dark shipment, boss." And Merry would stand there, all four feet of him, turning his hat in his hands.

"That's all right, Merry. We could use a dark shipment."

"The Board of Guardians at the Almshouse isn't happy."

"They never are," Uncle Valentine would say. "I'll talk to them later."

"Talk won't do it. They want more money."

"Then we ought to start calling them the Board of Buzzards."

Merry would nod his head vigorously. "But there's good news, boss. The procurement committee has intelligence on some new donations."

"Good, good, Merry. I'll be in touch with them this afternoon."

Sometimes Marietta dropped by early in the morning to have coffee with us. She'd talk to Uncle Valentine. About her children. She'd ask him what to do about their ailments. "Willie has the croup," she'd say. Or, "Florence is coming down with a cold."

Uncle Valentine would tell her what to do for them. Or, if it was bad enough, he'd tell her to bring them around.

Usually Maude lingered after she served Uncle Valentine

his second cup of coffee, and she'd go over plans for the day. "Funeral this afternoon," she'd tell him.

He'd ask who. It was never anybody important. Maude seemed to go only to the funerals of those who were impoverished or bereft of family. Many were at Potter's Field, which was the burying ground for paupers.

"They've caught up with John Wilkes Booth," Uncle Valentine read to me from the paper on Thursday, April 27, at breakfast.

"Where?"

"In Virginia. On a farm owned by a man named Garrett. South of the Rapahannock. Federal troops surrounded the barn and ordered the suspects out. He was in there with Herold."

"David Herold," I said.

He looked up quickly. "You never said you knew him."

"Herold is the friend of Johnny's who worked at Thompson's Drug Store. He was supposed to bring the medicine for Mama. He didn't."

Uncle Valentine nodded and continued reading. "Federal troops set afire the barn where Booth was hiding. He wouldn't come out. Then someone fired a shot and killed him. They're bringing his body back to Washington for identification and an autopsy."

"Why are they doing an autopsy?"

"They want to determine what killed him."

"A bullet killed him," I said.

Booth dead. It set me to thinking of Annie. What would she say? "Can I go to Annie's after school? I think she's going to need me."

"No," he said sharply. "I don't want you near that house!"

Then he softened. "Annie can come here anytime she wishes," he said quietly. "But there is no telling when the Metropolitan Police may search that house again. You must listen to me on this, Emily. Don't you see what happened to my friend Dr. Mudd?"

He was absolutely devastated by his friend's imprisonment. So I supposed I must humor him. Annie would come. She'd been around twice in the last week, to tell Uncle Valentine that her mother found the new lawyers most satisfactory. She'd also said her mother was not eating.

It looked to me as if Annie wasn't eating, either. She'd gotten thin. There was a stain on her dress the last time she was here. Her hair needed washing. She went, every day, to see her mother in prison. Then she'd go home to the empty house on H Street, without even a cat to greet her.

"Annie told me that her mother is manacled at the wrists and is in leg irons," I said.

"She is lucky. The others, including my friend, are on ironclads in the river, manacled, with hoods over their heads, in the heat."

"I'm sorry about your friend, Uncle Valentine," I said.

He sighed. "I'm sorry, too, Emily. We have something in common now, don't we? Friends involved in this nasty business. There is nothing more I can do for Mrs. Surratt, child. The rest is up to Mrs. Surratt's lawyers. And her son Johnny. If he would come home, likely they would let his mother go free. It's Johnny Surratt they want, not his mother."

I flushed and looked down at my tea. Nobody had heard from Johnny. But it was what people were saying, that if Johnny came back to Washington and gave himself up to authorities they would let his mother go. *Oh, Johnny,* I thought, *where are you? Have you heard about what's going on? Why don't you come home?*

"Now, let's change the subject," Uncle Valentine said. "This is dreary. What do you have planned for after school today?"

It was Thursday. I knew what he wanted. On Tuesdays and Thursdays he saw patients here at the house. They started arriving at three. And Maude was never here at that time. She was either at market or at one of the many funerals she attended. Usually nobody was home.

The first time I'd seen all the patients waiting outside the house I hadn't known who they were or what to do. Once they explained who they were, I let them in. It seemed the civil thing to do. But then they started crowding around me, telling me their names and their ailments, wanting to be first when the doctor arrived. There had been such commotion I did the only thing I could do. I took names and ailments. I decided which ailment sounded the worst and put that person down as first to be seen. I seated them in the small waiting room. I fetched water for the coughers, brought down some old soft toys I'd found upstairs for the children. One day I made tea for an old Negro woman with three children hanging on her. She was so grateful, she cried.

"You're wonderful," he said when he came home. "I never saw anyone make such order out of chaos. I've always dreaded coming home and having all those people yelling at me."

He asked me if I would do it every Tuesday and Thursday. I said I would. No one had ever accused me of making order out of chaos. I liked the charge. Perhaps if I did a little more of it I could soon make order out of the chaos of my own life. I was starting.

167

"I'll be home from school directly," I promised. "Do you want me to sort the mail?"

"If you would be so kind."

He got tons of mail every day. From students asking to be in his classes; colleagues all over the world; old friends in Edinburgh, where he went to medical school; suppliers from out of state; quacks writing to him of their cures; old patients he had made well again. There were bills, newspapers, periodicals. I kept a log as to what letter had come in from what place on what day.

It was on that very Thursday, the twenty-seventh, that I found the letter addressed to me in the pile of Uncle Valentine's mail. I had just finished ushering four patients into the waiting room and was sorting the mail out on Uncle Valentine's desk.

My heart jumped right up from my chest, like Puss-in-Boots jumped for a dangling string. It was on its way out of my mouth when I saw that the letter had no postmark. How had it gotten here?

I had to put my hand over my mouth to hold my heart in. There was no return address. It was Johnny's handwriting.

Dear Emily,
Burn this letter. Please, burn it as soon as you read it. I am taking a chance even writing to you. I cannot write to Annie. I suspect all the mail coming to our house has been seized. Tell Annie, please, that I am fine. I cannot tell you where I am. Just that I am in Canada. They have detectives here looking for me. I originally came north on orders from General Wilder, who directed me to go to Elmira, New York,

and learn about the fortifications of the prison where they are holding Confederate soldiers. I completed my mission and was traveling from Elmira on my way back to Richmond, when I heard about Lincoln's assassination. Then I read in the papers that they are offering $25,000 for my capture. So I took the next train north and crossed into Canada, where I've been hiding. I have employed a gentleman to go to Washington to put himself in touch with my mother's counsel and report to me if my mother is in any real danger. I have paid this man's expenses. He promised to find where you were living. But his presence is a secret. Even from my mother. You must keep it a secret. Promise.

Until I hear from him that my presence is necessary, I must stay hidden away. But my bag is packed. Up until now I have had only one report from him: "Be under no apprehension as to any serious consequences. Remain perfectly quiet, as any action on your part would only tend to make matters worse. If you can be of any service to us, we will let you know; but keep quiet."

Again, please tell Annie I am fine. Tell no one else you have heard from me. And burn this as soon as you read it. I do miss you, Emily. Canada is beautiful. I wish you were here with me.

Yours affectionately,
Johnny

My hands were trembling. I felt the blood drain from my face. Johnny's man had dropped this off at our house!

Johnny was alive and well. And hiding. But he was ready to come back if his mother needed him.

Tears flooded my eyes. My heart felt like an old rag wrung out in turpentine. It stung so. My legs were shaking with a life of their own that I could not control. In the next room I could hear Uncle Valentine's patients talking. I heard a baby whimpering. Then the front door opened and I heard Uncle Valentine come in. "Good day, good day to all," I heard him greet his patients. "Give me just one moment, dear people, and I shall be right with you."

Then his footsteps coming into the office!

I crumpled the letter up and stuffed it in my apron pocket.

"Emily. So there you are."

"You're early," I said.

"Yes, well, I settled things earlier than usual at the college today. Don't forget, this is Thursday, dinner party night."

"Yes. Who's coming?"

"A photographer fellow named Gurney, who took a picture of Lincoln in his coffin in New York City the other day. He brought the picture to us at the college. Lincoln is not holding up. I told them he wouldn't. His face is all shrunken in. He still must travel through Albany, Syracuse, Buffalo, and Cleveland, then into Indiana and Illinois. You look pale. Are you all right?"

"I have a headache."

"Go lie down, child. I'd like you to be at your best at dinner."

"I haven't logged in the mail yet."

"You can do it later. Go, go. I must see my patients. Get yourself a nice cup of tea and take it to your room."

I went. I got myself a nice cup of tea. I heated it on the fire on the stove in the kitchen. The fire was low, but it burned brighter when I put the letter from Johnny in it. Then I got some fresh sugar cookies Maude had just made that morning and went to my room to think.

Johnny's man had come here to our house. Would there be any more letters for me?

THREE LOSSES

I HAD SENT ANNIE a note the very afternoon I got the one from Johnny, asking her to dinner that evening. But she couldn't come. Our guests were Mr. Gurney, the photographer who took the picture of Lincoln in his coffin in New York, and Dr. Springer and his wife. He was a colleague of Uncle Valentine's.

Gurney told us that a large Newfoundland dog had walked under the president's hearse in New York City. Its owner said he'd been in Washington, met Lincoln, and had the dog with him. Mr. Lincoln had patted the dog and now, the owner said, the dog recognized Lincoln's hearse.

Mrs. Springer spoke about gentle things. The roses she was cultivating in her garden, her love of Shakespeare. Dr. Springer was doing experiments to prove that flies were the culprits in the transmission of hospital gangrene. He was in the Peninsular campaign in 1862. And he observed that troops in motion most of the time were healthier. "It wasn't because of exercise and better morale," he told us. "It was because they left their dirt behind them."

I enjoyed myself immensely. And I forgot about Annie. The next day, when she came to the house, we had a fight. And from there everything in my life turned sour as bad milk.

Annie and I were alone. As usual, Maude was off to a funeral. I lit some astral lamps and they made a nice glow in the parlor. I made tea and served applesauce cake. I told her the story about the Newfoundland dog in New York walking under the president's casket.

She didn't smile.

"Uncle Valentine's guests are always so interesting," I said.

"Well, I'm glad you're enjoying yourself here, Emily. I really am." She crumbled bits of applesauce cake in her dish with her fingers.

"I didn't say I was enjoying myself. I said things were interesting."

"It's the same thing. You know what I did yesterday?"

"You were invited for supper. You didn't come." I hadn't told her about Johnny's letter yet. I was waiting to surprise her at the right moment. It hadn't yet come.

"I went to visit my mother. They put her in a smaller cell. She has no bed but straw on the floor. One thin blanket. She has to relieve herself in a bucket, out in the open, in full view of the guards. My mother is a lady. How can she live like that?"

"I heard the others who were arrested are confined in iron-clads on the river," I said, "with hoods over their heads at all times."

"Are you telling me my mother is lucky?" She was spoiling for a fight.

"No."

"They won't let me bring her any supplies."

"Perhaps you can bring her something else," I said. And I told her about Johnny's letter. I didn't tell her about Johnny's man in Washington.

Her expression never changed while I recited the contents of the letter to her. I had committed it to memory.

"Let me see it," she said.

"I can't. I burned it."

"You *burned it!*" Now she really had something to pounce on me about.

"As Johnny directed."

"It would have meant so much to Mama!"

"It would have led them to Johnny."

"How? You said he didn't tell you where he was."

"It would have led them to me," I told her.

She looked at me. "Are you saying you're ashamed to know Johnny?"

"No. But they don't know the Johnny we know. They think he was in on the plot. Uncle Valentine doesn't want them thinking I was."

"Oh, I see. Because that would ruin all those lovely Thursday-night dinners for you."

Tears came to my eyes. "That isn't fair."

She didn't care. She kept right at it, hitting me one blow after another. "Or maybe he doesn't want the attention of the authorities on him. With what he does."

"What are you talking about, Annie?"

"You know. This doctor business. And what he does with dead bodies."

For a moment I couldn't speak. Then I found my tongue. "Whatever he does, it's all proper and legal. And he went to the prison and spoke up for his friend Dr. Mudd. That doesn't sound like he's trying to avoid the authorities. I think you're being hateful and mean, Annie. Uncle Valentine was good to you. Didn't he get the lawyers for your mother?"

"Oh, what do I care about dead bodies or what he does with them, anyway? The only dead body I care about is John Booth's. I'm glad he was shot. I'm glad they killed him. I'd have killed him myself if they didn't. All I care about is Mama. And the way I have to see her in prison every day. What do you expect?"

"I expect you to be reasonable."

"Who is reasonable in Washington these days? Find me one reasonable person. Everyone has a gripe, a fear, a hatred. And is looking for someone to blame it on."

"Exactly. And if they find Johnny, they'll blame it on him."

"Johnny shouldn't wait to be found," she said. "He should come home of his own accord."

"How can you say that?"

"He knows I'm in trouble. And Mama. He's read it in the papers. He should come home to be with us." She was crying, wiping her eyes with her sleeve.

"Then you'd have both a mother and a brother in jail," I said. "Would that help?"

"It'd help to know Johnny cared enough to come home and put himself in the line of fire for Mama. Or help me. I've got no one. Not even Alex. I've had no letters from him. Wouldn't you think he'd write? I go home to an empty house. Without even my cat."

"You can have your cat back if you want her," I said, "but you're wrong about Johnny."

"You always did favor him over me," she retorted.

There was no consoling her. She wouldn't be soothed with more tea or applesauce cake, words, or reminders of friendship. She left in a huff.

She took Puss-in-Boots with her, too. Just picked her up and went out of the house with the cat under her arm. In the rain. I sat alone, feeling hurt and confused. I wanted to cry. Annie was the only friend I had from the old days, the days when my mother and father were still alive, the days before the madness of the war came on us all like some sickness, turning us against each other. She was the only one with whom I could share common memories. And now she was gone. With Puss-in-Boots.

I waited for Uncle Valentine to come home. I couldn't tell him about the letter from Johnny, of course, but I could tell him Annie had been in a foul mood and meaner than a hen with its head chopped off.

I could tell him we'd fought, that she thought Johnny should come back.

I could tell him she took Puss-in-Boots. He would know what to say. He always did.

But he didn't come home that night. He sent a note around to Maude, who came in soon after Annie left. He had gone to a hanging.

"A hanging?" My mouth fell open as Maude read me the note. "Why a hanging?"

"He was invited."

Invited? People got invited to hangings? I was baffled, desolate.

"They need doctors to pronounce the people dead," she said.

"Was it a criminal?"

"Of course. Why else is anyone hanged?"

Oh, I thought. *So then he'll get the body for his medical school.* I felt sick to my stomach at the thought, but I didn't say anything. Maude served me dinner alone in the dining room. Rain slashed against the windows. The lamplight flickered. *A good night for a hanging,* I thought. I wondered what Annie was doing all alone in her house. Then I remembered she was not alone. She had Puss-in-Boots.

I missed the cat. She'd taken to following me around the house. When I pulled back the bedspread she'd hop up on the bed and roll over, waiting for me. Would Annie remember to feed her, with all she had on her mind?

I went up to my tower room and got into bed. I tried to read, but I couldn't. The whole house seemed to be filled with creakings and eerie noises. Outside a shutter banged. A tree branch scraped against a window.

Upstairs, in her room above mine, Addie was walking. She walked constantly, it seemed. Two nights ago I'd gone up and knocked on her door to see what was wrong. She'd said Uncle Valentine had her on new medicine. It stopped the coughing. "But I's restless," she'd said. "An' I keeps thinkin' it's a shame to let it go to waste. I could be out there helpin' my people."

If you'd help me escape. She had not said the words, but they hung in the dark between us. They fluttered around the glow of my candle, like moths drawn to the flame. And they followed me downstairs. Addie had become a recrimination to me. I felt guilty about her. As guilty as I felt about Annie. And there was nothing I could do for either one.

I listened to the sound of the rain against the windows. It lulled my thoughts. I supposed that Uncle Valentine had taken the body of the hanged man back to the medical school and that was why he hadn't come home. What would he do with it? Would the neck be broken? The eyes bulging out? Wasn't that what happened when they hanged people? What good would that body be to Uncle Valentine, anyway?

I fell asleep.

Toward morning I woke up. I'd been dreaming that I was in the creek back home, wading and waiting for Johnny Surratt, who was to bring fishing rods. We were to fish the morning away. Then my father appeared on Manfred, in his full-dress uniform of the Union Army. "Johnny isn't coming home anymore, Miss Muffet," my father said. Then of a sudden there was a terrible fog and my father rode off into it. I ran across the creek to get to the bank and call him back, but he was gone. All I heard was voices muffled in the fog.

I sat up in bed. I was awake, but the muffled voices were still in the house. Downstairs. I got up and opened my door.

Addie was standing there, like she'd been waiting for me the whole time. I jumped. I'd taken to locking my door at night after she'd come into my room a couple of times and I'd awakened to find her standing over me.

"You should knock," I scolded.

"And if a man has committed a crime punishable by death and he is put to death, and you hang him on a tree, his body shall not remain all night upon the tree, but you shall bury him the same day, for a hanged man is accursed by God; you shall not defile your land which the Lord your God gives you for an inheritance," she said.

"What?"

"Deuteronomy," she said.

I stared at her. This woman could not read. But then, all

Negroes know their Bible, even if they can't read. That didn't surprise me. What surprised me was that she'd said the words slowly, like a child reciting a verse, but in plain English, with no slave dialect.

She smiled. "I can speak in tongues when I want," she said.

I nodded.

"You know what that verse mean?"

I shook my head no.

"He do." She pointed to the direction of the banister and the downstairs. "Your uncle. He know full well." She was speaking like Addie again. "He know, and he goin' against that verse." Then she put her index finger to her lips, shushed me, and led me over to the banister.

I followed, thinking, *Dear God, somehow she's found out that Uncle Valentine went to a hanging and brought the corpse back to the medical college.*

"Listen," she said again. I peered down over the banister, listening. I must humor her.

Voices. One was Uncle Valentine's. Another belonged to Merry Andrews. And he was very excited. The other voices I didn't recognize.

Apparently Addie had already gotten the drift of the conversation. She was grinning widely. "You jus' listen. An' you'll know what I always tol' you 'bout him."

I sighed wearily. Were we to speak of this again? I was annoyed because I wanted to sit down and savor my dream, because my daddy had been in it. And even if it was silly to put so much store in a dream, the presence of my daddy was still strong with me.

"How many?" Uncle Valentine was asking.

"Hundreds," a strange voice said.

"What do you mean *hundreds*?"

"Hundreds were killed in the accident. All Federal soldiers. On their way home from Vicksburg, just out of Confederate prison camps." Merry's voice. "The name of the riverboat was the *Sultana*. On the Mississippi. Just north of Memphis, near Old Hen and Chickens islands. Word we got was that it was a burst boiler. Wreckage was strewn into the air. Men and horses and mules were everywhere in the water. Over two thousand souls were on board. They're saying at least twelve hundred were killed."

They were speaking in muted disembodied voices that seemed to float up to me like part of my dream. "There will be nothing left of them," Uncle Valentine said sadly.

"You're working on burns, aren't you?" Another voice. Whose?

Robert's.

"Yes, burns," Uncle Valentine said. "You're right. This is our chance to learn about burns! Of course, forgive me, Robert, I'm not thinking clearly. I've had no sleep. How quickly can you get there?"

"I can leave now," Robert said. "There's a train at eight this morning."

"Mole?"

"I'm on my way, boss. Just give the word."

"Spoon?"

"I'm all packed."

The Spoon and the Mole! I was awake now, all right. I heard Myra's voice in my head: *I'll bet that business at the cemetery was all a little farce. So you would never dream he was involved in body snatching.*

I had to hold on to the banister.

Uncle Valentine knew those two dwarf body snatchers he'd chased that night in the cemetery. They worked for him. What more proof did I need to know that Myra was right?

"Have you made contact?" Uncle Valentine was asking.

"Yes." It must have been one of the dwarves. "Our man in Memphis."

"How many do you think we should bring back, Robert?" Uncle Valentine asked.

"Two," Robert said. "Other doctors are sending representatives. So we should waste no time. Students from Winchester Medical College in Virginia are on their way there already."

"Have you a plan?" Uncle Valentine sounded like a teacher now, like Mrs. McQuade.

"It's always best to say you're family," Robert said. "I'll say I'm looking for a brother. And I thought I'd take Marietta with me. She could be a neighbor, looking for her husband. We've done it before. She's sharp and smart, with a level head and not given to silly feminine hysteria or scruples. She said she could get someone to take her place in school for a few days."

"Right," Uncle Valentine said.

Marietta. But of course, why not? I felt a stab of jealousy. *Sharp and smart.* Enough to be in on whatever it was they were doing. *A level head. Not given to silly feminine hysteria or scruples.* She worked in the lab, didn't she? Oh, it was like a knife through me, hearing Robert talk about Marietta like that. And the special note of pride in his voice when he'd said it, too!

"It's always better with a woman along. They invite less suspicion," Uncle Valentine said.

A woman. He considered Marietta a woman! And me a child. He wouldn't even let me go over and see Annie without permission. Because I hadn't gone last time, Annie had been put out with me. And we'd ended up having a fight.

"I want facial burns, if you can get them," my uncle was saying. "Also burns on limbs. And get them back as quickly as possible. Pay whatever you must. Come into my office. I'll give you money."

Their voices were receding. I slipped past Addie and down the stairs, staying close to the wall. In Uncle Valentine's office they were making plans, talking about money, train schedules, routes.

"My Maude should go with him," Merry was saying. "She could act as the grieving mother. You know how good she is at it."

"Yes," Uncle Valentine said, "but I need her here."

Grieving? You only grieved when somebody was dead. *Were they going to get dead bodies, then?* For a moment I'd allowed myself to think Uncle Valentine was going to have them bring back living burn victims.

Oh, I didn't know! *Think,* I told myself sternly. *Be sharp and smart. Like Marietta.* Addie didn't help, of course. She'd come down onto the stairs and was poking me and pointing and grinning "I tol' you, I tol' you," she said gleefully. "You sees now what I means? Now you believe old Addie?"

I looked back at her. "You'd best get back upstairs," I hissed.

Just then Robert came out into the hall, heading for the front door. I heard his special walk, with the little limp, turned my head, and there he was, staring up at me.

Me and my silly feminine hysteria. And scruples.

For one terrible moment that seemed to stretch into eternity, he and I looked at each other. And in that moment I knew what was wrong with me.

I loved Robert.

Not Johnny. Robert. With his limp and his Northern accent and his full mouth and long nose and determined thrust of jaw. With his passion for medicine and his dark brown eyes. Not Johnny's eyes anymore. But his own. His very own. There for me. Inviting me in. That's what he'd been doing all along. Only I'd been too stupid to know it. Instead I'd rebuffed him. And now he was going away with Marietta.

He was like Johnny, yes, in age and stature and a certain something about the cheekbones. But here was the thing I'd just this moment come to understand.

He was the good side of Johnny. The side that I'd seen fleetingly, been drawn to, and tried to draw out. The side that had eluded me. It was here in Robert. And it was not fleeting at all. It was real and constant and full-blown. Most likely it would bloom best in times of darkness, of trouble. And I wanted to be part of it.

I saw the surprise on his face. His mouth fell open. Then I saw understanding creep into his eyes. He knew I'd heard everything.

He slid his gaze in the direction of Uncle Valentine's office, where the others were still talking, then back to me. He shrugged his shoulders. He gave a little smile.

I did not breathe. Neither did I smile back. I would enter into no conspiracy with him now. And he wouldn't have seen my smile, anyway. Because somebody was there in the hallway between us.

The ghost of Marietta.

He knew it and I knew it. So I dropped my gaze to my hands in my lap. If I was to be perceived as having feminine scruples, well then, I would put them to good use.

I was angry with him. I had every right. For his being in on this, for keeping it from me so I was left eavesdropping like a naughty child. But most of all because I knew now that he'd traveled with Marietta before. And admired her for it.

He knew I'd heard *that* along with everything else. Now he expected me to smile at him?

I looked at him again. Was he going to tell Uncle Valentine I was here? *Well, go ahead, tell*, I thought. *See if I care*.

I saw the uncertainty in his face, the look in his eyes. As if he were pleading. For what?

For some kind of understanding.

In that moment I knew he would not give me away. He nodded his head at me, almost curtly, then turned without even a whispered word, and went out the front door.

I felt a great sob forming inside me. Something had just happened between me and Robert, but what?

And then I knew. A deal had been struck between us.

My understanding, for his silence.

I never said I'd give my understanding, did I? And I never asked for his silence, either. I turned with a strangled sob, pushed my way past Addie, and ran up the stairs.

"Now you know," Addie was saying, lumbering behind me on the wide upstairs landing. "Now you know, doan you?"

"Leave me alone!" I whispered savagely.

I knew nothing. I knew less now than before. Only that I'd been betrayed somehow by both Robert and Uncle Valentine; I did not even know the exact nature of the betrayal. I knew that everyone in the house but me understood what was going on.

I knew that Myra was probably right. But I had no proof. Everything that had been said could have two meanings. It was the way they talked to each other in this house. In codes.

I knew that I'd lost Robert, before I was even mindful that I'd wanted him. Just like I'd lost Annie. And Puss-in-Boots. I went into my tower room, where I belonged, like the miller's daughter, and closed the door.

I DIDN'T LIKE THE ARITHMETIC

FOR THE NEXT FEW WEEKS I walked around in a kind of daze. I took part in things but did not *feel* part of them. After a while I felt like Addie must feel and thought I must be going mad.

How does one go mad? Is Addie mad? If she is, she does not know it. If you don't know it, does it count?

One minute I'd be so sure Uncle Valentine and Robert were involved in the snatching of bodies. Everything pointed to it. The way Robert and the Spoon and the Mole had jumped so fast on that steamboat accident. Robert going there as a brother of one of the victims. And taking Marietta along as the wife of a neighbor. Why couldn't Robert have gone as an assistant for Uncle Valentine, if they were to bring back live bodies?

Uncle Valentine saying it was always better to have a woman along because they invited less suspicion. Suspicion of what?

Merry saying Maude should go along to act as a grieving mother. And how good she was at it. Was that why Maude went to so many funerals here in Washington? As a grieving mother? To claim the bodies? Was that why she went only to funerals of the impoverished or the forgotten?

It was all starting to add up, and I did not like the arithmetic.

Then the next minute I would look around me at the ordered rhythms of the house, at Uncle Valentine's casual and yet elegant demeanor; I would think of the good he was doing, and know I was wrong.

If he was engaged in body snatching, why did all those poor people who came on Tuesdays and Thursdays entrust themselves to him for treatment? I know he didn't charge them. I watched when he welcomed his patients. I saw the gratitude in their faces. One day I saw an old Negro woman kiss his hands.

Why had he taken Addie in instead of letting her die in the streets and using *her* body? Why didn't he let Marietta die after she was pulled out of the water? She'd been so sick, she had told me.

Why hadn't I found any evidence in the shed? Robert hadn't had time to remove it.

Was it possible that all the intrigue involved in his trip to Memphis was because Uncle Valentine simply wanted to treat two burn victims who might be left to die? And in order to get them here Robert had to pretend to be a relative?

Would he be good in his role of brother to one of the victims? I could see him doing it, limping a little when he walked across the room to speak to the authorities. With that old military bearing about him, proud and in command of himself, yet all respectful at the same time. Never giving away what he was thinking; guarded, yet polite.

Where did you get your war wound? they would say.

And he'd tell them, hesitantly. *Fredericksburg.* With that little hoarseness he got in his voice when he spoke of the war.

And they'd give him the two wounded. Or the two dead bodies. Or whatever he wanted. Because when he said *Fredericksburg* like that, when he looked down saying it, or across the room, as if he were still hearing the guns booming and the screaming men and crazed horses, when he got that look in his eye like he did remembering, they'd give him anything.

I'd given him my heart, hadn't I?

Thirteen days went by with me in this state. Somehow I got through them and managed not to make a brass-bound fool of myself.

"Don't ever act on your thoughts if you're confused, Miss Muffet," Daddy had told me. "Wait until your mind clears."

There it was. There was what I would do. I would do nothing. For now, at least. I would wait until my mind cleared. If it ever did. I would treat Uncle Valentine as I had always treated him, as if I suspected nothing. I would sit on my tuffet and continue to eat my curds and whey.

On May 1 President Johnson ordered nine army officers named to the military commission to try the eight accused in the assassination conspiracy. Of course Annie's mother was one of the accused.

Uncle Valentine read this to me from the newspaper at breakfast. "Federal authorities have ruled it be a military rather than a civil court," he said. "This might be a good topic for your Wednesday Discussion Group. Everyone in Washington is arguing the point. Does the military have a right to try civilians?"

It was a good question. But I did not bring it up for the Wednesday discussion, even though Mrs. McQuade gave us extra credit if we introduced a good topic. I was too involved in the whole thing. I didn't want Myra to get a whiff of my friendship with Annie and Johnny Surratt. Who knew what she'd do with that little tidbit, she and her newspaperman father. No one in my class knew of this yet. So far I'd managed to keep it secret.

Was I still friends with Annie? I didn't know. I hadn't seen her since our argument. Then that very Thursday, the fourth, when I was thinking of her, she came around again. It was downright creepy.

I had just settled the next-to-last of Uncle Valentine's patients in the waiting room and turned to see what the last lady in the hall was here for. Out of my eye I'd seen her lingering in the shadows with a shawl over her face. I had a pad and pencil in my hand.

"And what is your ailment?" I asked before turning.

"They're going to try my mother." She drew the shawl back.

"Annie!" I dropped my pad and pencil and we hugged. She felt thinner.

"You never noticed me," she said.

"You had that shawl on."

"I wear it all the time when I go out. I don't want to be recognized."

"Nobody here would recognize you. These poor people all have their own troubles."

"Still, I didn't want to put you in any danger. By association."

"Oh, Annie." I ushered her into the kitchen. I was flooded with guilt for having ignored her. "I don't feel that way about you," I said.

She sat down and peered at me. "I was watching you. You seemed a thousand miles away. I know the look. I feel that way myself most of the time. What's wrong?"

"Nothing. I was just busy. How have you been, Annie?"

"Terrible. I have bad news."

"I know about the military trial. Uncle Valentine says they won't dare convict her. He says they're only putting her on trial to try to bait Johnny out of hiding."

"It isn't that," she said dully.

I put the water on for tea. "What, then?"

"It's my Alex." She took a crumpled paper from her reticule. Her movements were like those of an old lady. "Alex has been killed."

"Killed?" I almost dropped a cup taking it down from the cupboard. "Killed?" I asked again. "The war is over!"

She shook her head sadly and pushed the crumpled letter across the table at me. She seemed awfully calm. I picked up the letter and read it.

She was right. Alex had been shot on April 25 at Durham Station in North Carolina, by a Southern sniper who had decided the war wasn't over yet.

"Oh, Annie!" I said.

She was either in shock or beyond grief. "It's for the best, I suppose. I never did tell him about Mama. Although I know he may have seen it in the papers. And that's why he stopped writing. I couldn't bear losing him because of that. I suppose it's better this way. I'll take that tea now," she said. "Things can't possibly get much worse." Her eyes were dull. She looked like a waxwork figure we'd seen once in the Smithsonian. "Except if they hang my mother."

"They're not going to hang your mother." I said the words fervently.

"People in Washington are thirsty for blood," she said. "They want culprits. They don't care who they are, innocent or not. They want someone to blame for the loss they have suffered. Do you know they're still dragging Lincoln's body around out there? The man's been dead two weeks and they haven't buried him yet. If they'd bury him and get it over with, maybe all this hysteria would stop and we could all get back to normal!"

She was right. The Lincoln funeral train hadn't reached Illinois yet. But I doubted if things would be back to normal when it did. I felt as if I didn't know what normal was anymore. And I hadn't lost a sweetheart in the war. My brother hadn't run off to Canada with a price on his head. And my mother wasn't in prison.

But I felt a deep and haunting sense of loss just the same. What loss, I asked myself, besides Mama? And she would have died even if Lincoln hadn't been shot.

I'd done nothing but gain knowledge since I'd come to Washington.

Now I knew that a girl could have been one-eighth Negro and still been sold as a slave. Now I knew that people rob graves. Now I knew that our medical hospitals were hopelessly behind the times. I knew that more men could have been saved if we'd had an ambulance corps earlier in the war. I knew that a young man can be shot by a sniper even after a war is over. While another can run off and not come out of hiding, even when his mother's life is threatened.

Now I knew that a matinee idol can kill a president.

I knew that my uncle may have been stealing bodies for research. So that maybe the next time a young girl's daddy got wounded in the stomach, they could save him. Or the next time a president got shot they would be able to keep him alive.

Would that be so wrong?

Were there degrees of right and wrong?

It *was* a loss I felt. The loss of my innocence.

On May 4 they finally buried Abraham Lincoln in Illinois. On the tenth they arrested Jeff Davis, president of the Confederacy, in Georgia. They said he was wearing a woman's dress.

On the twelfth a man came up to our door, took off his hat, and asked to rent a room. I was alone after school. He was in uniform. "We don't rent rooms," I told him. "I'm sorry."

I felt bad. He was thin and sunburnt and somewhat the worse for wear. He wore a loose shirt and held a soft hat. His boots were dusty and his mustache drooped. So did his eyes. "There are places that feed soldiers on their way home," I said. "I can direct you to one."

"Ain't hungry, miss. Or on my way home. Yet. Come for the review."

"Review?" I asked.

He must have thought me a noodleheaded flighty girl. "Hunnerts of soldiers in town. Ain't you seen 'em?"

I had. I nodded. There had seemed like an unusual

amount of soldiers walking the streets these last couple of days.

"Gonna be a lotta soldiers in Washington the next week or so. 'Bout a hunnert and fifty thousand of 'em."

"A hundred and fifty thousand soldiers?"

"Yes, miss. For the review of the Grand Armies of the Republic. On the twenty-third. They say it'll take us two whole days to parade. I was with Sherman."

"Sherman? Did you know a Captain Alex Bailey?"

"No, miss, sorry."

"Well, in any case, doesn't your regiment have a place to stay?"

"We're bivouacked near the unfinished monument to George Washington. But I had hopes of a clean room and a tub of water. Been a long time since I was in a house."

I directed him down the block to where Mrs. Waring, whose husband had been killed in the war, was talking about starting a boardinghouse.

"Much obliged," he said.

"Would you like something cold to drink?" It was the least I could do.

"That sounds good, miss."

I fetched him a glass of lemonade. He drank it quickly.

"Where are you from?" I asked.

"Indiana, miss." He wiped his mouth with his sleeve and handed the glass back to me, then put his hat back on his head. "Much obliged," he said again.

"Can I ask you something before you leave?"

He nodded briskly.

"Did you burn people out down South, like they say Sherman's soldiers did? Women and children?"

He hesitated. "You're Secesh," he said.

"No. I'm from Maryland, but we're Union. My daddy died fighting for it."

"I ain't never burned no women or children, miss," he said.

"What did you do, then?"

"I foraged. For food."

I smiled to show I believed him. But I didn't. Likely the food he'd foraged had been plundered from the larder of some Southern woman who had children to feed and no man left on the plantation. Mrs. McQuade said what Sherman's men couldn't take with them they'd slaughtered on the spot—chickens, hogs, cattle. Just to leave destruction in their wake. Was it wrong? They'd brought the war to a quicker end. Did that make it right? We'd had a whole Wednesday Morning Discussion on it.

The soldier smiled back at me. "Come see the review," he invited, as if he were in charge of the whole thing. "Gonna be cavalry and mules and wagons, infantry, Zouaves in their flashy uniforms, everything."

I told him I would, watched him walk away, and went back inside. I had some reading to do for class. It was the end of the term and Mrs. McQuade was giving tests. No sooner had I sat down than there was another knock. Another soldier? Again I went to open the front door.

It was Robert. He had a cat under his arm. A red cat.

"Was that soldier looking for a room?" he asked.

I found my tongue. "Yes."

"They're all over town. It's swarming with them."

"There's going to be a review."

"I heard. It'll bring disease, drunkenness, and fights."

"My, you're in a cheerful mood. I suppose things went well in Memphis."

"They did."

"Why did you knock? You never do."

"I have a friend who needs a room. I thought I'd ask politelike."

"Why don't you take your friend to the Young Men's Christian Association, where you live?"

"Because they don't take cats," he said. And he held out the fluffy red cat. "He needs a home. His name is Sultana. Will you give him one?"

We were uncomfortable in each other's presence. It was different now. I hadn't been wrong about that morning in the hallway. Something had happened between us and whatever it was, he'd felt it, too.

We sat in the parlor. I gave him some lemonade. He put the cat in my arms, and I carried on about it like I'd never seen a fool cat before. "Sultana?" I said. "You named him after the riverboat that blew up?"

"Yes."

I stroked Sultana. He purred in my lap, looked into my face, and gave me that unblinking stare cats give. "Where did you get him?"

"Found him abandoned on the docks in Memphis. I'd wired your uncle on a business matter and asked him what I could bring home for you. He wired back. 'A cat,' he said. That you were upset because you'd lost Puss-in-Boots."

"Annie took her back. Why did you want to bring me something?"

"To make up for things."

"What things?"

"Whatever it was that caused the look on your face the day I left here."

I stroked the cat's ears. "They'll give you undying loyalty for scratching their ears," I said. "Such a little thing to do to get loyalty."

"Yes," he said. "And humans require so much."

"You want me to say I want my ears scratched, Robert? You think that's what I want from you?"

"No, but I'd like to know what it would take, Emily, for you to trust me. I thought what I did that morning in the hall would do it. When I didn't tell your uncle you were eavesdropping."

"Is that why you didn't tell him?"

"Yes. I want you to trust me, Emily. What must I do?" He looked at me square. "Since the day I met you, you've been angry, defiant, bitter toward me, as if I'm to blame for everything in your life. I can't help it about Johnny. Or Annie. You have to stop blaming me. All I want is to be friends with you. I like you, Emily. I liked you the minute I met you."

"As a girl?"

"Well, you are a girl, aren't you? Yes."

I ducked my head. I could feel things bursting inside me. "I'm not blaming you for Johnny or Annie," I said.

"Well, then, what *are* you blaming me for? Would you do me the honor of telling me?"

I gave a great heaving sigh. "You mustn't tell my uncle any of this. Promise?"

"Trust me."

"I heard the conversation before you left for Memphis. You were to bring back two riverboat victims. Have you brought them back?"

"Yes."

"Are they dead or alive, Robert?"

He was not stupid. The understanding was there in his eyes. I could not catch him off guard. "They're alive, Emily. Burn cases. I dosed them with laudanum to ease their pain and brought them back. They're in Douglas Hospital. Why would I be bringing back dead people?"

"For specimens. What we talked about the night you showed me inside the shed."

More understanding in those eyes. "You suspect us of stealing bodies. That's why you were listening on the stairs."

"I can't help it, Robert. There's the Spoon and the Mole, for one thing. They were trying to rob my mother's grave the very night she was buried! Uncle Valentine chased them."

"He told me about that." He sighed. "He found out they were running a little grave-robbing business on the side. He's called them to account for it and made them promise to stop. They never stole bodies for him."

"Then what were they doing here that morning you left?"

"They work for your uncle. They do numerous odd jobs. They get around, as dwarves do. They scout around the city and tell your uncle of cases he might be interested in. They found him Marietta. And Addie. And their contacts got the news to us about the riverboat accident."

"Why did you have to lie and say you were a relative of the burn victims? Why not say you worked for a doctor?"

"Relatives get there first. Officials release victims only to relatives. I know it was a little dishonest, but we're concerned with helping the victims. Your uncle is doing research on burns. He's made progress."

"You have an answer for everything," I said. "It's so provoking."

"I'm sorry, Emily, if the answers I give you don't fit in with what you want to think of us. You're of an age where you have a lively imagination. We're not doing anything dramatic or exciting here. Our work consists of long, tedious hours, a lot of failures, and a few slow gains. I'm sorry to disappoint you."

"I'm a lot older than fourteen. Don't treat me like a child."

"I'm sorry," he said.

"And what about Marietta? Why did she have to go? Oh yes, I forgot. She's sharp and smart. She has a level head. And she's not given to silly feminine hysteria or scruples."

"You're jealous of Marietta," he teased. "That means you like me." Then he got serious. "Her not having silly feminine scruples makes it a lot easier, I admit. But I much prefer you, if you must know."

Something was stuck in my throat. My heart. Oh, it wasn't fair, him doing this now. I closed my eyes and clung for dear life onto the cat. But there was one more thing I had to know.

"What about Maude? And the way she's always going to the funerals of people who are impoverished or without family?"

"I can see where that might bother you, given what you've been thinking of us. But what can I say? Maude is just Maude. Have you ever known another like her?"

I had to agree that I hadn't.

He reached out and touched the side of my face. "You've got yourself tied all in knots. I know you haven't had an easy time of it in life. And all this business with the Surratts has likely made you mistrust everybody. And then from what your uncle tells me, your mother made you suspicious of him even before you came here. Isn't that right?"

"Yes."

"She was jealous of him, Emily. Your mama was an unhappy woman. Look at the things she said about your father. Do you believe them?"

I lowered my eyes. "Would you march into hell for Uncle Valentine?"

"Yes."

"Why?"

"Because I'm honored to be able to work for him. It's the chance of a lifetime."

He had the answers. All of them. I had nowhere else to go.

"I can't make you trust me, Emily," he said finally. "But I'm glad I'm the one you took your anger out on and not your uncle. He's a good man. He loves you. I don't want to see him hurt. If you have any more questions or doubts, come to me, will you?"

"I have one more question. If I were to ask you to take me to my uncle's lab at the college now, right now, are you telling me I'd find no burn victims there?"

"That's what I'm telling you," he said.

We faced each other. He smiled. "You want to go to the lab right now? There are not only no dead burn victims there, there are no dead bodies. We're winding up the spring semester and they've all been properly buried. You'd be disappointed. Well? Do you want to go?"

I felt so tawdry, so small. So full of silly feminine scruples. He'd just come home from a long trip with a cat under his arms for me. He was doing important work with Uncle Valentine. And I was acting like a spoiled child. "I don't want to go," I said. "I believe you."

"Good. Because there's someplace else I'd like to take you."

"Where?"

"To Gautier's. For some ice cream. What do you say?"

I said yes.

WALLS DO A PRISON MAKE

I WENT EVERYWHERE with Robert. When he had the time to take me.

We went to ball games on the old Potomac grounds, to hear the Marine band play on the White House lawn, to a hop at Willard's. For the first time in my life, I felt young and pretty.

Uncle Valentine insisted I have some new dresses made. I laughed. "I could make them myself," I told him. But he insisted I go to a dressmaker. I did, a woman recommended by Mrs. McQuade. It turned out the woman knew Elizabeth Keckley.

"What happened to Mrs. Keckley?" I asked.

"Happened?" She was kneeling, pinning a hem on a blue

dimity. "She's still in the White House with Mrs. Lincoln."

"Mrs. Lincoln is still in the White House?"

"President Johnson has let her stay until she can gather herself together. Word is, she is half-crazy packing. But she never finishes. Her son Robert is yelling at her that they can't stay forever, they have to get out. Elizabeth won't leave her side."

How terrible, I thought, walking home. Mrs. Lincoln was sure working hard at her grief. But she wasn't getting on with her life, as she'd told Maude we have to do. I was glad I'd stayed in school and didn't take the job with Mrs. Keckley. I was even glad I'd come to live with Uncle Valentine.

I was happy for the first time in my life. It was a beautiful spring in Washington, the war was over, the city was in a fever pitch of excitement about the upcoming Grand Review. I had a new cat, who'd taken immediately to me. I was at peace with myself. And with Uncle Valentine and Robert. I had the attentions of Robert, a handsome young medical student. So why then did I have this nagging little feeling that something might go wrong?

Because I did not trust happiness. You had to be a fool to do that. I'd never been a fool, and I was not about to start now.

On May 15 Robert and I met Annie outside the Arsenal Building at the foot of Four and a Half Street. The eight accused in the Lincoln assassination were to plead this day. Lawyers were taking testimony.

It was a day of bright blue, green, and gold, shot through with the white and pink of tree blossoms. We waited outside the gates for Annie.

When she came out the side door, her feet dragged. Her

dress was gray with black trim, her hair bound back in a severe twist. There were dark circles under her eyes. She smiled wanly and came through the gate.

"How did it go?" I asked her.

"Mama pled not-guilty. They all did, even your uncle's friend Dr. Mudd."

She showed us a paper with the charges. It said her mother had received, entertained, harbored, and concealed John Wilkes Booth, David E. Herold, Lewis Payne, who also called himself Powell, John H. Surratt, Michael O'Laughlin, George A. Atzerodt, and Samuel Arnold, with intent to aid, abet, and assist them in the execution of the president of the United States.

The paper looked awful, with all of it written out there in legal language. And the names of people I knew connected with it. Annie's hand shook as she held it.

"Worse, my mother has one of her migraines." She looked at Robert. Then the black bag he held in his hand. "Why have you brought that with you?"

"For you. In case you are in need of anything," he told her.

"You're not a doctor yet."

"I will be, soon. And I've accompanied Dr. Bransby on house calls enough to be able to administer if someone is in need."

"Do you have anything in there for migraines?" Annie asked. "And have you ever made a prison call?"

It took Robert only a heartbeat to say yes, he'd do it.

What surprised me most as we went through the underground corridor of Carroll Prison was the sound of water running. It ran down the stone walls in a constant trickle. Underfoot, everything was wet. I could have sworn I felt something scurrying on the floor beside me. I lifted my skirts.

Within ten minutes I'd forgotten the blue, green, and gold day outside. Here it was winter—cold, dim, and bleak, even with candles in sconces on the walls. Ahead of us the jailer shuffled, his shadow thrown against the wall. So this was a prison, then, not the tower of my fairy tales.

"Suppose it's all right to let you see her. But I should check with my boss," he said.

"Has a doctor been in yet to see her?" Robert asked.

"Prison doctor sees 'em all, regularlike."

"He hasn't helped my mother," Annie told the jailer.

"Don't know as anything could." The man's rough clothing and manner made him seem surly. But he could have turned us away at the door and hadn't.

Thanks to Robert. "Don't say anything," Robert had warned us. "Sometimes when you just act as if you belong, they're so taken by surprise, they don't know what to do. And rather than show their stupidity, they'll go along with you."

Robert was right. The jailer hadn't known what to do. But seeing Robert's black bag and officious manner, he'd agreed to let us in. Our bluff had worked.

"Suppose anythin's better than havin' to hear her puke up her guts in there like she's doin'." The jailer took his huge ring of keys out of his pockets as we approached the last cell.

"Where are the other prisoners?" Robert asked. The cells were all empty.

"This is the women's ward."

There were no other women prisoners. Mrs. Mary was alone at the far end of a dark corridor in a cell with straw on the floor and one small window that admitted a single shaft of sunlight.

She was kneeling on the floor over a bucket, throwing up. The sounds of retching echoed in the emptiness. The place smelled like an outhouse.

"Mrs. Surratt, you got company," the jailer said.

She looked up. Her hair hung in dank tendrils around her face, which was white and haggard. Straw clung to her black dress as she struggled to her feet. "Annie." She started to cry, then stopped herself, seeing me and Robert.

"Emily! Oh, I'm so ashamed that you should see me like this. But I've been so sick with one of my headaches. And cold." Then she saw Robert. "And who is this? Annie, you haven't brought friends."

"No, Mama, he's a doctor. He's come to attend you."

Robert submitted himself and his doctor's bag to a search by the jailer, then made all of us wait at the end of the corridor. From down the dank hall I heard him making conversation with Mrs. Mary, heard her plaintive replies, though I could not make out the words. After a short time he came out.

"I've given her a powder for the migraine," he said to the jailer, "and I'm leaving some with her daughter in case she needs more." He handed a small vial to Annie. "Are you staying now or leaving?" he asked.

"I usually stay until they make me go home at night," Annie said.

"Then I want hot water and soap brought immediately so the woman can wash," he told the jailer severely. "I want those buckets emptied, a fresh ticking for the mattress, candles in her sconces on the walls, and two warm blankets."

"I don't have the authority," the jailer said.

"Then perhaps you have the authority to tell your superiors

that if my instructions are not followed you will be reported to the Sanitation Commission. This place is a disgrace. You're in charge, aren't you?"

The man nodded.

"Well, your head will roll if your superiors get a citation from the Sanitation Commission. Don't think for a minute they won't blame it on you. Or perhaps you'd like the conditions here reported to the *Intelligencer*. Her case is being followed by newspapers all over the country, you know. Do you want to be written up as the jailer of a hellhole?"

The man was terrified. "No, sir. I don't need no trouble."

"Good," Robert said, "then we understand each other. Is there a place to make coffee?"

"My office down the hall."

"Then let Miss Surratt make her mother fresh coffee. I expect you to supply it." Robert drew some money out of a billfold. "Coffee will help her migraine. I'm going to keep tabs on things here. Remember what I said."

"Yes, sir."

When Annie saw us out the door she looked at Robert as if he were God. "Thank you," she said.

I looked at him with a little less admiration, maybe as an avenging angel. I was so proud of him! But my feelings were warring inside me. The horrors of the prison, the smells, dankness, clanging gates, had shaken me. How terrible to think of Mrs. Mary in a place like that! I shivered in the warm May sun. And then I looked around at the prettiness of the day. How wonderful to be out in the sunshine again, walking with Robert! Was I wrong to feel that way?

"I feel like I've come out of a tomb," I said to Robert.

"You have." His face was grim. "And it makes me wonder how the other prisoners are faring. I'm going to ask your uncle if maybe I can get onto the ironclads in the river to see them."

It was Myra Mott's birthday on the twenty-second. There was to be a big party at school. I did not want to go. But when you live with a doctor you can't very well say you're too sick to go to school. Unless you are sick. So I went. I made fudge to bring, and Uncle Valentine gave me money for a present. I bought Myra a book of poetry, *Leaves of Grass* by Walt Whitman.

Of course Myra simpered and preened and held sway over all of us that day. Lessons were shortened all morning so that we could have the party in the afternoon. It was a tea. Mrs. McQuade insisted we make a formal tea and mind our manners.

But a tea, presents, and being fawned over weren't enough for Myra. She wanted more. She wanted to be looked up to as the most clever, daring, and exciting girl in the class. And that day, for her fifteenth birthday, she had found a way.

Satisfied that the tea had gone off properlike, Mrs. McQuade left us to ourselves and went down the hall to her office. The minute she left, Myra looked at each of us in turn. "The presents are beautiful, but this is boring the life out of me. Who's for a bit of fun afterward?"

"What have you got planned?" Stephanie Wilson asked.

"You must swear, all of you, that even if you're afraid to be part of it, you won't tell anyone."

The girls exchanged glances and giggled and promised.

"That goes for you, too, Emily," Myra said. "Because it involves a story my father is pursuing. You know what story I mean. Now, if you can't promise to keep it secret, you must leave the room before I say what it is."

"I thought you were finished with all that, Myra. I showed you everything you wanted to see. I thought I'd satisfied you."

"Something else has come up. My father has a new lead."

"There are no new leads. You'll be dragging everyone on a fool's errand."

"Then that should make you happy."

We locked eyes across the room for a minute.

"What is all this?" Melanie Hawkes asked. "Let the rest of us in on it."

I shrugged. What did I have to lose? Robert had convinced me my uncle had nothing to hide. I had put the matter to rest. Let Myra make a fool of herself.

"Just one thing before you speak," I said. "You're not going to bring everyone into my uncle's yard and poke around that shed again. I can't allow that. It's trespassing." I knew nobody would be home. Uncle Valentine had taken the train to Baltimore this morning to give a speech at the University of Maryland. Maude was off to one of her funerals. But I still couldn't allow it.

"Who cares about the old shed?" she retorted. "We're going somewhere more interesting." Then to the other girls. "What do you say? Want to see some dead bodies?"

I'd never been on the grounds of the National Medical College, where Uncle Valentine taught, and I was surprised to find out how easily anyone could just walk around there. Once in the front gates, no one bothered you. "Most of the guards are away helping the police because of all the soldiers in town for the review," Myra told us.

A block from school her older cousin Jason had been waiting for us. He was down from Baltimore with his mother, visiting. He was seventeen, had bright red hair and freckles.

His father had served on the North's ironclad *Monitor*, and Jason was soon headed for the Naval Academy at Annapolis.

Myra was so puffed up with herself I thought she would burst. She clung to Jason's arm as we walked across the campus. It was near the end of the semester. Windows of the buildings were open and we could hear the droning voices of professors inside. With Jason leading us, it looked as if we were a passel of girls on a tour. No one paid us mind.

Myra had promised everyone dead bodies. Where they expected to find them, I did not know. But I could not have refused to come along, or it would have looked as if I had something to hide.

If some other professor had "subjects" in his lab, I didn't know. I would have liked, somehow, to get in touch with Robert. But as luck would have it, this morning he had succeeded, after persistent tries, in getting aboard the ironclad *Montauk*, which was anchored in the Potomac alongside the *Saugus*. Both housed the male prisoners in the conspiracy. Robert was to see to the conditions of the ships and the health of the prisoners.

I followed the others reluctantly along the quiet paths of the college. Up ahead, Jason and Myra seemed to know where they were going. We went through a grove of trees, down some stone steps, through a sort of dingy tunnel, and then came to a courtyard below the street level.

On the ground lay a ladder. Immediately Jason set it up against the old brick building. The girls gathered around, *ooh*ing and *aah*ing and asking silly questions.

"Where are the bodies? Inside?"

"Who told you they were here?"

"You mean, if we climb up that ladder we'll be able to *see* them?"

"Will they be cut up?"

"Will they be men or women?"

"Will they be naked?"

That, of course, started a whole other set of conjectures. Who had seen a naked man? Who wanted to? Giggles and whisperings. Then silence as Jason removed his coat and climbed the ladder while Myra held it.

The girls stood around bug-eyed, watching him make his ascent to the second floor. I stood back, blinking in the warm May sunlight dappled by lacy trees overhead. Birds sang. The sky was as innocent as a newborn's eyes. From above the wall of the courtyard could be heard street sounds, carriages passing by, people talking. Yet we were sealed off here. No one could see us.

Jason stopped climbing and peered into the window.

"Well?" Myra called up softly. "Can you see anything?"

"I sure can."

"Was my daddy right?"

"He sure was."

"What do you see?"

"Two of them," Jason reported. His voice sounded a little weak. "Lying on tables. Covered with sheets. All I can see are the faces. Men, I think."

"Don't say another word," Myra ordered coldly. "Come down this instant!"

Jason climbed back down, then held the ladder for Myra. She got onto the first step, then smirked over her shoulder at me. "Do you know whose classroom that is up there?" she asked.

"I have no idea," I said. "I've never been here before."

"It's your uncle Valentine's."

"You're lying, Myra. You just don't know what to do anymore to make yourself important. I don't know whose laboratory that is, but I do know that if you don't get everybody out of here soon, we can all get into trouble."

"Trouble?" She was climbing the ladder, unafraid. "We aren't the ones in trouble." Then she stopped and peered in. "Oh, my God." She groaned.

"What, what?" the girls on the ground called up. "Tell us, what do you see?"

"Two men, just like Jason said. Dead. Oh, my God, I was right. My daddy was right. I have to tell him." She scrambled down.

On the ground she was immediately surrounded by the other girls, all asking to be next climbing up the ladder. "Wait, wait," she said. Her face was white. She looked at me. "I'm not lying. I swear to you, Emily, there are dead men up there. And it's your uncle's classroom. My daddy knows it is. I've been here in this courtyard with him before. He's pointed it out to me."

"If it is," I said, "any specimens they have up there are legal. Donated. Or executed prisoners. And you've got no right poking around here today. Nor did your father."

She looked dazed and thrilled with herself all at the same time. "Listen, everybody," she said breathlessly. "My father talked to Dr. Bransby two weeks ago. Because he got wind of the fact that Bransby had two dead burn victims shipped in from that riverboat explosion on the Mississippi. There were victims of that tragedy missing. Their relatives were looking for them. And somebody told them about my daddy and how he was investigating grave robbers."

She paused breathlessly and met my eyes, then continued.

"My daddy was in this very laboratory talking with Dr. Bransby. The doctor invited him in and showed him around.

At that time he said there were no dead burn victims. That he had no more legitimate specimens because the semester was at an end. Well, what I just saw wasn't live people. And their faces had burns."

"Lies," I hissed. I made my way through the other girls and stood toe-to-toe with Myra. "Lies. How do we know this isn't all a trick? That maybe your daddy told you those relatives of the victims got in touch with him, and you made the rest up to feed your need for excitement? How do we know there really are dead bodies up there?"

I don't know where I got those words. I was trembling. They just tumbled out of me. But they sounded good. And they fit the occasion.

Myra tossed her head back, raised her chin haughtily. "Why don't you climb up the ladder and see?" she challenged.

Silence. I heard street sounds. Birds chirping. They sounded far away.

Myra's eyes glittered. "Well? Are you afraid? The others are all going to do it. Do you want them telling you? Or do you want to see for yourself?"

"I'll do it," I said. And slowly, I began to climb the ladder.

First rung. *She's lying. When I get up there, I'll tell her so.*

Second rung. *Robert invited me to come and see if there were any burn victims here.*

Third rung. *He said there were not only no burn victims here but no dead bodies. That they'd all been disposed of because it was the end of the semester.*

Fourth rung. *He promised that he'd brought live burn victims back from the accident.*

Fifth rung. *I believe Robert. He wouldn't lie to me. Johnny lied to me. Not Robert.*

I was level with the window now. I stopped and looked in.

"Well?" Myra was calling up from below. "Well?"

"Tell us," the other girls were saying, "tell us what you see."

The faces were horribly burned. You could scarcely make out the features. The hair was singed. One man had an ear missing. Their cheeks were sunken in, like Abraham Lincoln's must have been when he got to New York City after having been dragged around for a week. Their bodies were wound in sheets. And they lay there as if they were sleeping.

I felt sick. It seemed as if the ladder swayed. But Jason was holding it steady.

"Why would I bring back dead people, Emily?" I heard Robert asking.

Oh, Robert! A sob formed inside me, a great heaving sob.

I wanted to die. I wanted to be lying on that table instead of those men. "No!" I screamed. "No, Robert, no!"

"Get down, Emily." Myra's voice. Then Jason's urging me down.

Then another sound. A whistle and a cry. "You there! What are you kids doing down there in that courtyard?"

"God's teeth," Jason mumbled. "A guard. You told me they were all elsewhere. My God, if I get caught...I can't get caught. I can't get in trouble. Or it'll be the end of Annapolis for me."

"Let's get out of here!" Myra cried. "Come on, everybody, he's on the hill above the steps. There's a door over there. And steps to the street. I went that way with my daddy. Come on!" Her voice was hoarse, yelling it.

They ran. "Come on, Emily!" Melanie yelled.

The ladder was unsteady. Nobody was holding it. It jiggled

and I nearly fell. But somehow I made it to the second bottom rung and jumped.

The ladder fell crashing to the ground. I ran. Out of the corner of my eye I saw the guard running through the tunnel toward me. I followed the others across the courtyard, through the door in the wall, and up the steps to the street.

20

ALONG CAME A SPIDER

THERE IS NO FEELING in the world worse than betrayal. I felt cheated, laughed at, shut out of the lives of all around me.

I went home. Maude was there, puttering in the kitchen.

"Well, where were you? Your uncle won't be home this night. I thought I'd just serve leftovers."

"All right," I said, "but I have to go out a little later, on an errand. I'll be home about six." I went to my room. There was so much to do and not enough time.

First I had to decide what I was taking with me and what I was leaving behind. I stood in the center of my blue-and-white room. I wanted to take everything and I wanted to take nothing.

I would take nothing that Uncle Valentine had given me,

I decided. Not clothes, books, or even food. I would buy food before I got on the train. I would take nothing from anybody in this house. I would go to Aunt Susie's in Richmond as poor as I'd been when I'd come here.

Except the cat. I'd take Sultana. Because it was as plain as the nose on your face that he couldn't live without me, poor thing. And already he'd been kicked around from pillar to post, worse than a freedman.

Only, first I'd change his name. Sultana was a girl's name and he was a boy. What would I call him then, Sultan? No, it had to be far removed from the name Robert had given him.

No, don't think of Robert.

I threw some things into a portmanteau. *Oh, Lordy*, I thought, *if I go to Richmond I won't be able to finish at Miss Winefred Martin's.* And there would go my daddy's money. What would my daddy have said? *Miss Muffet had been frightened away.* I felt a great sadness cut through me at the thought of Daddy. And another for Mrs. McQuade. "There was one I thought had so much promise," she'd say. "You never can tell." I'd disappoint her. Well. How many people had disappointed me?

I ran around my room throwing things into that portmanteau. All the while I tried out names on Sultana, who was sitting in the middle of my bed watching.

"Arnold," I said. "How would you like to be called Arnold?"

He blinked at me.

"Look, it's not after Benedict Arnold or anything. I just thought it had a nice solid ring to it. Well then, what about Sad Stock? It's a new plant Marietta got for her garden."

He licked his paw, feigning disinterest.

"No, you don't look sad enough. Maybe I'll call you Custer. You know, he's the boy general and he has long blond curls. Don't like that? Too dandified for you? Well then, what about Ulysses? Nothing dandified about him."

I decided on Ulysses. Maybe when I got to Richmond I'd change my name, too. No more Emily Pigbush. I'd start over when I got there, new name and everything.

After I finished packing I went under my bed, where I'd hidden the twenty gold pieces from Johnny. I took two out of the little velvet sack. That ought to be enough for a ticket to Richmond and a wire to Aunt Susie. I knew she was still at the same address. Hadn't she written to Uncle Valentine, "This is my home. Here I shall stay. Richmond will re-build"? So what if Richmond was a mess now? I'd thought I was safe coming *here*.

And what did it get me? Two dead bodies lying on a table, and Myra Mott snickering up the ladder at me. My uncle was a body snatcher. How could I show my face back at school? That was what trusting people and wanting to be safe got you. I'd gone from the frying pan into the fire.

Oh, I couldn't bear the thought of it. Every time I closed my eyes I saw those two dead bodies on that table. And heard Robert's voice. "Why would I be bringing back dead people, Emily?"

How could I have let Robert sweet-talk me out of my suspicions? Oh, what a simpleton he must think me to be! My face burned with the shame of it. And what about Uncle Valentine? How many times had my suspicions been aroused against him? And always I'd found an excuse for him. He'd helped Annie. He'd given me a home. He had warm brown eyes and his voice healed me.

Well, I wasn't healed now. I was betrayed, naked, and used.

I felt like those bodies on the table. Like my face was all burned off.

First I went to the telegraph office and wired Aunt Susie. I told her I would be down to see her in a couple of days. Then I went to the railroad station and purchased a ticket. Both errands took me the rest of the afternoon.

I would leave tomorrow morning, early, before Maude even got here. Uncle Valentine wouldn't be home from Baltimore until tomorrow evening. I'd leave a note for Maude saying I'd been invited to have breakfast with Mrs. McQuade. By the time they missed me I'd be halfway there. Then, once in Richmond, I'd wire Uncle Valentine and tell him I was staying with Aunt Susie.

I felt a mite better walking home. I was filled with a sense of purpose and determination. I'd go home and grab a plate of food from the kitchen and take it to my room. Tell Maude not to bother with supper. I'd help myself. She'd be glad of it, an evening off.

There were just two more things I had to do first.

"What do you *mean*, you're leaving?" Annie stood in the open doorway of her mother's house, her hair disheveled, her sleeves rolled up, and white flour on her hands and arms.

"Tomorrow. On the ten o'clock train to Richmond. I have to leave, Annie. I can't live in that house anymore. Something bad has happened."

Her eyes darkened. "It's Robert, isn't it? You've been seeing a lot of him. He hasn't been playing free with you, has he? You're not in trouble?"

"Oh, God, Annie, no."

"Well, what else could be so bad?"

I stepped inside the hall. Immediately I felt dizzy. Memories can do that to you, make you dizzy. It was all too familiar—the textures, the light, the smells. "It smells good in here," I said.

"I'm baking," she said. "Come into the kitchen."

"Are you having company?"

"No. I'm baking to keep from going insane."

We sat in the kitchen. She reheated some coffee and gave me a cup, then went back to kneading her bread. "Now tell me," she said.

"You must promise not to tell anyone."

"Oh, in heaven's name, Emily, who would I tell? Who talks to me?"

"Well, you were right. About Uncle Valentine. He *is* stealing bodies."

She went on kneading. I told her the story about Myra, the trip to the college, the burn victims. She kept right on kneading. I sipped the dark, sweet coffee. For a moment or two after I stopped talking, she said nothing. A clock chimed somewhere in the far reaches of the house. Puss-in-Boots came into the kitchen and rubbed against my skirt, recognizing me. I picked her up.

"And so that's why you're leaving?" Annie asked dully.

"Yes," I said.

"You want to know what I think?"

"You know I do, Annie."

"I think you're spoiled and selfish, Emily. I think you don't know when you have it good. I think you're like your mother."

If she had slapped me, I couldn't have been more shocked. "Annie," I said, "don't you understand what I just said? He's a body snatcher. All of them—Robert, Maude, Marietta."

She never stopped kneading that bread. "Have you ever had a burn, Emily?"

"Not really."

She picked the bread up, threw some more flour on the board, and slapped it back down. She wiped her hands on her apron and poured herself a cup of coffee. She was getting thinner than ever, but her back was very straight in the old calico dress, and she did not turn around from the stove as she spoke. "Wouldn't you like to think that if you were burned someday, doctors would know how to treat you?"

I did not know what to say. "Yes."

"I've seen my mother suffer so with her migraines. Wouldn't it be wonderful if someday doctors knew what caused migraines? I understand Mrs. Lincoln gets them. And wouldn't it be wonderful if the next time a president got shot in the head they'd know what to do for him? Think of it! If they could have saved him, Mama wouldn't be in jail."

"Maybe she still would be," I said.

"But not in danger of being hanged."

I could say nothing to that.

"What's so bad about what your uncle has done? How do you think doctors got to know everything they now know? By working on dead bodies. My God, Emily, stop being a child. Look how your mother died. Coughing her lungs out. Maybe he'll cut into these men while he's at it and find out about lungs!"

"It isn't that," I said. "It's that they all lied to me. I can't live with people who have lied to me."

"Oh, my Lordy." She raised her eyes to the ceiling and gave a bitter laugh. "They lied to you, did they? Well, what do you think my brother Johnny did to us? What do you think my mother did to me? But I still love her. I'd give my eyes to have her back here in this house living with me right now. And Johnny, too! My God, Emily, they're going to hang my mother! They've got all the evidence against her. This trial that's coming up is just a formality. They want to hang people and they're going to hang them. Now, *there* is trouble. Not the fact that your uncle Valentine is trying to find a better way to treat burns and lied to you."

Silence in the kitchen. Except for Puss-in-Boots. She was purring.

"You're measuring everybody else's problems by your own," I said.

"That's right, I am."

"It isn't fair. The yardstick for measuring doesn't work anymore if you do that."

"That's right," she said. "If they hang my mother we're going to have to throw the yardstick away. Because nothing will be more unfair, Emily. So I would advise you to thank God there are men like your uncle Valentine and Dr. Mudd, who care so much for humanity that they are willing to take chances and break the stupid laws."

I set the cat aside and stood up. "There's no talking to you anymore, Annie. You don't care about anyone else. All you care about is your own problems."

"Because I *have* problems. And they aren't imagined."

"Other people do, too, Annie. Next to yours they may not seem important. But mine are. And I'm sorry you can't see them as I do."

She shrugged and started kneading the bread again. "I've been through too much," she said.

"Does that mean you don't want to be my friend anymore?"

"No. It means I've been through too much. Johnny's gone.

My mother's in prison. Alex is dead. My home is up for sale. I have to sell it."

"I lost my daddy in the war and my mother died. I don't *have* a home."

"You have your uncle!" she snapped. "And a good home, and Robert paying court to you. You want advice? Go home. And forget about what those noodleheaded girls at school are playing at. Your whole life is ahead of you. Mine is finished."

"Annie." I moved toward her. I touched her arm. "You're still young. Your life isn't finished."

"Isn't it?" She drew away. "I'm a Surratt. I have to live with this name forever. Who will want anything to do with me?" Her face was taut, white, ugly.

For a moment I felt sorry for her. Then in the next moment I didn't. She hadn't listened to me, to my troubles. And they were real. She didn't care about anybody but herself. "No one," I said, "if you continue on as you are."

Then I left the house.

I felt bad about Annie, but there was nothing I could do. I'd helped her. Robert had helped her, and so had Uncle Valentine. It wasn't my fault if her mother went and got mixed up with John Wilkes Booth, was it? Besides, I'd needed Annie. Always in the past she'd been there for me. Now she just wasn't anymore. I went home.

There was one more thing I had to do. Tonight, before I went to bed. The idea of it was so gratifying it put all the other bad feelings out of my mind.

Maude was waiting for me in the kitchen. "Well, I was ready to send for the Metropolitan Police. Where have you been!"

"I had an errand. And the streets are crowded. For the Grand Review tomorrow."

"Exactly. Which is why you shouldn't be out alone, with all those soldiers hanging about."

I filled my plate at the stove. Leftover chicken and beans. She'd made fresh muffins, though. I was hungry. "I'll just take it to my room," I said. "I have some studying. You deserve the night off. Why don't you leave now? I'll put the food away."

"I have to bring a plate up to Addie."

"I can do that."

She looked doubtful. "All right, but don't forget to lock the doors. I'll be over in the morning to make breakfast for you and Addie."

I'll be gone by then, I said to myself. *And so will Addie.*

"Leave?" Addie wiped the gravy in her plate with a muffin and put it in her mouth. Her old eyes were wary. "You wouldn't be funnin' me, would you, little missy?"

"I wouldn't do that to you, Addie. It's what you want, isn't it? So you can have a chance to do something with the freedom Mr. Lincoln gave you?"

" 'Xactly," she said. "But you always say no. You get inta that shed out there? You find out what's in them barrels that say PICKLES? You find out they be dead bodies in them barrels?"

Dead bodies! Pickles! Of course! How could I have been so stupid? I could hear Robert's words to me that night in the shed. *Rum, arsenic, and corrosive sublimate.* It was what they preserved specimens in. Likely what he'd used to preserve the bodies from the *Sultana* disaster. *Not from out of state, I hope. The doctor wants no out-of-state pickles.* Of course not. Except for the *Sultana* disaster they did not want to traffic in out-of-state bodies. It was too risky.

"Yes, I found out, Addie," I said sadly. "And so now I'm leaving. And I want to help you leave, too. If you want to. You're better, aren't you? No more coughing?"

"Medicine make me better."

"Well, then, do you want to go, or don't you?"

"I wants to go."

"Good. We leave in the morning, early. I have some money. I'll give you some. But you must promise to use it to get settled, and not for rum."

"I doan drink no more. Fer sure."

"Where do you want to go? I'll take you."

"Go?" She stared at me. She got dreamy for a minute. "I gots a place," she said.

"Where?"

"Can't tell."

"Then how can I take you there in the morning?"

"You take me to the Relief Society. Twelve an' O Streets. So's I kin pick up my things."

My God, I thought, *the outskirts of the city. How will I get her there? But I must.*

"Reverend Nichols," she said, "he runs it. I wuz workin' fer him before. Gotta let him know I's arright. He think I's dead. Gotta let him know I's arright and pick up my things."

"All right," I said. "You get some rest now. I'll be up to wake you at first light. I'll hire a carriage. And take you to Twelfth and O Streets. Tomorrow you'll be a free woman, Addie."

AND FRIGHTENED
MISS MUFFET AWAY

EVERYTHING WENT WRONG.

Addie had to wear two petticoats, two skirts, an apron, two blouses, and one vest. She would have worn her shawl, too, but I said it was too warm. I got her downstairs for a quick cup of tea.

"We really goin', little missy?" she must have asked me a dozen times while we sipped our tea. Birds were already chirping outside. I heard the *clop-clop-clopp*ing of the milkman's horse down the street. The light was a soft gray now outside the windows. And, of course, it was foggy. For once I welcomed the fog. I counted on it to shield us.

"Yes," I said, "we are really going, Addie. Hurry now, finish your tea and biscuit. Last evening I arranged for a hack to meet us down at the corner."

"One thing I wants afore I go," she said.

"What? What is it?" She wasn't going to balk on me now, was she?

"I wants one o' them flowers." She smiled sheepishly. "I always wanted one o' them flowers. The kind that hangs down like bells at rest. And turns right up at night."

"I suppose I could get you one before we leave, Addie."

So there I was, stumbling around in the fog in Marietta's eerie garden. I cut a yucca flower on a long stem. Addie stood waiting. Beside her on the stone walk was my portmanteau, a basket of food, and another basket with Ulysses the cat. At least he was cooperating. He'd curled right up in the bottom of the basket and gone back to sleep.

I wrapped the flower in wet paper and presented it to Addie. "Come on, now, let's go."

We must have made a strange procession going down the street, me with my bundles and Addie with her flower. I heard church bells chime across the city. Six o'clock. I heard and smelled the horses before they appeared out of the fog, waiting at the head of the carriage.

"Twelfth and O Streets," I told the driver.

"That's a long way, little lady. Across town."

"I know. It's the Relief Society."

"It ain't a good neighborhood. And the way the streets are clogged with the Grand Review today, I'll have to charge extra."

"How much?"

"Twelve dollars."

I sighed and settled my things. The war was over, but people were still price-gouging. "All right," I said. "Just get us there, please." Thank God for Johnny's gold pieces. It seemed like a hundred years since the morning he had given them to me.

To get to the Relief Society we had to travel through the most terrible areas, past shanties and swampy land along the lower stretches of the Washington Canal. People were just getting up, bending over cooking fires outside their shanties. In the fog they seemed like creatures from another time. I knew that these were the freedmen who had tried Elizabeth Keckley's patience so. There were forty thousand of them in Washington now, needing schooling and homes and jobs.

Sometimes Addie gave one of the figures a wave of recognition. And they'd wave back. Then she told the driver where to stop, in front of the old army barracks.

I got out. I helped Addie down from the carriage.

"Best do your business quick and get outta here," the driver was mumbling. "These places are known for breeding disease. 'Specially smallpox."

"I'll be right with you," I told him. "Wait." Would they want Addie here? Suppose they didn't and I had to find someplace else for her. What would I do?

My worries were short-lived. A figure came out of the fog. "Addie? Addie Bassett, is that *you*? Lord awmighty, we thought you were dead!"

"Well, I ain't. I's alive."

The old, white-haired Negro reverend embraced her. "You look good, Addie," he said.

"I's better. Been livin' wif a doctor. He take care o' me." She chuckled. "I's free. And gonna use my freedom right that Mister Linkum gave me."

Others came forward to greet her. The fog gave an unreal quality to the voices and scenes. I saw a woman in the distance stirring something in a huge pot. Another stacking clothing on a table in some kind of order. I smelled breakfast cooking.

"Are you staying with us, Addie?" the reverend asked.

"I come to let y'all know that I's alive and kickin'. And to pick up my things. Then I aims to git myself to the depot and be on my way. This very afternoon."

"Where?" the reverend asked.

"Home. I's goin' home, Reverend. To help my people, now that the war be over."

There was much murmuring over that. Then the reverend thanked me for bringing Addie. I took two gold coins and gave them to her. "This will get you a hack to the depot," I said, "and buy your ticket. Where is home, Addie?" I was thinking that if it was Richmond she could come right along with me.

The reverend laughed. "She won't tell you that," he said. "She's never told anyone that."

Addie smiled. "Long ways," was all she said. "You doan worry your head none 'bout that. You jus' go along now."

I hugged her. "You do good," I said. "Make Mr. Lincoln proud." We drove away. When I turned to look back I saw her standing there, holding the yucca flower against her bosom.

The sun had burned through the fog by the time we got across town to the main part of Washington. The streets were clogged with people and soldiers. On every corner there were regiments of the Grand Army of the Potomac, holding their battle flags, quieting their horses, being formed into lines by grand marshals. I heard muffled drums.

As we came near Pennsylvania Avenue, I gasped. The whole stretch of it, right to the Capitol, was lined on both sides with a river of people who had come to wait for the parade. They had staked out their places, brought chairs, set out great buckets of water. Enterprising people were already selling cold lemonade. Others were hawking flags or buttons with General Grant's or President Lincoln's face on them.

Civilians held banners. WELCOME HEROES OF THE REPUBLIC, HONOR TO THE BRAVE, said one. HEROES OF GETTYSBURG, said another. And still another, SHERMAN TO THE SEA.

Horse-drawn trolleys were decorated with bunting. Some horses from a cavalry unit were bedecked with white satin ribbons. Flags dripped from front porches, store canopies, rooftops. Brass band instruments gleamed in the sun. Hundreds of schoolchildren seemed to be running about wearing red-white-and-blue rosettes and carrying small flags.

We couldn't get out onto Pennsylvania Avenue. All traffic had come to a standstill.

A group of white-gowned ladies walked right in front of the carriage, carrying a banner that said, WITH MALICE TOWARD NONE.

"Well? What are we going to do about this, missy? There are gonna be a hundred and fifty thousand soldiers marching here today." The driver had plenty of malice toward me. He acted as if the whole mess were my fault.

"How far is the train depot?" I asked.

"Two blocks west."

"I'll walk." I paid him and got out, pulling the portmanteau out after me.

The excitement all around me was working to a fevered pitch. I could see them coming way up at the end of Pennsylvania Avenue. Thousands of men in blue. At the same time I heard church bells ringing and the boom of mortars from the ironclads on the river.

A cheer went up from the crowd. "They're coming, they're coming." The bands all began to play "The Star Spangled Banner" on cue.

"Look, the flag at the White House is at full staff for the first time since Lincoln's death."

"Have you got those flowers? Good, I want to throw them. General Meade's men are coming."

I pushed my way through the crowds. Only two blocks to the train depot. It might as well have been a dozen. My hat was knocked off. I dropped my portmanteau once and had to stop and get a better grip on the basket with Ulysses in it. He had gotten a hint of the excitement and was meowing, afraid. I shushed him and continued on.

It must have taken me fifteen minutes to go one block. My head reverberated with the sound of marching feet as a swarm of blue men marched on Pennsylvania Avenue. Out of the corner of my eye I saw their regimental colors snapping in the breeze, their musket barrels gleaming. The epaulets on the shoulders of the officers shone in the sun. Their faces were lean and brown, their eyes hard. I wondered what my daddy would have looked like if he'd come home from the war. Sword hilts flashed. Horses high-stepped to sharp commands. Mules, laden with equipment and wearing the blankets of their units, trudged along. The crowd cheered. "On to Richmond!"

"Don't forget the Wilderness!"

"Three cheers for the Twentieth Maine!"

The sun was hot already. I trudged along. My train would leave at ten o'clock. I stopped and asked a dignified mustached man what time it was. He drew out a pocket watch. "Nine-fifteen," he said.

I had time to rest. But where? Then I saw my place. On the nearby green lawns that sloped down to the Capitol building in the distance. The slope was crowded with schoolchildren and their teachers. But there was also a man there selling lemonade. I was parched.

I set my portmanteau, basket, and shawl under a tree. I purchased a cup of cold lemonade and took it back under the tree to watch the goings-on. The band music was bright and sassy. They were playing "The Girl I Left Behind Me." A group of schoolgirls dressed in white and wearing red, white, and blue ribbons rushed forward up the slope carrying a long garland made of flowers.

"There he *is*. There he *is*."

Who? I craned my neck and went up the slope to see. A gallant-looking officer with long yellow curls and a wavy mustache was leading the next contingent on a high-stepping horse.

"General Custer, General Custer! Hurray for General Custer!" the girls yelled while they ran right to the curb of Pennsylvania Avenue. Then they threw the flower garland at Custer.

Everything happened at once. Custer's gloved hand went to his hat. Just as he was about to raise it, his beautiful horse got hit in the face with the flowers. It reared and neighed in terror.

Caught off balance, Custer did his best to reign his mount

in. But the frightened girls screamed even more, adding to the horse's fear. At the same time a gigantic snare drum boomed. The horse was out of control. He came charging right at the schoolgirls, down the slope. I saw Custer's hat fly off, his blond curls whipping in the breeze. I saw the girls run. All but one.

She stood there, paralyzed, and the horse was coming right at her.

"Out of the way!" Custer was yelling. He mouthed the words, but the brass band drowned them out. I saw the wild look in his horse's eyes and, without thinking, rushed forward and dived at the dumbstruck girl who stood there with her mouth open staring into certain death.

As my body hit hers I felt the wind knocked out of me. Together we rolled over on sweet spring grass, a tangle of dresses, arms, and legs. I felt a pain in my left wrist as I landed on it. Then I rolled over and my head reverberated like a snare drum as the back of it hit the ground, hard.

For a moment I couldn't think. Everything went black. Then I was looking up into a bright blue sky through the leaves of a tree and all kinds of faces were peering down at me.

"Is she all right? Who is she? Did you see what she did? If it hadn't been for her, Elvira would have been stomped to death."

"Where is Custer? Does he even know what he almost caused?"

"He's gone back to the head of his column. He's a wild one. They say it's typical of him. Did somebody send for a doctor?"

"Yes. Miss Chauncy went." It was the girl I'd pushed aside.

She stood over me. "I'm beholden to you," she said. "You saved my life. My teacher has gone for a doctor."

"Are you all right?" I asked.

She nodded. She was white-faced and tear-streaked, but all right.

I sat up, with difficulty. My head hurt. My wrist hurt. "I don't want a doctor. I've got a train to catch."

"I've found a doctor! Would you believe it! He was right over there on the edge of the slope. He has a bag and everything!" A woman in a white lawn dress with red, white, and blue streamers that made her look like a sailboat, was coming toward us. I felt my face go as white as her dress. She was pulling someone along by the hand.

"I don't want a doctor," I said again. I started to get up but had to sit back down again.

"It's all right," he said softly, "it's all right. Get her some water, somebody. In God's name, Emily, I've been looking all over for you all morning. And then someone just came up to me yelling for a doctor and I came to help. I didn't know it was you. My God, what happened?"

I started to cry then, and they were hard put to stop me. His voice did it. And his eyes. And the way his hands touched the lump on my head and picked up my hurt wrist. I had hoped never to see him again. "Oh," I sobbed, "I've made a mess of everything."

"You sure have," Robert agreed, "but we won't talk about it now."

I sat there blubbering while he bound up my wrist. "I want my cat," I sobbed. "Where's my basket with my cat? If I lose Ulysses, I'll die."

The girl who claimed I saved her life ran and got my

basket. Ulysses was crying fretfully. "He needs some water,"
I told Robert. So Robert gave him some.

Then Robert made sure Elvira was all right. Her teacher
insisted we exchange names. Robert gave her mine. And
Uncle Valentine's address. "It's where Emily lives," he said;
"it's her home. Come and see her."

22

$\mathcal{H}$OW CAN
I EXPLAIN THIS?

"It isn't where I live," I told Robert. "It isn't my home. And you had no right to invite them to come and see me there."

He was guiding the chaise away from the crowds and the traffic. He had all he could do to manage this and was not listening to me.

I waited until we were away from the push of people and carriages and finally on a side street. "My train, at this very moment, might be coming into the station. My seat is waiting for me. Paid for. I have to get out of this chaise!"

He did not answer.

"You have to stop," I said. "I have to get out. Stop the horse now, I say! Robert!"

We were on a side street now, the crowds were thinning,

the horse *clip-clop*ped at a steady pace, its mane stream-
ing out, the cobblestone street whizzing by under its feet,
making me dizzy. I started to stand up. He pushed me back
down.

"Stop, please, I'm going to throw up."

"Then do it and get it over with."

"How can you be so mean? Robert, stop now, I say, or I'll
jump out."

"Then do it. I'll not pander to you further."

"Pander? *Pander?* What does *that* mean?"

"Everyone's pandered to you since you first got to your
uncle's house. And look how you repay him."

"How? How do I repay him?"

"By setting the police on him."

"Police?" The breeze was blowing his hair about. And I
noticed he was growing a mustache. "What are you talking
about?" I felt a sense of dread in my bones. "What happened?"

We were driving past a park now. He slowed the horse
down. "Do you care what happened?"

Myra, I thought dismally. *She went and told her father
about the dead bodies in the laboratory.* "Yes," I said.

"Your uncle's work was near ruined. If I hadn't gotten rid
of the evidence before the police arrived at the college with
the reporters, it would have been. And he might now be in
jail. Just because you and your silly friends had to go on a
lark. Couldn't you have thought of something else to do?
Gone to the Soldiers' Home, maybe, where you could have
laughed at the veterans who are half blind and can't walk
anymore?"

"Stop it, Robert, it wasn't like that."

"What was it like, then? I want to know how a bunch of silly schoolgirls can get the notion to ruin the lifetime work of one of the finest doctors we have today in Washington."

Oh, dear God, I thought, *how can I explain this?* But I had to try. So I told him. The words sounded so lame, so inept, the reasoning so selfish. But I told my whole sad tale, starting from the party at school for Myra and ending up with how we ran from the courtyard.

"And you never gave a thought to what this little Myra witch would do when she got home. Because you were busy thinking of yourself. And your own shocked little sensibilities. Am I right?"

Tears crowded my eyes and my throat. "No," I said. "My feminine scruples."

He said nothing to that. But he was angry. He had every right to be, yes, but he was missing something here, overlooking something. What was it? Then it came to me. "If you hadn't lied to me, I wouldn't have allowed them to go to the college. I'd have found a way to keep them from it."

He said nothing.

"Didn't you tell me the bodies you brought back from Memphis were alive? And when I asked you if I would find dead bodies at the lab if I went there, you said no. That it was the end of the semester and they were all gone. Isn't that right, Robert?"

"Yes," he said hoarsely.

"I *believed* you, Robert. I was convinced Myra would make a fool of herself."

He'd allowed the horse to slow to a walk. "How long ago did you know Myra's father was doing an investigation?" he asked.

"I've known it for a while, but I've been able to keep her at bay."

"Why didn't you tell us?"

"Because I wasn't supposed to know what was going on."

"You suspected. You admitted that to me the last time we had this conversation. You should have told us."

"You should have told me things, too."

"Could you have been trusted? As soon as you found out, you decided to run away."

"Because I was betrayed. Not because I found it out."

We rode in silence for a minute or two. We were a block from Uncle Valentine's house. "Where is Uncle Valentine?" I asked.

"Home, waiting for you. He arrived at about eight this morning. Traveled on the cars all night. The minute he found out you were missing, he sent me for you. And I haven't slept all night. I was tipped off yesterday afternoon, just as I returned from my trip to the ironclad, about the police raid on the lab. I got there first, with two other students. Just in time to get the bodies out."

"So the police and reporters have nothing to go on, then."

"No. Only you have. You know now what we're doing. And you can turn us in anytime you want to."

"How dare you! Do you think I would do that?"

He didn't answer.

"How did you find me? How did you know where I'd be?"

"Annie. She came around to see your uncle and told him—the train time and everything—so I knew you'd be in the vicinity of the depot. You can thank Custer for the rest."

"Annie." I fumed. "A fine friend she is."

"Yes, she is a fine friend. You're lucky to have her. She was worried about you running off to God-forsaken Richmond.

There's hardly any food in Richmond. There's military rule. Annie felt she owed your uncle that much. I wouldn't criticize Annie. She knows what she's about."

"And I don't, I suppose."

He drew the chaise up in front of the house. "Did you let Addie go?" The brown eyes pinned me. I could tell he was hoping I would say no.

"Yes," I answered.

"Well, you've really repaid your uncle for all his kindness. I don't know why he puts up with you. I think he should put you in a convent school."

"I'm not Catholic."

"Well, maybe you'd learn right from wrong."

I gave a bitter laugh. "Like Johnny Surratt did?"

He was decent enough not to elaborate on that thought. He fell silent for a moment.

"The Spoon and the Mole have been working for my uncle all along, haven't they?" I asked. "And that night at the cemetery, when he chased them from my mother's grave, he planned it all so I would be indebted to him, didn't he?"

"Because he wanted you to live with him. He knew your mother had turned you against him. She knew about the body snatching. He wanted to make you think he was opposed to it, yes. But you wanted to live with people who were planning on assassinating the president."

"That is unfair, Robert!"

He sighed. "I'm weary of this. My head is spinning. I need to go home and sleep. . . . Go into the house and face the music. He's waiting for you. I wish you luck."

I clambered down from the chaise. He handed down my portmanteau and the basket with Ulysses in it. "For your information," I told him, "I wanted to get in touch with you yesterday afternoon, when Myra sprang her plans on us. But I couldn't."

He nodded briefly. "A lot of good it does us now," he said.

I picked up my things and moved away. "I hate your mustache," I said.

23

$\mathcal{N}$OTHING AND NO ONE,
HE SAID

I WAS TREMBLING when I went into the house. I set my things down in the hall. Ulysses meowed again, poor dear, and I opened the basket and let him out. He ran scampering off, right up the stairs. I wished I could follow him and jump into my bed and pull the blankets over my head.

Where was everybody? Except for the ticking of the tall clock, the house was as silent as the inside of a marble vault. Was Maude out? I hoped so. I didn't need her around, chiding me. It was enough I had to face Uncle Valentine.

What would he say? I knew how he could cut you with his words, like he was doing surgery. Like he was cutting the bad parts out and throwing them away. Would he cut parts out of me now? I'd seen people he'd done it to. They walked away limping. Or all white in the face, like they were bleeding and didn't know it.

"I'm in here, Emily." The voice came from the parlor, muffled and sad.

I went down the hall. He was seated in a large wingback chair, reading. He looked up. I was a sight, all right, with grass stains on the skirt of my dress. It was torn at the hem, too. My arm was in a makeshift sling, my face dirty.

He stood up at the sight of me. The book dropped to the floor. "Are you all right? What happened? You look as if you were run down by a carriage."

"No. A horse, almost. It's a sprain, Robert said. And there's a bump on the back of my head."

He came over to me and felt my head with expert hands, knowing hands. "That's quite a bump. You've got to get some ice on it. But you don't have a skull fracture." He went to the kitchen next and I heard him fussing around out there. He came back with some ice tied in a rag. "Sit down and put this behind your head." He gestured to the wingback chair. I sat. He did, too, across from me.

"Emily," he said, "we have to talk." He looked so sad.

I said, "Yes."

"Why did you run away from me, Emily?"

"Because of what I saw yesterday." I wished his voice wasn't so kind. I wished he would scold. But he didn't.

"The bodies in my lab?"

"Yes."

He leaned forward. "You have suspected the true nature of my work all along, haven't you?"

I told him yes again.

"Then why didn't you ask me outright? Don't you think I deserved at least that?"

"I wanted to. But every time I set my mind to it something happened. You did something good for Annie. Or me. I was thrown off the track and thought I was being silly."

"I meant to throw you off the track. I couldn't have my work compromised. And it *was*, yesterday. It was more than compromised. It was almost ruined. I was almost ruined. If Robert hadn't been tipped off about the police raid and gotten the bodies out, I would have been arrested."

"Uncle Valentine, I didn't lead those girls there. They forced their way. The only reason I went along with it was because Robert told me there were no bodies at your lab. I never meant to hurt you."

"You discussed all this with Robert?"

"Yes, but he wasn't honest with me, either. Any more than you were."

"Don't call me to account, Emily." He turned sharp.

"I'm not calling you to account, sir."

"This has nothing to do with honesty. It has to do with research. With treating shattered bones and torn muscles. With head injuries and ghastly injuries of the face, the spine, the chest. The war taught us all we do not know about the human body. But we must now apply what we have learned in the war. Only, there are not enough available legal cadavers. We need Anatomy Acts to provide us with legal cadavers. New York has one now. Pennsylvania is working on one. I am authoring a pamphlet telling of the need here for such an act. When it is passed, the traffic in bodies will end. Until that time, I shall continue my practices. It is not a pleasant business. I do not profit from it, and I will not purchase a cadaver from anyone who profits from it. But it is my work, the most important thing in the world to me. Do you understand?"

I understood. "It's what caused the argument between you and Mama," I said.

"Yes. She found out what I was doing. She did not approve."

"I would have approved," I said, "if you'd given me the chance."

"I don't want your approval, Emily. All I want, if you wish to continue living with me, is your promise that you won't interfere again. If you can't promise, you may go to Aunt Susie in Richmond. I will pay for your ticket."

I stared at him. "You'd let me go?"

"I don't want you to go. I think you know that by now. But I will let nothing and no one interfere with my work, Emily. Ever. I will put nothing before medical science."

"I won't interfere," I said.

He sighed. "Now that we have that cleared up"—and he waved his hand to dismiss the matter—"tell me. Did you let Addie go?"

The question was so abrupt, the brown eyes so accusing. "Yes."

"Why?"

"She begged me. Ever since I've been here. All she wanted was to be free. I didn't think it right that she was a prisoner."

"You didn't think it right?" Tears came to his eyes. He couldn't speak for a minute. And he was white-faced. "Do you think that was your decision to make?"

"Uncle Valentine."

"Do you know what you have done? Letting that woman go was more an act of betrayal than going with those girls to my lab."

I was confused. He was more distressed about Addie being gone than about the police raid on his lab. There was something here. But what? It came to me then that if I could figure it out, I would understand my uncle Valentine.

Maybe I would even understand the secret of life.

"Do you know how long I've been working with Addie? How far I've come with curing her of the Wasting Disease?"

"She was better," I said. "She wasn't coughing anymore. That's why I let her go."

"She was better because she was on my medicine." He turned and picked up a bottle from a nearby table. He set it down, none too gently, on another table before me. "This medicine."

The bottle was dark. Or was that the medicine inside?

"Pick it up and open it," he said. "Smell it."

I did so. It smelled terrible. Like camphor. Yet at the same time like rotten fish. "What is it?"

"I call it Purple Mass. President Lincoln took something called Blue Mass for his nerves and other ailments. Until I find a better name for this, it is Purple Mass. It clears the lungs. I have been working on it since my wife died. It is a mixture of my own making. Made in part from crushed leaves of devil's tongue, a flower Marietta grew in my laboratory. A nightflower."

I remembered the flower. Remembered Marietta saying what trouble she had growing it. Remembered how the flies were drawn to it, how she'd told me it would smell of decayed fish.

He gave a great sigh and took the bottle back. "My wife always had a cough," he said, " 'Valentine,' she would say to me, 'can't you find something to cure this cough?' Only I was too busy becoming an important doctor. I had no time for her. I thought she was being petulant because I wasn't pay-ing her much mind. 'Keep away from damp air,' I told her.

245

'Take hot tea. Soup.' She got sicker and sicker. Then she got bad. Her lungs filled up. I knew nothing about lungs. I still don't know enough about lungs. She died."

He fell silent. He set the bottle down. "I went on being an important doctor. I worked to overcome my grief. Then Marietta came along. She is very knowledgeable about slave medicine, folklore medicine. One day I told her the story of my wife. It was she who told me about the devil's tongue flower. She had all these decoctions written down from before she came north. I thought devil's tongue was worth a try for congested lungs. Marietta grew the flowers in pots in my lab at the college. I experimented with them and added my own ingredients. It was working for Addie. She was getting better. But her treatment wasn't finished. And without her medicine, she will sicken again and die."

I stared at him. "She was better," I said.

"No. She was on her way to being better. I explained to her how long the treatment would take. She agreed to it. Oh yes, every day she'd ask to leave. Every morning I'd talk with her, reassure her, tell her, 'Just a little while longer.' And she believed me. Until you spirited her up to be free. You have interfered, my girl. In a most dastardly way. With medical science!"

"I didn't, Uncle Valentine. She kept telling me she was a prisoner."

"I told you when you first came here not to listen to her, that she was a patient, not a prisoner. One of the effects of the medicine is that it makes people feel persecuted, mistrusting of others, and addle-headed. Even dizzy. They are plagued with dark thoughts. Lincoln's death didn't help. It brought her guilt over her past drinking to the fore. When these moods struck, she played on your sympathy."

I said nothing.

"Where is she, Emily? Can you tell me that?"

I met his inquiring look with a dumbstruck one of my own. "Gone," I said.

"Gone? Where? Where did you take her?"

"I took her to the Relief Society at Twelfth and O Streets this morning. It's where she wanted to go."

He started to get up out of his chair.

"No," I said. "She's not there, Uncle Valentine. She's gone by now. Long since gone. She just stopped by to tell the reverend there she was all right and to pick up some things. She was leaving this very day."

"For where?"

I brightened. "Home," I said. "You can likely fetch her there. Or get some medicine to her."

He shook his head sadly. "She never told me where home was, Emily. She never would tell me. Did she tell you?"

"No," I said miserably, "she didn't."

24

THE FERRYMAN

THINGS WENT back to normal. Uncle Valentine wanted it that way. "It is over and done with," he said when I told him I wanted to do something to make up for the loss of Addie. "I just want life around here to get back to normal. Do you understand?"

I said yes. But I didn't believe it. Some matters are never over and done with. They just seem that way, is all. If you wait long enough, they pop their heads up again when you least expect it.

Uncle Valentine didn't believe it, either. He acted differently toward me. He acted polite.

I could have stood anger, I think. Even being punished. But in the days that followed he was so carefully polite I thought I would die. I went back to school and decided I would wait for a chance to make things up to him. It would come to me.

Myra Mott did not speak to me. Which qualified as normal, I suppose. I could bear that. But I could not bear the fact that Robert didn't speak to me, either, when he came around. And he came most every day. He actually sat at our breakfast table and didn't speak to me. He spoke more to Ulysses the cat. He acted so superior I couldn't bear it. I sat paralyzed in his presence, tears in my eyes. How could a person's silence say such terrible things to you? And when he left, I felt so stricken I wanted to die. Uncle Valentine noticed, of course. But all he said was, "He'll come 'round, be patient."

I didn't want to be patient. And I didn't want Robert to come 'round. I wanted to show old, superior Robert that I was not the stupid, noodleheaded, no-'count, inferior insect he thought I was. I didn't want him to like me anymore. I didn't even know if I still liked him. It had nothing to do with such insipid feelings. It had to do with respect.

Robert would know I was someone to be reckoned with before I was finished with him, or I'd know the reason why. And if I could make things up to Uncle Valentine at the same time, why, I'd die happy. That was all I knew.

In spite of my troubles, life went on. President Johnson granted amnesty and pardon to all who'd participated in the "existing rebellion," with a few exceptions. On Saturday, June 17, Annie came around. She looked wild eyed. I'd had it all fixed in my head how I wasn't going to talk to her because she snitched about my running away. But I don't think she even remembered that, that's how crazy-acting she was.

They were getting ready to sentence her mother. The

249

government's man, John Bingham, was summing up his argument for the convictions, she told us. "He's been talking three days straight and shows no signs of stopping."

"The press has condemned your mother from the start," Uncle Valentine mused.

"Oh, what will I do?" Annie was pulling at her hair.

I hadn't thought about Johnny in a long time. But now I wondered what had happened to his "gentleman in Washington" who was supposed to let him know if his mother was in danger. And what about the stories in the press? Hadn't Johnny seen them? Funny, I had no more feeling for him except anger. Same as I had for Robert. I was fourteen and finished with men.

"Don't lose faith," Uncle Valentine told Annie. "A last-minute act of executive clemency is always possible. We are a civilized nation. We don't hang women. If they sentence her, I'll go myself with you to the president, on her behalf."

Annie left, plied with food and comfort. But she still looked wild eyed. "He's a good man," she said of Uncle Valentine. "How could you ever have wanted to run away from him?" So. She did remember.

School let out. I made myself useful around the house, minded my business, and kept my eyes and ears open. You can learn an awful lot that way. I helped Maude, greeted Uncle Valentine's patients, did some baking, and sorted out Uncle Valentine's mail daily. Bills came from Aiken and Clampitt, Mrs. Mary's lawyers. There was correspondence from the Almshouse. Did Uncle Valentine go there and visit the poor? Another bill from the Board of Health. It fell out of the envelope.

It was not a bill but a permit to bury material from the dissecting room in Washington Asylum Cemetery. Quickly I put it back in the envelope and sealed it as best I could. Why had I never paid mind to this stuff before?

I even weeded Marietta's garden, for she hadn't been around in a week. Uncle Valentine said he hoped she wasn't sick. She wouldn't tell him if she were. She was afraid of his medicines. Merry still popped his head in the dining room door every morning to tell about shipments. There hadn't been any in a while.

I started reading a book called *The History of Anatomy*. It told how Michelangelo and Leonardo da Vinci studied dead bodies hundreds of years ago to learn anatomy for their artwork. And how they had trouble getting the bodies.

It was better than the Brothers Grimm. I kept thinking of Michelangelo getting bodies sneaked to him in a garret someplace. Not so he could cure the Wasting Disease. But so he'd know how to paint pictures on the ceiling of a church in Rome.

On June 30 all the conspirators in the Lincoln assassination were found guilty. Herold, Payne, Atzerodt, and Mary Surratt were sentenced to be hanged. Spangler was given six years. The others got life sentences, including Uncle Valentine's friend Dr. Mudd.

Annie's mother to be hanged! I couldn't believe it! Mama's girlhood friend from that fancy school that gave them notions. I'd wager Mrs. Mary had no notions now.

Uncle Valentine was having an uneven time of it with this news of Dr. Mudd. "They're putting all doctors on notice," he said. And I know he was talking about more than a doctor's decision to set the leg of a man in pain who came to him in the middle of the night.

He brooded. But he kept his promise to Annie. He

arranged to go and see the president with her. And he was so busy arranging things that he never even noticed it when my chance came along to make things up to him.

On Saturday, July 1, we were at breakfast. Uncle Valentine was awaiting Annie's arrival. They were to go and see President Johnson today.

Merry popped his head in the door. "Shipment tonight, boss."

"Where?"

"The Almshouse."

My ears perked up.

"Is it a good one?" Uncle Valentine asked.

"Robert's been in touch with our man inside. He says it's just what you need."

"Is the Board of Guardians cooperating?"

"No. We gotta pick it up ourselves. Robert's ready, but we haven't heard from Marietta. He's too busy to call at her house. He wants you to write a note."

"All right. This is a devil of a time for it, I'm so busy. But then maybe it's a good time. Most of Washington is taken with the trial and sentencing. Go along, Merry. Help Robert. I'll get a note to Marietta."

He asked me to fetch paper, pen, and ink from his office. I did so. Then he wrote the note and asked me to deliver it. Marietta lived in a small roominghouse on L Street. He seemed distracted. "She must keep this appointment tonight at the Almshouse. It's all here in this note. She is to meet Robert. We're depending on her," he said.

"Isn't there anything I can do to help, Uncle Valentine?"

"Yes. Come directly home after delivering the note, and stay in the house. From the meeting with the president, I'm going to see Dr. Mudd before they take him away.

Washington is in an uproar over the prospect of hanging a woman. I don't want you out on the streets. Go along now."

I went, glad to be out of the house. I wouldn't be here when Annie arrived. It was cowardly, I knew, but she didn't want me. She wanted only Uncle Valentine. There was nothing I could do for her now, anyway.

I found Marietta in bed, upstairs in her small neat room. She was sick. And her landlady was concerned. "She's been coughing all week," she said.

She was not only coughing but feverish. "I'm all right," she told me. "I've got my cough syrup with Balm of Gilead."

"Why didn't you tell Uncle Valentine?" I asked innocently.

"He's got enough worries now. I read where Dr. Mudd and Mrs. Surratt were convicted. I know he's in a state."

I sat down on a chair. Maybe her "knowing" was a special power. But I'd found out something. Every time you knew something about another that they didn't know you knew, you had power. I gave her the note. She read it and had a spell of coughing, took a drink of water, and looked at me. "I don't think I can go. The medicine makes me sleepy. And nights, my head hurts. I must apply feverfew to my temples. You must tell him to make other arrangements."

"Is it a fresh body at the Almshouse?"

She looked at me in surprise.

"I know all about everything," I told her. "Uncle Valentine told me. And he trusts me."

"When?"

"He decided I can be trusted," I said simply. I must appear strong to her, like she did to me. "What do they want you to do?"

"The usual." She shrugged. "The Board of Guardians at

the Almshouse has been charging too much for bodies. They're not supposed to sell them in the first place. But they do and they've been constantly raising their prices. Which is why Robert and your uncle started calling them the Board of Buzzards. Uncle Valentine has a man inside there. He is called the Ferryman and attends to the burials at Potter's Field behind the Almshouse. He informed your uncle of the death of a young man who lived there. I am supposed to claim him tonight, as a long-lost female relative."

"Like you did in Memphis," I said.

"Yes. When I appear for the burial, the Ferryman has to release the body to me. That way your uncle outwits the Board of Buzzards and the Ferryman is protected. No one can help it if a relative appears at the last moment."

"Don't they recognize you by now?"

"I have many different disguises. Sometimes I'm a sister, sometimes a wife. I can even look like an old lady."

"What would you be tonight if you could go?"

"Likely a sister," she said, "who just found out about the death of a long-lost wastrel brother."

I felt the blood pounding in my temples. "I could go in your place," I said.

"You?" She had an immediate fit of coughing. I poured her fresh water from the pitcher. "You?" she said again when she recovered herself.

"Yes. Uncle Valentine said I can do it if you're sick. He said I should let him know and he'll come around with some medicine." I looked at her innocently. "Of course, I don't have to tell him you're sick. I could just go in your place. What with all the worries he's got, going to see the president."

She met my eyes. I don't know if she believed me about Uncle Valentine saying I could go. But she saw me as someone strong, someone in charge. And someone who could tell Uncle Valentine she was sick. I was someone to be reckoned with. That was all I wanted from her. All I wanted from anybody, when it got right down to it.

"All right," she agreed. "Over there in that closet. I have several outfits. Let's see which one is best for you."

We went through the clothes. They were all black, of course, and smelled worse than Uncle Valentine's Purple Mass medicine. I tried on a few things and settled for a black silk dress with lace ruffles at the neck and long sleeves. There was a darling velvet hat with netting that came down over the face. Even a little black satin reticule with a scented handkerchief in it. And black kid boots. They were too large. We had to stuff old copies of the *Intelligencer* in them.

Marietta coughed a lot.

"Why don't you take some of Uncle Valentine's Purple Mass medicine?" I asked her.

"Foul stuff," she said. "I prefer my Balm of Gilead. But speaking of that medicine, this shipment is very important to your uncle. Do you know what the man died of?"

"What?"

"The Wasting Disease. Dr. Bransby will be able to study his lungs."

I could scarce contain my elation.

"Now, as for you. Your story is that you come from a wealthy Maryland family. You are high placed. Your wastrel brother ran off when the war started because he didn't want to fight for the South. In Maryland they call it skedaddling. What with the war and all, nobody could locate him, but they've been on the trail. Your father is failing, so he couldn't come. He wants his son home, though he's been a drinker, a gambler, and an all-around bounder. His name is Johnny."

Fitting, I thought.

"Johnny Collins. He must be buried with honor on the family land in Hagerstown in western Maryland. And not in Potter's Field. Hagerstown is about thirty percent Rebel. Here are some coins to give to the Ferryman. Robert will be waiting with a wagon, on the east side of the Almshouse. He'll be your faithful family servant. Dressed as an old man."

Robert. What would he do when he discovered it was me behind the black veil? Refuse to speak to me? Send me home? Well, I would have to count on the element of surprise. And the fact that it would be too late to stop things set in motion.

"But you must meet the Ferryman alone. He'll know you're from Dr. Bransby; but never falter in your act. Someone from the Board of Buzzards may be watching. You don't want to get the Ferryman in trouble. Anyway, he may have to go inside and ask their permission to release the body to you. They may come out to meet you. Play the part well if they do. It will be all right. Most men can't abide a weeping woman."

I thanked her and took up my bundle of clothing.

"Be careful," she said to me as I went out the door. "What you are doing is illegal in the eyes of the law. You could be arrested."

I hadn't thought about that.

"And if you are, there is one rule we hold firm. You must not tell them who you are doing this for. You must never mention the name of Dr. Bransby."

I went home with her ominous words in my ears. Still, I was more excited than frightened. Uncle Valentine was out.

So was Maude. I went right to my room and showed my outfit to Ulysses. He approved.

I read *The History of Anatomy* until five. I was to meet Robert at seven. I heard Maude come in and start to fix supper. Maude could be a problem. But when I went downstairs to tell her I'd take a plate in my room, I could tell she had something else on her mind.

"I'm so upset about this Dr. Mudd thing. It sits ill on your uncle. It's wearing him down. Not to mention the business with Annie's mother. To think that they are going to hang that woman! What is the world coming to? There's a group of protestors uniting in front of the White House tonight, with torches. I've a mind to join them."

"Why don't you?" I said.

"You'll be all right?"

"Yes. I'll keep a lamp lit for Uncle Valentine."

She left. Merry was going with her, she said. Thank heaven for the women protestors. Thank heaven that Merry wouldn't be at the Almshouse. One less person to worry about. I left at six-thirty, dressed in black, to meet Robert.

I paid the driver of the hack a block from the Almshouse, which was at Nineteenth and C Streets, and set off on foot. A mild drizzle was coming down; fog from the Potomac wrapped the houses in a premature dusk. The cobblestones on the street were slippery. Was this the east side of the Almshouse? Yes, in the near distance, through the fog, I saw a wagon.

I felt awkward in the black silk dress. The hem was a bit too long and I had all I could do to keep from tripping on it. The veil obscured my vision, but I dared not remove it.

The musty smell of the clothing was giving me a headache, even in the open air.

Was that man leaning against the wagon smoking a cheroot Robert? He had long gray hair, a shabby jacket, and a soft-brimmed hat pulled down over his eyes. He stood up straight when he saw me approaching.

"Marietta?"

I made a sound of acknowledgment in my throat.

"Thank God. Are you all right? Where've you been all week? Dr. Bransby was worried. You haven't been sick, have you? I wanted to come 'round but couldn't get the time."

"I've not been sick."

"You sound like you are. What is it, your throat? I knew it. You shouldn't be out on a beastly night like this. Well, let's get it over with. I can see Potter's Field from here. I'll walk you up there. I understand it's a young man. The Wasting Disease. A good specimen, fresh. Since that brat of a niece of his let Addie go, he really needs this one. He was making such progress with Addie . . . I can get this specimen right over to the lab tonight. It's a good thing about the hanging, in a way, don't you think? Everyone is up in arms over that. Maybe they'll leave us alone for a while." He took my arm. "Here, just in case anyone's watching. You're grieving, re-member."

I felt the gentle strength of him supporting me. We walked like that for a few paces and then I tripped on the hem. If Robert hadn't been holding my arm, I'd have gone down. "Oh no!" I cried. I said it sharp and clear.

He stopped. Still holding my arm, he turned to look at me. "You're not Marietta." He said it calmly. Then he took the veil by its edge and lifted it from my face.

"It's *you!*"

"Don't be angry, Robert."

"By God!" He grabbed me by the forearms. "What in hell are you doing here? Are you crazy? Where did you get these clothes? This isn't a joke! We could get caught. Does he know you're here? Who sent you?"

All the while he was talking he was pulling me into the shadows of some high hedges. He still gripped my arms.

"Robert, you're hurting me."

"Explain," he said.

"Marietta is sick. I went there with a note from Uncle Valentine. She couldn't come."

"He let *you* come?"

"No, he doesn't know I'm here. He went with Annie to the White House to beg for her mother's life. Then, after, to see his friend Dr. Mudd."

"Who gave you those clothes?"

"Marietta."

"Marietta would never consent to let you come, sick or not."

"I told her Uncle Valentine agreed to it."

"You little lying brat. You're trying to ruin us, aren't you?" He released me. He moved away like I was something not to be touched. "Those clothes were taken from a corpse, you know," he said. "Did Marietta tell you that?"

I felt a new sense of revulsion at the smell I'd been breathing in.

"That dress was worn by a dead woman! All the clothing we wear on these excursions is. That dress was in a grave. Removed from a cadaver."

He was angering me, trying to scare me like that. I tossed my head and rallied. "Well, I can't get squeamish now, can I?" I asked him.

I saw something come into his eyes, for just an instant. Some glint of admiration, quickly concealed.

"Robert, please," I tried to sound bored. "This is wasting everybody's time. I want to help. I *can* help. Marietta told me what has to be done and I can do it. Please, Robert, cooperate."

He waved his hands at me in disgust.

I thought quickly. "I'm here now, Robert. You can hate me all you want. But if we don't do this now, you'll lose this specimen. And nobody's paying attention tonight. Everyone's at the protest in front of the White House. Even Merry and Maude. They're all fixing on the hanging of Mrs. Mary. Marietta coached me. I know what to do. Then you never have to speak to me again. Or see me. As long as you live."

"That isn't long enough," he said.

I felt a great heaving sadness inside me. Did I still care for him, then? But there was no time for that now. I started walking away from him, down the street to the cemetery gate.

"Where are you going? You come back here!"

"I'm going to do my job, Robert," I said. "I'm going to get the specimen. You can stand there and nurse your own feelings, or you can accompany me, the way you're supposed to. Either way, I'm going."

"Come back here!" His whisper was loud and savage.

"There are some people over there across the street," I whispered back in a singsong voice. "Do you want to attract attention?"

In a moment I heard his odd, shuffling gait behind me. Then felt the grip on my arm again. This time the fingers tightened on me, hurting. "I'm going to tell him about this. You're finished when he finds out. You're off to Richmond for good."

"You do what you have to do, Robert." We were nearing the cemetery gate. I could see a man inside holding a shaded lantern. I could see a coffin on the ground beside him. I fumbled with the gate latch. It came loose. I swung it open. "Now, I'm counting on you to go and get the wagon," I said sweetly. And I walked inside.

The man was starting to dig a grave. I walked down a path, around some burial plots. There were no headstones, I noticed, just crosses crudely put together from sticks. Of course. People who died in the Almshouse couldn't afford headstones.

The man was digging slowly. He'd raise a shovel full of dirt, set it aside, and rest on the shovel, like he had all night. Like he was waiting for someone to come along and relieve him of his task. When he saw me approaching, he stopped.

I took the handkerchief out and put it to my nose. The fragrance was thick and sweet. I felt nauseated. Tears came to my eyes. Good, I needed the tears. "Are you the Ferryman?" I asked.

"Who wants to know?"

"My name is—" I hesitated. *What is my name?* No one had told me. I thought quickly. "My name is Maria Collins. I was told to come here tonight. That you were burying my brother."

"Brother? This poor soul's got no family. That's why he's been livin' here. This is the Almshouse, miss. You sure you got the right place?"

"Yes, oh yes!" I remembered Marietta's words: *Never falter in your act.* I knelt down beside the coffin. "Is his name Johnny Collins? From Hagerstown, Maryland?"

"Name's Collins. Don't know where he hails from. Don't

think any of them in the Almshouse know where they hail from, either."

"Oh, Johnny!" I embraced the old wooden coffin. "I've found you at last! Oh, to think I'm too late. I've been looking for you so long." Still kneeling, I peered up at the Ferryman's face. It was an old face, deeply lined but kindly. And the eyes twinkled at my performance.

"He's been a wastrel, a scoundrel, and a ne'er-do-well," I explained, "estranged from the family. Daddy just never forgave him that he wouldn't fight for the Cause. So I suppose that's why he never came home. But Daddy is failing fast. And all he's longing for now is that Johnny come home. Am I too late? Can't you just let me have him, sir, so I can bring him home and have him buried in honor on our land?"

He took off his hat. He wiped his brow. "I'll just go inside a minute and make it right with the Board," he said. "Oughta be somebody inside from the Board. You wait." He set down the shovel and walked through the stick crosses to the door at the back of the Almshouse.

I looked around me and shivered. His shaded lantern was on the ground next to the coffin, casting a weak, flickering light. It was raining lightly. What was I doing here, all alone in this sad little cemetery with stick crosses, wearing musty, evil-smelling clothing from the grave? From a nearby tree I heard a hooty-owl calling to its mate. Where was Robert? I peered through the fog out onto the street. Was he angry enough to desert me?

Suppose someone from the Board came out to question me? Suppose my answers didn't satisfy? Would I be arrested this night? Hauled off to jail like Annie's mother, where I'd have to use a smelly old pot in full view of everybody?

For one terrible moment panic seized me. I wanted to run.

Then the back door of the Almshouse opened and the Ferryman came out. At the same time, from the street I heard the *clip-clopp*ing of a horse. Then the outline of a wagon just outside the gates. Relief washed over me. Robert had not deserted me!

The Ferryman took his time. He had all the time in the world, I minded; all night. He ambled back to me.

"Well?" I asked. I wrung the handkerchief in my hands. "What did they say?"

"They said it's awful peculiarlike that you showed up just now."

My heart fell. My knees were trembling.

"They asked if you had any identification."

"Identification?"

"Yes. They require proof of who you be. Or who you come for. They want a paper."

"Paper?" I asked stupidly.

"You know, a paper." He shrugged and winked at me.

I looked into his eyes. They were warm and kind. *I hope you have it,* they seemed to be saying. *Robert,* I thought. *He has the paper. He wouldn't have let Marietta waltz in here without it.* "Give me just a minute, sir," I said, "and I'll fetch it. I left it with my servant."

I would kill Robert for not giving me that paper. I walked back to the gate. "Robert," I whispered savagely, "the Ferryman wants a paper."

"You did it, then." He sounded unbelieving.

"Of course I did it! What did you think I was doing in there with him? Inviting him for tea? Give me the paper. And I hope my name isn't on it. Because you didn't tell me what it's supposed to be and I said it was Maria."

He reached inside his coat pocket and pulled out two papers. "No, your name isn't here. It's a letter from John Collins, Sr., from Hagerstown, Maryland, requesting the body of his son. The second paper is permission from the Board of Health to take said body across state lines. Both counterfeit, of course."

"Why did you let me go inside without them?"

He had the decency to look shamefaced. "I forgot."

I took the papers, walked back, and handed them to the Ferryman. He inspected them. "Good," he said, "good. This will satisfy the Board. I'll keep the one from Mr. Collins. You'll need the other to get him across state lines. I suppose you want help getting the coffin into the wagon?"

"Yes, please."

He swung the lantern twice. A signal. Robert came in the gate. They lifted the coffin down the path and loaded it onto the wagon. "Get in the carriage, Miss Maria," Robert said.

I drew some coins out of my reticule and handed them to the Ferryman. "Thank you so much, sir. Your kindness will make my daddy happy in his old age."

"Have a safe trip, Miss Collins."

I got into the wagon. Robert walked the Ferryman back to the gate. They huddled in conversation for a minute, then Robert shook his hand and came back to hop up beside me. I was shivering. Robert reached for a blanket. "It's not from the grave," he said.

I wrapped myself in it. My teeth were chattering. I ripped off the lace mitts and rubbed my hands together in my lap. He reached out and put a hand over mine. I pulled my hand away.

"I'll take you right home," he said. "You'd best have something hot."

"You'd best take said body to the lab first," I snapped.

He gave a quiet chuckle. "All right. I'm sorry I gave you such an uneven time of it. Sorry I slipped up. But you covered my mistake. I never realized you were such a spirited little thing."

"There's lots you don't realize about me, Robert."

"You were good back there. The Ferryman said you were better than Marietta."

"If you're trying to make things up to me, don't. Not at the expense of Marietta."

He gave me a quick glance of admiration. I looked away.

"So, then? Are you going to tell Uncle Valentine about tonight? So I'll be off to Richmond for good?"

"I thought you wanted to go to Richmond."

"I don't. Not anymore. But don't let a little thing like that stop you."

He looked at the reins in his hands. "If you stay, I suppose you'll keep getting in my hair, won't you?"

"Yes," I said, "and I still hate your mustache."

"Don't push me too far, Emily Pigbush," he said. "I still haven't made up my mind whether to tell him about tonight yet."

"You do what you have to do, Robert," I told him.

25

$\mathcal{F}$IRECRACKERS
ON THE FOURTH

ROBERT DIDN'T TELL.

He came to breakfast the next morning and bade me a polite hello. He even directed some conversation at me. Though he was careful not to be too nice. I had to give him credit for decency. Uncle Valentine wouldn't be suspicious. And later he told me he'd sworn Marietta to secrecy about my escapade, too.

My escapade. I was happy and unhappy. Uncle Valentine would think Marietta had gotten the cadaver of Johnny Collins for him. He would never know that if I hadn't gone it would have been lost to him forever. I'd made up to him for the loss of Addie. But I couldn't let him know it. Isn't that always the way of things? Sometimes our best deeds need to be kept secret. I wondered if there were a lesson anywhere in the Brothers Grimm about that. Surely there must be.

There seemed some sweet sense of justice, though, in the fact that I couldn't tell Uncle Valentine what I'd done. Like I was doing additional penance for the loss of Addie. Johnny Surratt had told me all about Catholic penance. You had to do it or you went to hell for your sins. Addie was going to die because she didn't have her medicine. That was my sin. Certainly additional penance was needed. I'd probably be seeking it out for the rest of my life.

I didn't have time to think about it that morning, though. Uncle Valentine told us at breakfast that he had failed at the White House. President Johnson had refused to see either him or Annie. "He sent us a message," Uncle Valentine said. "He said that Mrs. Surratt kept the nest that hatched the eggs."

A *serpent in the breasts of those people,* Elizabeth Keckley had said. And what about Ella May? A *curse on this street,* she'd told me. And even Uncle Valentine had sensed something. *Evil is brewing there,* he'd told Mama.

"So what will happen now?" I asked him.

"They're going to hang the woman," he said. "There is nothing anybody can do about it."

Robert and I both fell silent. "And Dr. Mudd?" Robert asked.

"He's been sentenced to life. My dear friend. They are taking him to Fort Jefferson military prison in the Dry Tortugas."

"Where's that?" I asked.

"It's a hellhole," he said. "A sun-fried island a hundred miles off the coast of Florida."

"Marietta said he won't serve a life sentence," I told him. "She told you that he'd be in prison a while and then be released. And she has powers, you know that, Uncle Valentine."

He looked at me. "Well, we're all going to need all the powers we have to get through this next week. The hanging is on July seventh. We're going to have to stand by Annie."

That afternoon I found myself at loose ends. Maude had the afternoon off. It was Sunday. Uncle Valentine was working in his office on his pamphlet about the need for an Anatomy Act. The house was quiet and cool. Outside, the heat was oppressive and unyielding. I was trying to read, but I had to keep getting up to answer the door clapper.

Messages for Uncle Valentine. Three of them. "Thank you," he said each time I brought one in to him. Then he went back to work.

"What's happening, Uncle Valentine?" I finally asked.

"Not enough, I'm afraid." He smiled bleakly. "Friends informing me that Mrs. Stephen Douglas, wife of the dead senator from Illinois, is going to petition the president this week for Mrs. Surratt's life. Also Thaddeus Stevens, a radical Republican congressman."

"Why are they sending notes around to you?"

"I asked Mrs. Douglas and Stevens to help."

"You never wanted me to live in Mrs. Mary's house," I said.

"Don't let's dwell on that now, Emily."

"Do you believe it was the nest that hatched the eggs?"

"Yes. She opened her doors to them. She gave them comfort. But then, Dr. Mudd opened his doors to Booth, too, and treated him. It doesn't make him guilty."

I nodded. Uncle Valentine was fair. I went back to my reading.

The next time I answered the door clapper, it was Annie. She seemed not to know me, or care. She was dressed neatly now, her hair done up in a bun. She carried a small portmanteau.

"Is Dr. Bransby in?"

I ushered her into the cool dimness of the house. Uncle Valentine got up from his desk, came forward, and took her in his arms. "There is always hope for a last-minute reprieve," he told her. "People are telling me that wherever they go, in hotels and on the streets, people are saying they shouldn't hang your mother."

"You've been kind. I shall not forget it. I came to tell you, I'm going to spend every night from now until the seventh with my mother in her cell in Carroll Prison."

"Are you sure you want to do that, Annie?" he asked.

"Yes. My mother needs me."

"What can we do for you?"

"Just be there on the seventh. Stand with me, if she doesn't get a reprieve."

"We'll be there," he said.

She picked up her portmanteau and turned to me. "Puss-in-Boots is with a neighbor until I can return home again."

I nodded mutely.

She started to leave. I wanted to put my arms around her, too, before she left, but she walked right by me, head held high, shoulders straight. She had a carriage waiting, she said.

I couldn't let her go like that. I must do something for her, but what? Then it came to me.

"Annie, wait," I begged.

She turned. "I haven't time."

269

"Just a minute. Wait right there in the hall. There's something I must give you." I ran through the kitchen, took a knife off the counter, and ran out into Marietta's garden. The heat was beating down unmercifully. Where were they? Oh yes, there. The night-blooming cereus. I bent to cut two on long stems and brought them back into the kitchen. There I wrapped them quickly in wet paper and brought them into the hall where Annie was waiting.

"What are they?" she asked.

"Night-blooming cereus. They are nightflowers. Bring them into your mother's cell."

"Thank you," she said.

"Tell your mother hello."

She nodded, thanked me again, and went out the door.

That was Sunday, July 2. Somehow we got through the next few days without losing our senses. On the Fourth, Robert took me sailing on the Potomac. We were not as friendly as before. We were wary of one another, yet at the same time bound by secrets, shared experiences, and concerns. And he had a newfound respect for me. I could not ask for more.

He was a very good sailor. Maude had a supper of cold chicken, hot biscuits, jellied shrimp, and ice cream when we got home. There were fireworks afterward, down by the Sixth Street wharves. Robert took me, but when I looked up to see those colorful bombs bursting over the water I took no joy from them. And a couple of times when an especially loud one went off I saw Robert wince.

We walked home in silence. Robert left me at the gate and walked home. When I got inside, Annie was there, in the parlor with Uncle Valentine. Neither of them looked up as I came in. I took a chair and listened.

Annie was begging. "I need you to use your influence with Dr. Porter, the jail physician, to get them to release my mother's body to me. They don't want to let me have her."

"Why don't we wait and see what happens on the seventh before we talk about this?" Uncle Valentine said.

"I know what's going to happen on the seventh. They're going to hang her. Neither Mrs. Douglas nor Thaddeus Stevens could get anywhere with the president. She's going to hang."

"There is always hope for a last-minute reprieve, Annie. I heard that the president's secretary is going to keep a fast horse outside the White House door, in case Johnson changes his mind at the last minute."

Then of a sudden Annie stood up. "Dr. Bransby," she said in a clear firm voice, "I'm going to be standing outside the prison gates on the seventh. Stanton has told all the relatives of the condemned that he will not release the bodies. He wants them buried in pine boxes by the jailhouse wall. If you use your influence with Dr. Porter, if you get my mother's body released, I'll give it to you. For medical research. My mother gets migraine headaches, you know."

Uncle Valentine looked up at her, disbelief on his face.

"I mean it, Dr. Bransby. You can have my mother's body. I know you use the bodies of executed criminals. It's legal. I know that, too. My mother is no criminal, but I'd rather give her to you than have her buried on the penitentiary grounds."

My uncle nodded and sighed, got up, and walked across the hall to his office. I got up, too. I saw him penning a note. Then he gave it to Annie. "For Dr. Porter," he said.

"Thank you, Dr. Bransby," Annie said. Then she looked at me. "Mama liked the flowers," she told me. Then she went out.

"Uncle Valentine, are you going to take the body?"

He was on his way into the kitchen. He stopped. "What do you think, Emily?"

"I think of what you told me. That you would put nothing and no one before medical science. So then, if they give Annie her mother's body, are you going to take it? Is that why you wrote the note to Dr. Porter?"

He smiled at me, a slow sad smile. "No, Emily," he said. "No?"

"This may be the first time in my life that I let someone come before medical science. But no, Emily, I am not going to take the body. I wrote the note to Dr. Porter to appeal to his humanity. To try to get Annie's mother's body released to her for a proper burial. Now I'm on my way to the kitchen to see if there's any chicken left. I need something to eat."

I thought I heard firecrackers. It was still the Fourth, wasn't it? I felt them exploding inside me. "I'll get you some chicken," I said. "You go and finish your work."

26

I WISH I COULD BE
MISS MUFFET AGAIN

"MY GOD, they're not going to hang the woman, are they?"

He looked like a newspaperman. There were so many of them around. He had pad and pencil. He pushed his way through the crowd at the gates of the prison yard. It was eleven in the morning and already the sun was beating down like some kind of a great white bird suffocating us with its wings.

"Nobody knows yet," a man behind us said. "Ask that one there, why don't you? She's the daughter."

The reporter looked at Annie. His face lit up, not believing his luck. "Are you Annie Surratt?"

"Yes."

"Can I ask you some questions?"

"You don't have to answer if you don't want to, Annie," Uncle Valentine said.

Annie said it was all right and went off with him a distance away from us and the others crowded at the prison gate. "How long have you been keeping this vigil here?" I heard him ask. And Annie's murmured answer, "Since I came out of my mother's jail cell and bade her good-bye at six this morning."

We'd been here since ten. Uncle Valentine hadn't wanted me to come. "A hanging is no place for a young girl," he'd said. "What has the world come to?" But his argument was no good. He knew what the world had come to.

There were a lot of young girls present. There must have been about two thousand people pressed against the wrought-iron fence that surrounded the prison yard. Inside were about a thousand soldiers. And some civilians.

Annie had told us they had special tickets.

The crowd was in a festive mood. Inside the gates the carpenters were still hammering at the gallows. Every once in a while we could hear the crash of a trapdoor as it was tested. The sun rose higher in the sky. Everyone waited.

Annie came back with the reporter. "They can't find anybody to dig the graves," she was telling him. "All the prison employees refused, because they are hanging my mother."

He scribbled very fast. "Thank you, Miss Surratt," he said. "I wish you luck. I heard that General William Hancock is at the back door of the prison waiting for a messenger from the president." Then he lifted his hat and motioned for a guard. While he waited, he looked at me. "Those flowers you're holding are wilted, miss," he said.

"No," I told him. "They're nightflowers."

"Nightflowers?"

"Yes. They will bloom tonight."

He tipped his hat at me. "How appropriate," he said. Then he flashed a card at the guard, who opened the gate and let him into the prison yard.

Annie followed him with her eyes. She gripped the iron bars of the gate. Uncle Valentine put a hand on her shoulder and drew her back. She was hollow eyed, white-faced. She looked ten years older than her seventeen years this morning.

Propped up in a corner, where the gate met the fence, she had a casket. A plain pine casket. She'd brought it, just in case.

Now we saw a short man in a captain's uniform coming across the dusty yard toward us. Two soldiers with carbines were with him. Everyone else saw him, too, and a murmur ran like a ripple through the crowd. He drew some keys out of his pocket, opened the gate a crack, and motioned Annie to the other side. The soldiers stood by the opening, rifles poised to hold back the crowd. Annie went in.

A distance away she conferred with the man. His face was close to hers. From our side of the gate the people shouted at the soldiers. "Let the woman go! Stanton doesn't need to hang a woman!" The soldiers stood guard, stone-faced, carbines poised across their chests. A distance behind them I saw other soldiers approaching.

Annie was conferring with the captain. I saw her nod and smile weakly, then he led her back to the gate. The soldiers opened it and slipped her through and locked it.

She walked and spoke like someone in a trance. "That was Captain Rath. He's the hangman," she said dully. "He said Generals Hancock and Hartranft, who are running things, want him to stall as long as he can. They're still hoping for a messenger from the president."

Uncle Valentine drew her aside and pulled a flask out of his pocket. "Have some water, Annie," he said. She took some. I saw her lift the flask and the water dribble down her chin. Then we waited some more.

Robert drew me aside. "Are you sure you want to see this?"

"I must stay with Annie," I said.

He nodded and took my hand. He squeezed it.

"If it were my mother, I wouldn't be able to be like Annie, Robert," I said. "I don't know how she's holding up."

"We never know what we can do until we have to do it."

There was something I needed to say to him, something important. But I couldn't think of what it was. Time and the sun beat down on us. People were opening umbrellas, holding them over their heads. *Why don't they just go home,* I thought, *to their cool, safe houses? Why did they have to come out here to see this?*

In what seemed like a short while I heard church bells down the street. Twelve chimes, soft and musical on the summer air. Birds twittered in the trees overhead. Across the street some children were playing. How could this be? How could life go on like this when they were going to hang my best friend's mother?

Then the back door of the prison opened and they came out.

Four of *them.* Three men and a woman. Accompanied by two priests and three ministers.

A unified gasp went up from the crowd. Then silence.

Mrs. Mary was wearing her good black bombazine dress, the one with the satin ribbons. *How could you wear your best dress to be hanged in?* Her head was veiled. The priests were on either side of her, supporting her arms. Under the blazing impersonal sun the sad procession walked across the dusty prison yard and the prisoners went up the steps to the scaffold. Atzerodt, Herold, Payne, Mrs. Surratt.

Thirteen steps. *Had they planned thirteen steps?*

It was in that moment that I thought of Johnny Surratt. My Johnny. I wondered if he still had the handkerchiefs Annie had made him with the days of the week on them. I remembered the night he took me to Ford's Theater and we sat in the president's box.

A hundred years ago. Another time. *Where are you, Johnny? If you'd come back they wouldn't be hanging your mother. Couldn't you have come back?*

I wondered if Annie's mother were thinking of him. I wondered what she was thinking just now.

The prisoners sat on chairs on the platform. General Hartranft read the execution order. Then the clergymen said their prayers, each in turn. Then more waiting.

"Oh, God!" Annie moaned. "They're holding an umbrella over my mother. She must have one of her headaches!"

"Hold on, girl," Uncle Valentine told her. "A stay of execution can still come."

"How can they be so cruel, Dr. Bransby? How can human beings be so cruel?"

Uncle Valentine put his arm around her and held her close. I clutched the stems of my nightflowers. Robert gave me a tight smile of encouragement.

Then we waited some more. Mrs. Mary was kissing her crucifix.

Nooses were slipped over the heads of the prisoners. Then Captain Rath made them stand up while soldiers tied their hands behind them. He himself knelt and tied a rope around

Mrs. Mary's dress, just below her knees. Then white hoods were placed over the prisoners' heads.

Just before the hood was placed over Payne he shouted, "Mrs. Surratt is innocent and doesn't deserve to die!" Then the voice was muffled by the hood.

Emboldened, Atzerodt cried out, "Good-bye, gentlemen. May we all meet in the other world!"

Annie moaned. "Don't look," Uncle Valentine said. He drew her head against his chest. Her face was to his jacket front. I saw him cast an eye to Robert, saw Robert nod.

Captain Rath wasn't ready yet. He walked up and down the platform behind the bound and hooded prisoners, checking ropes and hoods. "He's stalling for time," Robert whispered.

Time. I looked up at the white heat-laden sky. Cicadas were singing in the trees, their song an upward spiral. Then the back door of the prison opened and everyone gasped again.

I craned my neck. Was it a reprieve?

General Hancock stood there. "Go ahead," he said.

Captain Rath stood motionless. "The woman, too?" he asked.

Hancock nodded.

Annie had turned her head to see, but Uncle Valentine turned her face back into his jacket front again. "No more looking, Annie," he said. "No more, child."

In a like manner, Robert put his arm around my shoulder and drew me to him. Like a brother. Or like Johnny would have done. Had there really been a Johnny? Or had I dreamed him?

I looked up into Robert's face, remembering what it was I

had to say to him. "I was so silly, Robert. I thought, these past months, that what Uncle Valentine was doing was wrong and bad. I wasted all my energies on it. And it wasn't wrong or bad. All he was trying to do was help people."

I heard the loud clapping of someone's hands. A signal. I heard a chopping sound. I supposed it was the soldiers under the platform, axing the props.

"Annie told me what real trouble was. And I wouldn't believe her. How could I have been so young and so silly, Robert? My daddy used to call me Miss Muffet. Did you know that?"

"No, I didn't," he murmured.

Then a snapping sound as the trapdoors went through. And a *whoosh*. And a heightened murmur from the crowd. Some people near us started praying.

"Do you know what, Robert?" I asked.

"What?"

"I wish I could be Miss Muffet again."

And then I turned and looked. And I knew I could never be the way I had been before. None of us could. Miss Muffet was dead. My daddy was dead. The world as we had all known it before the war and the shooting of Lincoln, that innocent world, was dead. This was the world now, as we had brought it upon ourselves to be.

Four hooded bodies swinging under the trapdoors of the scaffold. One of them a woman.

This is what the crowd had come to see this day, the official death of that old world. They had come to bear witness to it. I could do no less than look, could I?

One body swung harder and longer than the rest. Someone was struggling. Who was it? Mrs. Mary?

I knew I would, forever after, see those bodies every time I closed my eyes. And hear the terrible silence of the crowd in the pressing heat that sat on us in its white-hot fury.

They wouldn't give Annie her mother's body. Uncle Valentine and Robert did all they could. "I can't," Captain Rath told them. "They won't let me."

So we left, then. Annie left the casket. Robert and I asked her where she wanted to go. Uncle Valentine wanted her to come home with us, but she said no, she was all packed and leaving, going home to Surrattsville. "Even though they've changed the name," she told us. "They aren't going to call it Surrattsville anymore. Can they do that? Change a town's name?" She seemed more worried about that than anything.

"Why is she talking about this now?" I whispered to Robert.

"She has to," he answered. "She has to focus on something. Talk about anything she wants. The price of tea in China. Anything."

"Well, I changed my first name," Annie was saying, "and maybe now, I'll change my last one, too. They'll give me no peace if I don't. Help me find a new name, Emily."

So that's what we did, all the way home. We thought of new last names for Annie. We had to walk. Robert couldn't get a hack. The press of people was terrible leaving the prison. Hacks were all over, people yelling for them, drivers yelling at each other. The mood was vicious and the heat didn't help any.

Annie was selling the house at 541 H Street. She needed the money. We went inside. It was musty smelling and all the furniture was covered with sheets. It was eerie. I didn't look at the stairway for fear I'd see Johnny coming down, all gussied up for a night at the theater. I didn't look at the piano, either, for fear I'd see Mrs. Mary just sitting down to play.

I was in the nest that had hatched the eggs. And it was already haunted.

Annie was all packed. Except for Puss-in-Boots. I hunted her up for her. She knew me and purred. I kissed the top of her head and told her to be a good girl, she was going home to Maryland. Then I put her into the basket for Annie and we went out front, where Robert was trying to hail a carriage. He finally got one and paid the man himself. Then he put all Annie's portmanteaus in.

H Street was quiet. The houses all shuttered. Yet I felt eyes peering out at us, at Annie. In front of her house I kissed her good-bye. We promised to keep in touch, but like it was the day Johnny walked out of my life, I knew I'd never see Annie Surratt again.

The last thing I did when she got into the hack was give her the nightflowers. Tears came to her eyes. "You've been a good friend," she said.

"I haven't been, and I know it," I told Robert as we watched her drive off. "I haven't been a good friend or a good niece or a good daughter or a good anything. Have I?"

He shrugged. "You were a good sister to Johnny Collins," he said.

"That you can joke at a time like this," I admonished.

"It's called gallows humor," he said.

"Robert!"

He thrust his hands into his pockets and stood there on the deserted street smiling at me. "No disrespect intended. Soldiers have it. Doctors have it. It gets us through the terrible times. Or we'd go insane."

He was perfectly solemn. "And you were good at the cemetery that night, too."

"Good enough to do it again?"

"No. Good enough to do something better."

"What?"

"What do you want to do?"

"I've been giving it a lot of thought. Don't laugh. Promise."

"It hasn't been a day for laughter," he said.

"Maybe it's been living with Uncle Valentine. And reading his books. But I'd like to be a nurse. Like Clara Barton."

He nodded. "What about a doctor? Like Mary Walker?"

He was serious. I felt something swelling inside me in the place where I supposed my heart to be. On the deserted street, I smiled at him and the moment held for us, healing and full of hope. "You won't ever tell Uncle Valentine about that night, will you?" I asked.

"Do you want to ride home or walk?"

"Ride. It's too hot for walking. But you'll never get another hack. They're all busy taking people home from the hanging."

"Trust me," he said.

AUTHOR'S NOTE

In 1639 an apprentice in Massachusetts was dissected after his death, and his master, Marmaduke Percy, was arrested for causing the young man's skull fracture. This was one of the first legal postmortems in America. Such dissections were conducted all through our early history in this country. Many led to the arrest of perpetrators of murder. Many were done so doctors could simply determine why a patient died. Today we call them autopsies.

The acquisition of bodies for medical research became a problem in the eighteenth century in both England and America. At that time executed criminals were the only legal source for physicians. The first medical school in America was in the University of Pennsylvania's medical department, established in 1765. Dissection was allowed on the bodies of executed criminals, unclaimed bodies and, in Massachusetts after 1784, on victims of duels. Thus the practice of dissection became associated with criminality in America. It was said that the horror of dissection was additional revenge on criminals. And the blame was laid on surgeons and anatomists.

Back in those days, however, medicine was still half folklore, half magic, and half art. Medical training was acquired by the apprenticeship method. A young man followed a doctor around for several years and learned by watching and assisting.

It was different in England. Medical education required five years of study. Students had to take courses, attend lectures, do autopsies. So, many young men of means in America went abroad to study medicine, to London, Dublin, Edinburgh, or Glasgow.

Anatomy courses were the main reason for the establishment of medical schools. But both in England and in America there was a shortage of cadavers for dissection.

The acquiring of dead bodies for study goes back to the fifteenth century. Antonio Pollaiuolo (1431–1498) was the first painter to study the human body. Michelangelo (1475–1564) was able to do his paintings on the ceiling of the Sistine Chapel in St. Peter's in Rome because he spent years studying the human body through dissection. Leonardo da Vinci (1452–1519) has been hailed as the best anatomist of his time and did many illustrations of the human body, besides being known as a painter and sculptor.

During the American Revolution more men died in hospitals than on the battlefield. Hospitals were where you went to die. By the 1850s medical schools had sprouted up all over America, but the quality of education was poor. And vying for the attention of the sick were the herbalists, those who practiced slave medicine and folk medicine, and those who peddled bottled "cures," as well as just plain quacks. There were also midwives, who did more than deliver babies, and who sometimes knew as much if not more than the local doctors in far-flung regions.

In my book *The Blue Door*, which takes place in 1841, I have Ben Videau giving his girls "blue pills" to ward off "hot fever." He rolls the pills himself from the decoctions supplied by a slave herbalist on the South Carolina island plantation. In *The Second Bend in the River*, which takes place in Ohio in the early years of the nineteenth century, I have a doctor visiting a young dying woman and bringing "Bateman's drops, Godfrey's cordial, Anderson's ague pills, and Hamilton's worm-destroying lozenges." Both incidents are accurate depictions, gleaned from research.

In 1847 the American Medical Association was born and some control was exerted over medical practice. The profession in America upheld new techniques, put new focus on anatomical knowledge, and soon the torch was passed from Europe to America in medical education.

From 1768 to 1876 about eight thousand dissections for medical science were done in medical schools in Pennsylvania alone. There was a constant search for bodies. Between 1820 and 1840 more than sixteen hundred medical students were in school in Vermont. Four hundred cadavers were needed for dissection. Only two bodies a year were made available legally.

The American Civil War highlighted our physicians' abysmal ignorance and, at the same time, taught them so much. Surgeons just off the battlefields, where they'd dealt with carnage unbelievable to mankind, knew what they had to learn, and they weren't about to shilly-shally anymore about learning it.

Washington, D.C., at the end of the Civil War had more problems than any other city in the North. Change was happening so fast nobody could keep up with it. The war was ending. Thousands upon thousands of "freedmen" (freed slaves) had gathered there since Abraham Lincoln's Emancipation Proclamation in January of 1863. They were living in hovels, needing food, education, a new start. Photographs of the dead lying on the battlefield of Gettysburg were available to the public for the first time in the art galleries, the toll of dead was six hundred thousand in both the North and the South, African Americans were armed for the first time to fight for the North, women were entering new fields— nursing, writing, speechmaking. We even had an occasional woman doctor or two.

Officials were making a graveyard of General Robert E. Lee's front lawn at Arlington, which would eventually become our National Cemetery; the telegraph, cameras, and newspapers were making news available quicker than ever before; and what I call "the hysteria of celebrityhood" was fast taking hold.

State legislators had not yet made up laws to deal with supplying bodies for teaching. Resurrectionists, those who dug up and sold bodies, were rushing to Washington. Grave robbing became a lucrative activity. Handbooks were written on it. Wealthy people posted guards in cemeteries to protect the final resting places of their loved ones. There were four colleges in the District of Columbia. Three had medical departments. But there were a lot of cemeteries, as well as the Washington Asylum, and the Washington Almshouse (poorhouse). There were many derelicts who had nobody to claim their bodies. There was a potter's field and a good rail line, which made feasible the interstate shipment of bodies to Virginia and Michigan, where there were more good medical schools. (Back in 1859, when John Brown made his raid on Harper's Ferry to free the slaves, students from a medical school in Winchester, Virginia, rushed to the scene on hearing that the raid failed. They stuffed the body of Watson Brown, son of John, into a barrel, packed it in ice, and took it back to the college for dissection.)

In 1865, Washington was a boiling pot of confusion and constant turmoil. It had a peculiar mixture of educated and uneducated African Americans, well-placed citizens and transients, captured Confederate soldiers, Confederate sympathizers, political power grabbers, visiting dignitaries, do-gooders establishing new social agencies, architects finishing the Capitol building and the Washington Monument in the midst of pigs wandering in the muddy streets, a newly organized Sanitary Commission (precursor of the Red Cross) rushing to organize hospitals, the first women nurses in America, barrooms, dance halls, Willard's Hotel, the Smithsonian Institution, as well as people in the vanguard of our culture establishing museums, theaters, and art galleries.

It also had John Wilkes Booth.

I felt that the assassination and the mayhem that accompanied it was the perfect backdrop for my book. And Annie Surratt, the perfect friend for Emily. Only Annie Surratt could show Emily, who thinks she knows horror in her suspicions of her uncle's body snatching, what horror really is.

Emily Pigbush, Dr. Valentine, Maude, and Robert deGraaf are characters I created. Merry Andrews, the Spoon, and the Mole really lived and were involved in body snatching, though not in this time and place. Everything that happened to the Surratts is as I depict it.

It is true that Mrs. Surratt didn't have lawyers and someone supplied Mr. Aiken and Mr. Clampitt. No one knows who. Three doctors did attend Lincoln at Ford's Theater the night he was shot. Two are known. I made Dr. Valentine Bransby the third, who was unknown.

Lewis Thornton Powell also called himself Wood, and sometimes Payne. He did hide away in the Congressional Cemetery the Sunday night after the assassination, as I have him doing. And he did arrive at the Surratt house just as detectives were about to take Mrs. Surratt and Annie away for questioning.

Johnny Surratt's "career" and background were exactly as I depict them. He did take two young ladies to Ford's Theater on the night of March 15, 1865, and they did sit in the president's box, and John Wilkes Booth did stop by. Everything about Elizabeth Keckley, dressmaker and personal confidante of Mrs. Lincoln, is true.

There seems to be a controversy over Annie Surratt's age. Louis J. Weichman, author of *A True History of the Assassination of Abraham Lincoln,* has her age as twenty-six in the text and twenty-two in his chapter notes. Although his book is in my bibliography, I do not consider him a reliable source. He was a member of the cast in the Surratt house and the trial that followed. It would be like taking the word, a hundred and thirty years from now, about the "true story of the O. J. Simpson trial," by any one of the witnesses who gave dubious testimony. Other authors are more accurate about Annie's age. Gore Vidal has her eighteen in his *Lincoln.* Jim Bishop has her seventeen in his *The Day Lincoln Was Shot,* and in another book in my bibliography, *The Assassination of Lincoln*, Lloyd Lewis has her in convent school in 1863. That would hardly make her twenty-six years old in 1865. There also seems to be controversy about whether Annie was released immediately from prison after being taken for initial questioning. My sources tell me she was released within a day. We know she constantly visited her mother in Carroll Prison.

Of course, the fate of Dr. Samuel Mudd is well-known to all. Only within the last decade or so has his name been cleared in the assassination of President Lincoln. Mudd was sent to Fort Jefferson Prison on Dry Tortugas, an island a hundred miles off the coast of Florida. There he remained until 1868, when yellow fever broke out in the prison. Dr. Mudd offered his services and got the epidemic in hand. Officers of the fort appealed to President Johnson, asking for a pardon for Mudd, and this was done on February 8, 1869. Mudd took up his old life and died in 1882. I made him a friend of Uncle Valentine.

The *Sultana* riverboat disaster happened exactly as I depicted it, on April 27, 1865. And the accident with General George Armstrong Custer's horse in the Grand Review parade really happened, too.

Yes, they did hang Annie Surratt's mother. Annie did wait outside the gate for her mother's body, and they did refuse to give it to her. Johnny Surratt did stay away. Since his friendship with Emily is of my making, so, too, is the letter he wrote to her when he was in hiding. He did, however, have "a man in Washington" who was supposed to keep him informed about his mother's trial. This information was taken from a lecture Johnny Surratt gave on December 6, 1870, at Rockville, Maryland, on the conspiracy and assassination of Abraham Lincoln.

While his mother's trial was going on, Johnny was hidden by priests in Canada, then fled to Liverpool, England. From there he went to Rome, where he enlisted in the Papal Zouaves under an assumed name. In April 1866 he was recognized, and in November he was sent back to America. Some sources say Annie was living back in Washington and visited him in prison while he was on trial, and brought food. Their brother Isaac was at the trial, too. He was older than both Johnny and Annie, went south to join the Confederate army at the start of the war, did not return home, and was not in contact with his family until after his mother's hanging. I saw no need to bring him into the book.

Johnny Surratt's trial went on for sixty-two days. In the trial, a diary of John Wilkes Booth was introduced. Nobody had ever known before of such a diary. It proved that neither Mary Surratt nor her son, Johnny, knew of the assassination attempt. They knew only of a plot to kidnap Lincoln and hold him for ransom until Confederate prisoners held up North could be released.

The jury could not agree. Johnny Surratt was held for a new trial, but months later he was allowed out on bail and there never was a new trial. Johnny tried lecturing for a while, but it didn't work. He spent the rest of his life as an obscure clerk and died in 1916.

Annie Surratt does not appear in any factual accounts after the trial of her brother Johnny. Nobody knows what happened to her.

As for the nightflowers: My research tells me there are four hundred fifty members of the cactus family that bloom at night. The night-blooming cereus is one of them. The author of *The Evening Garden*, Peter Loewer, writes, "I have seen it bloom in September at Mohonk Manor, New York's famous resort hotel on the Hudson River." He furthermore writes, "These plants are native to every state in the United States with the exception of Maine, New Hampshire, and Vermont." Of the yucca, he says, "During the day, the white, six-petaled blossoms hang down like bells at rest. At dusk, they turn up to the evening sky, open wide, and release a sweet soapy smell to the night air."

When I started writing this book, I didn't know if I would find even one flower that bloomed at night. Thanks to Peter Loewer, I found a book full of them.

After all is said and done, I am writing fiction here. Writing, just like medicine in Lincoln's time, is half magic, half art, and half hard work. And my story is *based* on the hard, dry facts that I have taken pain to substantiate.

So then, what happened to my fictional heroine, Emily Pigbush? I like to think she stayed with Uncle Valentine. Perhaps she became one of Mrs. McQuade's star pupils. Perhaps she sat in the courtroom at Johnny Surratt's trial. Did he see her there? Did their eyes meet? Did they speak?

I like to think she finished her schooling and went on to become a woman doctor.

Body snatching declined by the 1890s. The medical profession succeeded in getting decent anatomy laws enacted and scientific methods made it possible for cadavers to be preserved for a very long time. By the twentieth century body snatching had all but ceased.

BIBLIOGRAPHY

Adams, George Worthington. *Doctors in Blue: The Medical History of the Union Army in the Civil War.* New York: H. Schuman, 1952.

Bettmann, Otto L. *A Pictorial History of Medicine: A Brief, Nontechnical Survey of the Healing Arts from Aesculapius to Ehrlich.* Springfield, Ill.: Charles C. Thomas, 1956.

Bishop, Jim. *The Day Lincoln Was Shot.* New York: Harper & Row, 1955.

Campbell, Helen Jones. *Confederate Courier.* New York: St. Martin's Press, 1965.

Green, Constance McLaughlin. *Washington: A History of the Capital 1800–1950.* Princeton, N.J.: Princeton University Press, 1962–1963.

Keckley, Elizabeth. *Behind the Scenes: Thirty Years a Slave and Four Years in the White House.* New York: Arno Press, 1968.

Lewis, Lloyd. *The Assassination of Lincoln: History and Myth.* Lincoln, Neb.: University of Nebraska Press, 1994. Originally published as *Myths After Lincoln*, New York: Harcourt, 1929.

Loewer, Peter. *The Evening Garden.* New York: Macmillan, 1993.

Long, E. B., and Barbara Long. *The Civil War Day by Day: An Almanac 1861–1865.* Garden City, N.J.: Doubleday, 1971.

Russell, Pamela Redford. *The Woman Who Loved John Wilkes Booth.* New York: G. P. Putnam's Sons, 1978.

Shultz, Suzanne M. *Body Snatching: The Robbing of Graves for the Education of Physicians in Early Nineteenth Century America.* Jefferson, N.C.: McFarland & Co., 1992.

Weichmann, Louis J. *A True History of the Assassination of Abraham Lincoln and of the Conspiracy of 1865.* New York: Alfred A. Knopf, 1975.